Through High Waters

A Revelation Novel

Allison Paige

Copyright © 2022 Allison Paige
All rights reserved.

Published in the United States by Finnegan Publishing Group
Printed in the United States of America.
First printing edition 2022.

No part of this publication may be reproduced, distributed, or transmitted in any form or by any means, including photocopying, recording, or other electronic or mechanical methods, without the prior written permission of the publisher, except in the case of brief quotations embodied in critical reviews and certain other noncommercial uses permitted by copyright law.

Any references to historical events, real people, or real places are used fictitiously. Names, characters, and places are products of the author's imagination.

ISBN: 979-8-9865593-1-5 (Paperback)
ISBN: 979-8-9865593-2-2 (ebook)

Cover art by India-Lee Crews

www.finneganpublishinggroup.com
www.authorallisonpaige.com

For everyone that believed in me.

I

A jacket covers my face. I can't see anything, but, slowly, feeling returns to my body. I breathe in. The air that fills my lungs sparks a fire throughout my body that would have made me cry out had I a voice. I wiggle my fingers, trying to find the strength to push the fabric away. I think it's still light out, though it's dimmer than I remember. How much time has passed?

Dying is one of the most horrific events I have ever experienced. It's hot, sharp, stifling, and dark. The only thing it isn't is lonely. I should have felt alone whenever the bullet struck me, but I am the exception to the rule. I am bonded with a demon and, even in death, he could not let me go. I could feel Raum with me as he flew away. Abandoning me, but selfishly holding onto me simply because he could.

I wish he would have let me die. I have suffered enough pain over the last few years, the most recent having been inflicted by his hand. He made me do unspeakable things, most I am still not certain were entirely influenced through his control. I'll never forgive Raum for marking me. I'll never forgive him for waking me from what I surely thought was eternal death.

He is crueler than any demon I have come across. I thought my time with Leyak had been the most horrendous experience of my life. I thought that until I woke up, just a few seconds ago. Now I am certain that Raum is not only the cruelest but the most dangerous demon that walks this earth.

The leather heap falls from my face as I sit up. The front of my shirt has been ripped open. It's stained with damp blood. I touch a dark mark over my chest where the bullet hit me, but already the wound has sealed itself shut. I press my finger against it, trying to reopen the wound. Beside me is the bloody slug Sebastian or Devon must have pulled out of me. Picking it up, I rotate it between my fingertips.

Thick smoke billows across the sky with a sense of urgency. The bees are few and far between. I only count six, which is far less than when I'd been dying, and they'd faded like little black and gold orbs. The sight of them is no longer comforting. I feel even more uneasy when I realize no birds grace the sky either. Where is the raven?

I tuck the bullet in my pocket as I stand, stumbling to the side. What sick joke is Raum playing this time?

They've abandoned me, humans and demon alike. I don't blame Sebastian and Devon for departing. They did what they could and still they failed. No one could have guessed that I would wake from death's embrace.

I yell at the top of my lungs, calling out Raum's name. My voice fades into the distance, moving on the shallow wind that stirs my hair. Not a sound answers.

I know he is close. I don't believe he healed me for the sport of it. There is always a reason to his madness.

I fling the dust from my jacket and set it over my head. The sun is halfway down the horizon, but it's hot enough that I need the shade. What I really need is water. My throat is raw like sandpaper. How long have I been dead? For all I know, it has been days since I was left here.

Did I actually die? I don't remember anything from being dead. The last thing I saw was the bees flying overhead, and then there was nothing. There was no white light or flames of damnation. Just absolute darkness; completely devoid of good or evil.

I turn slowly, taking in the cracks of the dried ground and wilted growth. Raum led us for days into the desert. I could turn back, seeking shelter in the mountains he stole me from, or I could keep going forward. My eyes settle over a pair of footprints leading away from me.

I curse under my breath. I shouldn't trail Devon and Sebastian, but what if Raum went after them? Were they able to escape his wrath? If they are alive, they won't be as welcoming. They'd nearly shot me the first time I came up on them. They tried to save me, though, and that counts for something.

Decision made, I follow the direction of their footprints, careful not to cover them with the sand from my own steps. I can't have been asleep for days if I can still see their tracks. The wind would have blown most of the evidence away.

It feels strange to be tracking them. They're careful, but not thorough enough. When I lose their footprints in the sand, I pick their trail up from broken branches cracked by footfall, burnt kindling, and smooth patches in the ground where they might have laid to rest. The biggest tell is a single strand of blond hair that catches the light against a thorn bush.

It's well into the night before I finally stop to rest. There is no shelter where I'm at and they took my kukri knife, so building anything would be difficult, even if there was anything to be forged. They didn't know I would still have need for it. I lay on my back staring at the stars between the bands of smoke that still stretch out from the compound. What had once been a sanctuary is many miles behind me. The trace of the fire is a damning reminder of what I helped Raum do.

The brutal murder of five people clings to my memory, so vivid it's like a horror movie is on a loop in my mind. I still can't recall what happened to Liam, but I know I must have had some hand in it. I'd put the count to six to include Anna, but I noticed three sets of tracks before I laid down to rest. If they belong to her, I hope she makes it.

I find it surprisingly easy to fall asleep, though monsters with long talons torment me in my dreams. They claw at my clothes, laugh mockingly in my face.

The frigid midnight air hits the beads of sweat forming on my skin when I wake, and I clench the neck of my jacket together with a shiver. Sitting up slowly, I arch my back that has stiffened from lying on the hard ground.

This is madness. Why did Raum wake me only to abandon me? If I do not freeze to death, then I will starve.

My body creaks in protest as I stand. The only thing for me to do is keep moving.

After a day and a half of wandering around, I lose the humans' trail. I knew it would happen sooner or later, but it is disheartening nonetheless. At least there are no signs of blood. I tell myself that Raum hasn't eaten them, but lack of evidence doesn't mean it didn't happen. I'd like to think they got away and are holed up somewhere safe. As safe as they can be in this world.

The sun is blistering hot, yet I don't tire. It would be so tempting to lie down, but I know I won't die. Raum won't let me. I feel like the walking dead stumbling around aimlessly. I lick my cracked lips to keep them wet, but there is no moisture in my mouth to soothe the pain.

Movement catches my eye, drawing my attention from the horizon to the sky. There is a massive cloud of birds circling through the air. They're far enough away I can't tell what kind they are. I scan the horizon once more. What are they circling? My stomach tightens as I get a clear image of human remains lying somewhere ahead of me. Is it Sebastian and the group? Or is it a more horrific scene like at the Boise Zoo?

What I had witnessed at the zoo had been a monstrosity. Humans, mostly women and children, had been mutilated and caged like wild animals. Others had been put up for show on the carousel and strung in trees.

Though, the desert isn't the sort of place to display such a horrendous exhibit.

That can only mean that Sebastian, Devon, and Anna are somewhere ahead of me. I hope the body the birds are stalking isn't one of them, but it is too far ahead for me to investigate.

The barren ground opens to sparse foliage. It's not much, but the hint of green here and there keeps me motivated. Golden blades of grass sweep between the thorny brush and rough boulders.

Everything is dead or dying. I stumble on a shriveled cactus that looks anything but promising. I scour the ground until I find two decent-sized stones and use them to cut into the spiky plant. There is not even a drop of water in it to quench my thirst. I gnaw at the brittle hide in desperation. The wilted flesh gives way, turning to thick gray ash in my mouth.

I spend the rest of my daylight hours collecting debris in my coat to make a fire. There's enough that will last maybe an hour. The land is too dry that, even if I do collect more, it won't make any difference. I curse under my breath as I set to making a fire.

It's been a long time since I've had to start a fire by hand. Before, I had the luxury of owning a flint stick and a couple of lighters. Once I met Raum, he started everything for us. I'm a bit out of practice. I curse again as I rub the two sticks together to no avail. It takes me well over an hour to get a spark.

Dark clouds, thicker than the smog, roll in from the west. I take shelter against a small rock shelf in preparation for the rain. I dig into the ground while I wait, making a divot in the sand. My nails chip and bleed, but I keep at it. Once the hole is big enough, I take off my jacket and shape it into the bowl I've dug in the dirt.

When the rain comes, it pours. I scrub the grime from my face before lapping at the ground like a dog. The dirt that clings to the leather and water taste like chalk, but it doesn't matter. It's water. If bliss has a taste, it is what I drink now. Sweet and delicious, it burns its way down the back of my throat.

I drink as much as I can, hating the way that my stomach clenches as the water hits it. I know I'll be sick, but it's worth it. I roll on my back and close my eyes. I savor every raindrop that splashes across my face.

***

Two more days of wandering the desert finally takes its toll on me. Raum's power has kept me together for the most part. He must be weakening, too. I hit the wall about thirty paces from something abnormal. What is that?

A dark mound lies up ahead. It's not a boulder, nor is it a plant. I look around, but there are no signs of life save for the birds that are still miles away. A mountain range is off to my right, but it is as barren as the rest of the land. I clench my jaw as I press forward. Even before I see the fabric flutter in the wind, I know that the mass is human.

There is no blood. The only sign of a struggle are scuff marks beneath Anna's boots. Her once sharp eyes are now bloated and white. I push her hair away. On her neck is dark bruising from where she was strangled. I sit back on my heels with a sigh.

The stench is bad, but it's not enough to drive me away. She hasn't been here more than a few days. Dried fluid pools from her eyes and nostrils; her skin is as pale as her eyes. Three days maybe? Maybe less with this heat. Her hair is damp from the rain.

It's my fault she's dead. It was Anthony who shot her, but it was I who led the raid back in the compound. Her wounds no doubt slowed Sebastian and Devon down, but I can't really see either one of them killing her for it. I chew off a piece of dried skin from my lip in contemplation.

My stomach growls. One bite wouldn't hurt… Maybe a few. If I had survived death, then I could survive whatever spoil is decomposing her body. It would ease the hunger, and her belly is so soft. I jerk my hand from the bottom of her shirt and stumble to my feet as soon as the startling thoughts slide into my head. I won't desecrate a human body, especially not one that I knew. God forgive me that I even considered it.

I continue my way toward the birds in hopes there is food somewhere close by. I glance back at Anna once. I'm surprised the birds haven't picked her apart yet. Whatever lies ahead must be better. It looks as if the cloud of birds is moving. The closer I get, the farther they fly.

Is Raum leading me somewhere? He must be. I haven't seen birds in a long time. Why hasn't he shown his face yet? It feels like a dark cloud follows me. I find myself longing for Raum's company if only to keep my wits about me. I feel like I'm losing myself.

***

Days and nights meld together like the turn of a kaleidoscope. Sebastian and Devon's path has long since become lost to me. I wish I could have found them, but I tell myself it is for the best. They are safer if I don't find them. If Raum is close by, and I suspect he is, then he will only kill them.

I can't shake the image of Anna, though. Who killed her? A demon would have eaten her, and the idea that either of her companions would have done it seems impossible. She'd been half dead the last time I saw her; maybe it had been done out of mercy. Though she would not have kicked for her life—as evidenced by the condition of her boots—had it been done out of kindness.

A warm wind tangles around me, and on its back is the stench of death. The grotesque odor burns its way through my nose, down to my stomach where it clenches so forcibly, I think it might expel the liquid I've consumed. I press my tongue to the roof of my mouth and fight back the bile and water.

Another body sprawls on the ground ahead. What is left of one. An arm lies two feet away from the torso it belongs to. Dried blood is spattered across the ground. The flash of blonde hair brings tears to my eyes. I don't want to walk closer to it, but I must. I have to confirm with my own eyes that the woman in the dirt is Devon.

I fall to my knees when I reach her. She's nearly unrecognizable. Her clothes are torn, and her body is covered in oozing lacerations made by claws or a large knife. A dark presence falls over me, tightening my chest. I suck in air, only to release it just as quickly.

My friend. My sweet friend.

I touch her face gently, running my thumb beneath where her blue eyes had once been but were now crimson pools. The color of them had reminded me of my home. Devon, above all others, had been my sanctuary. The hollow sockets stare up at me, blaming me for her death. It is my fault that she and all the others are dead. A strangled sob escapes me and then a series of them follows.

I close my eyes, wishing this nightmare to be over.

A hand presses into my shoulder. "Ah, Leah, don't cry," Raum croons.

II

I make a final wish before opening my eyes again. Raum's hand slides from one shoulder to the next as he circles me, coming to my front so he can pull me to my feet. His black eyes are framed by the crinkles he gets whenever he smiles. A broad grin touches his face as he looks at me. He looks happy, relieved.

He's as beautiful as when I last saw him. Incredibly tall and wickedly handsome. His bronze skin shines with a thin layer of sweat. His cashmere hair is knotted behind his scalp, revealing dark feathers at the base of his neck. They've grown longer, once brushing the collar of his shirt, now fluttering across it with a blue-black sheen.

"What have you done?" I whisper.

He runs a dangerous caress across the side of my face. "I saved you," he says.

Fire boils through my veins, turning my vision scarlet. I throw up my left fist and then my right. Raum catches my left, but I manage to strike him in the throat with a right hook before he grabs that hand, too. His fingers constrict, threatening to break my hands.

"This is not salvation!" I screech.

Raum's smile softens. He pulls my hands into one of his so he can stroke the side of my neck with the other. The curve of his nail grazes the vein that pulses beneath his touch. Demons are obsessive creatures. Once they're attached to someone, it's near impossible for them to let go. Never had I seen one so possessed like Raum is with me, though. What demon is insane enough to bring a *human* back to life?

Raum pulls me against his chest, wrapping his strong arms around me. I pull one of my hands free and strike him as another trickle of tears fall down my face. He tenses, but he makes no move to harm me.

"You don't feel love, but surely you don't hate me so much," I say.

Raum tsks. My hair presses against the back of my neck as he smooths it down. "I could never hate you." He grips the back of my neck as he lowers his lips to my ear. "Did you really think you would escape me? I told you that when you die, it will be by my hand. I will not let a bullet cheat me from the opportunity."

I wince under the pressure of his fingers. It would be easy for him to snap my neck like this. I think that's what he has planned before he shoves me away.

"Why did you do this to her?" My voice breaks. I resist the urge to look back at Devon. It's not her; it's just a body.

The shift in Raum's countenance sends chills down my spine. It's like I've challenged him. His eyes narrow. "She had a hold over you. They all did."

"The only thing holding onto me is you."

I want to scream. Time has not changed my ability to reason with him.

"Did you not miss me?"

A feeling to be closer to him calls to me. I'm too tired to sway one way or the other. I ignore the feeling and allow my gaze to drift into the distance, to the birds.

"Are those demons?"

Raum chuckles. "They're just crows."

Just crows. I don't believe him. Raum has lied to me from the beginning—from marking me, to the change of power amongst the demons, as well as his own abilities. I've always wondered what Raum could do. Turning into a crow is just one of the many things he kept hidden from me until the last minute. I suppose I should have suspected something the first time I felt the feathers at the nape of his neck. I never knew demons had the ability to shift into animals, though. I've seen their hands turn into talons, looking more like leathery paws than any human appendage, but I assumed it was because they were monsters outside of our skin.

"I thought you turned into a raven. You seemed a little big to be a crow."

He sneers. "Is that a compliment?"

Vile creature he is. I walk away from both him and Devon's remains. The rank smell of death and sulfur trail after me. Both of them burn a foul taste on my tongue.

"Come, Leah."

I sit down in response, tired of walking. I had gone in search of my friends and, one by one, I found them dead. I can't bear to find Sebastian on the path Raum leads us. He is the last of them, and I'd like to stay in the dark over what has become of him. If I never see his body, I can pretend he made it someplace safe.

"Leah."

"I'm not going anywhere."

"I did not wake you for nothing."

I scoff. "I don't have the strength to fight you." I look him over then, back toward the horizon. "Neither do I have the strength to succumb to you."

His anger ripples down the cord of our bond. It's more prominent now that I know it exists. Though, if my body was not so spent, I'm sure I would feel it less as I did before. His anger doesn't scare me. There is nothing he can do to me that he hasn't already.

"You think I can't hurt you?" A low growl whispers at the edge of his words.

"You've done everything you can to break me. You woke me and left me to wander for weeks with no food or water. I feel like I am dying, yet for whatever reason, you keep me alive. What is worse than this?"

Has it been weeks? I'm probably exaggerating. Despite Raum's influence over my health, it feels like my head is full of glass. Sharp pain clashes together, sounding like that insistent ringing I can't stand. I press my fingers against my temple. Everything burns, my skin, my throat, my stomach. What is worse are my eyes that are so dry that I can't even cry anymore.

Raum crouches on the balls of his feet. His heat used to comfort me, but the strength of it burns my cheeks in a way that hurts more than what I'm already feeling. "I have always been kind to you, Leah, even when I hurt you. You would do well to remember that."

The familiar touch of fear he has always been so good at instilling runs a quivering line up my spine. I learned quickly that it can oftentimes be foolish to stand up to him.

If this is kindness, I can't fathom what it would be like for him to be unkind. His countenance gives no trace of what that might be. I look at myself in his glassy orbs, but the only thing that peers back is darkness.

"What do you want?" I finally ask.

He smirks. "There is shelter not far from here. We will talk when we get there." He stands, stretching his long legs. I do the same and look back to Devon. Why did he have to take her eyes?

"Are you just going to leave her?"

"Yes."

I bite down hard, tensing the back corners of my jaw. "When I met you, you made me build a pyre for your friend. Will you not help me bury mine?"

Music rumbles deep within his chest before spilling over his lips. When Raum smiles, it is with heartbreaking beauty that draws me to him. I hate how much I love the sound that escapes that perfect full mouth.

"No," he says. "Her body will lie there and rot for what she has done."

The only thing Devon and all the others had done was live.

I can't tell if the sudden change of air is from the wind or the heat that still rolls off his body, but it feels thicker. Almost like a weight drapes over my back, dragging my shoulders down. I say a silent prayer to whatever power is in control for the safety of her soul. It is the best I can do for her.

I follow Raum to a shelter made up of rocks aligned in a circle, bedded with a thin layer of grass. It's a nest. I lean against one of the stones. A jagged edge digs into my ribs but at least it takes my mind off the other pains. Raum tosses me a strip of dried meat. I look over it tentatively, wondering if it's come from him or Devon. I take a hesitant bite, dismissing asking the question entirely. I don't want to know.

In two hours, the sun will set. I watch it creep down the horizon as Raum approaches me. A line of pain flashes across his face when he sits down.

"What's wrong?" I ask around a mouth full of food.

I didn't notice before that he isn't wearing the bloodstained, smoke-filled black shirt from last time. The olive t-shirt he wears now is too small for him, and it covers a lump in his abdomen.

"I am tired from maintaining you," he says irritably.

I scoff. Liar.

He cocks his head. "It is good to see you."

I look at the ground with a shake of my head.

"Are you not grateful?" His upper lip curls when he speaks.

I bite off another piece of the meat and chew it slowly, ignoring him. Out of all the feelings impressed upon me, gratitude is not one of them. Anger, hate, attraction—*those* have not changed.

"I brought you back to give you freedom," he says.

That gets my attention. I turn. "No," I say softly, looking down at his mouth then back to his pitless eyes. Death is the only form of freedom one can acquire in this world, and he cheated me from it. "Tell me the real reason you brought me back."

The sun drops a little lower before he finally answers. The amount of time spent together has taught me to read Raum better. I can see the wheels turning behind his eyes as he mulls over whatever it is he has to say to me. Perhaps he is doing it to be dramatic. The suspense makes my chest tight.

"I want you to bring the boy to me," he says.

A wisp of air stirs a piece of hair across my face. Raum brushes it behind my ear.

"Sebastian?"

Before I can ask why, the answer comes to me. Dark shadows hang on the underside of Raum's eyes. His sharp bone structure looks like it has been trimmed. I can't find any other differences in his appearance, but I know something in him has changed. Raum has always healed quickly, and never has he shown signs of weakness unless it was after he consumed honey. My eyes fall back to the lump under his shirt.

"You need his body," I say quietly. He pulls his hand away from my face. I look away, biting the inside of my lip. I shake my head when I look back at him. How dare he play on my sympathy and ask me to turn on another friend.

Raum stares back, unblinking.

I swallow. "Let me see." I feel guilty for asking, that a little bit of concern creeps into my voice. It would be easier to not care at all, but I can't help it. I've never been able to help myself when it comes to him.

Raum pulls up the hem of his shirt. A thick, bloodstained bandage wraps around his gut. It needs to be changed. "It has been difficult to heal since waking you."

"Then why did you? You could have taken him without me."

This is what he brought me back for? Blood flows across my tongue when I bite my lip harder. I curse him under my breath.

Raum pulls his shirt down. "He is the one that did this to me. He might be as good with a knife as you are."

His subtle play to humor me doesn't make me smile. "You should go ahead and kill me because I won't do this for you."

Raum's brow arches. "You will do whatever I want. I would prefer to give you the choice, but I will take it from you if I must."

"Choice? You've *never* given me a choice. Either way, you destroy me."

He shrugs.

"No," I say firmly. How easy it is to say the word now, but I have never known a way to phrase it before.

"Leah." A warning growl leaves his throat.

"I killed everyone else for you. If Sebastian escaped, then he deserves his life. If you die because he was protecting himself, then you deserve just as much."

As quick as I blink, Raum is looming over me. "I need his body, and you are going to get it for me."

Involuntarily, tears burn the back of my eyes. It hurts worse now that they're wet.

"You let me die," I say through gritted teeth. "You left me to rot until you needed me. You can't use me whenever it suits you." I lean harder into the rocks as he leers toward me.

"I do suit you. I was made to haunt you."

Our noses brush together. The taste of him is on my tongue when I breathe in. Hot ash and liquid gold.

"Take hold of me, because there isn't any other way I'm going to help you."

"My pleasure," he growls.

Raum moves with impossible speed. One second, we are close enough to kiss and the next I am on my stomach, my face grating into the dirt with him pinning me down. The blow of his fangs is like a gunshot. I cry out as they sink into the back of my shoulder.

When he releases me, the pain does not stop. The poison of his bite spreads across my neck and down the length of my back. He shoves my hair away from my face and leans down. I recognize the familiar metallic scent of my own blood when his wet lips brush against my ear.

"Do not think you can defy me just because you died. My venom still runs in your veins. You are mine," he hisses.

I whimper, trying to turn my face away, but he holds me firm. His thumb presses into the wound on my shoulder and a new wave of fire spreads beneath it.

"Say it," he snaps.

My teeth make a high-pitched sound as they grind together. My skin sheaths his thumb to the knuckle as he pushes it deeper into the wound.

"Say it!"

"I'm yours," I gasp.

His lips curve into a smile against my ear. When he draws back, the density of the air thins, growing cold. I gasp again, sucking in like a fish yearning for water. My back is on fire. It's easier for him to cull me when I'm wounded, when he knows I will not fight or run from him. I sit up, eyeing his stomach. It would be stupid to attack him, but it's an opportunity I'd be foolish to pass on.

"Where is he?" I ask, leaning back. I'll wait a little longer.

Raum licks his lips, cleaning the crimson stain in a single sweep of his tongue. "Not far. Maybe a day or two at most; ground we can cover quickly."

I nod. "What makes you think he is going to listen to me? If he sees me, he'll know you're behind it. How did he even manage to hurt you?"

"He got lucky" is all he says about it. I roll my eyes. Here we go with the secrets again. "He will listen to you. He has tried to save your life on multiple occasions. What is one more? All I need is a few seconds. You distract him that long and I can overpower him."

I don't know what is worse, what I did in the compound or what I'm about to help him do. I shouldn't even be contemplating betraying Sebastian, but neither can I turn my back on Raum. Aren't all evils the same?

I've seen a possession once. Leyak had taken James so quick I didn't even notice what was happening. Would Sebastian go the same way? Would he still be present when Raum overpowered him?

I meet Raum's eyes.

No. He would be a hard demon to overpower. I think if he seeds himself in Sebastian, he'll have total control. It will be Raum wearing Sebastian's skin and Raum alone.

"If I help you, you'll cut me free? How? Isn't the bond irreversible?"

"I can sever the tie," he says simply.

I snap my fingers. "Just like that?" A mockery of a laugh escapes at the end of my question.

Raum nods.

He has a way of making even the best lie seem honest, but I know when he isn't telling me something. My gaze drops down to his hand that has found a place on my thigh. Deep down I know there is no way to cut our bond. For the rest of my tormented life, it will be just the two of us.

I think of driving my fist into his stomach but dismiss the idea as quickly as it comes. Leaning against him instead, I turn my head into his shoulder to settle in. Fighting him has only ever wounded me.

I sigh. Whatever my fate, it feels good to be close to him again.

Raum reaches beside him and pulls out another piece of jerky from a leather bag that reminds me of the one I used to have before he found me. I wonder if it also holds a collection of knives. I wish he hadn't been so careless with my blades.

"Eat and sleep as much as you can," he says. "Once we start, we will not stop until we find him."

I stretch out beside him, resting my head across his lap. He strokes my head the way that I like, coaxing the tension and anxiety from my body. When his fingers catch on the knots that have tangled in my hair, he takes the time to unravel them. I hate to say that I've missed this, this part of us. But I have. The war inside me to fight him evaporates. I feel at peace.

It doesn't take me long to drift off. Between the comfort of his heat and touch, I'm lulled into a dreamlike state. It is the first night we fall asleep together without a fire.

III

Raum is in the same position whenever I wake up. I don't think he has moved all night, or slept for that matter. The rings around his eyes are darker. The light looks the same as it did when I fell asleep. It casts an indigo hue across his features.

Raum hisses when I sit up. At first, I think he is doing it *at* me, then I realize it's *because of me*. I've grazed his wound. He stands behind me, righting himself stiffly. The blood from the bandage has seeped through his shirt.

"Why can't I feel it?" I ask.

"You will likely pass out from the pain. I do not want to carry you," he says irritably, his voice hoarse.

"Can I see it?" I motion toward him, but he is already shaking his head.

"Let's go," he says.

"You should at least cauterize it."

The smell of sulfur is stronger now.

Raum rolls his shoulder as if brushing the comment away. "This body is past salvaging."

Despite his state, we make up lost time quickly. I only notice a difference in his strength on the third day when the sun burns my face. I don't remember when it stopped, but when it starts to hurt again, it's with a vengeance. I stay close to his side, brushing against his elbow whenever he stumbles. Relief and fear grip me.

If we don't find Sebastian in time, we'll both perish. Now that I'm alive, I don't want to die, but I would be free. Raum would not be able to bring me back in his weakened state. Sebastian's attack solves everyone's problem. He could escape. He could make it.

"Leah," Raum says, sounding choked. "Your thoughts are loud."

I bump against his shoulder. "They're only thoughts," I say. "Have you always been able to hear them?" I knew he could sense things and I feel emotions through the bond, but I had no idea he could point blank hear me. I've never been able to read his mind.

"I am always one step ahead, am I not?" Raum flashes me a sharp smile.

"How does it work?"

"I am the only one that benefits from it."

I scoff. I already knew that.

"Did you know when I left, before you found me in Boise?"

He frowns. "No," he says quietly. "No; I could not hear you."

I wonder if that had anything to do with distance or if the bees had something to do with it. Before I can ask, he gets a strange look in his eye. His mouth turns up again, revealing a fanged smile.

"What?"

"You have not considered what might happen should this body fail me before we find the boy." I look at him blankly and his smile grows more sinister. "I will take yours."

I come to a stumbling halt. "You wouldn't," I whisper.

He follows me, closing the space between us. Fear coils in the pit of my stomach when he laces our fingers together and pulls me back to his side. It wasn't that long ago that he broke the same hand he holds. I'm afraid he'll do it again, but the touch only lasts for a second before he trails his fingers across my palm and up my arm, roving over me like a spider.

"You know I would," he says. "It might take some time, longer than most. You are so small, it would be difficult to fit inside of you, but not impossible." His words bring a blush to my face, reminding me of another time he called me small. A dark chuckle rings from deep within his chest. "And I promise that if that happens, I will allow you to remain. It will just be us, forever," he hisses.

I want to scream. I want to fall to the ground and beat my fists into the dirt until it cracks open and swallows me whole. Mostly, I want to cry. I touch the invisible collar around my neck that Raum has had on me ever since we met. I will never be free of him. Not unless we find Sebastian.

I lick the sweat from my upper lip. The bit of moisture stings the cuts on my tongue that I've made after biting it repeatedly. The salty tang twists my stomach harder. God forgive me, but please let us find Sebastian. I hate myself for wishing it, but it can't be me. I link my arm through Raum's to support his weight as we continue our hunt.

Whether Raum has a hold over me or not, I am condemning myself to Hell, to the rot of the world. My actions alone are enough to do it, but it's the choice I make to preserve my life over Sebastian's that brings the heat of the flames so much closer.

The fourth day comes and goes with no visual sign of Sebastian's whereabouts. I find it highly unlikely that he would be returning to the coast, since that's where he'd come from. The wilderness is no longer safe with the demons going into hiding. Perhaps he thinks the cities are like Boise and free of demons.

One of those cities stands before us in the distance. It's a large obstructive black mass that looms against a muted sunset. Around it is a massive wall with broken-down buildings outside of that. I find myself pressing closer to Raum, using his body like a shield to protect me from the monsters that might be waiting for us.

Raum's head snaps up and he straightens. A jolt of pain runs through me that nearly takes my breath away. I clench my own stomach to steady myself. It's gone as soon as I gasp, and he gives an annoyed growl.

"Do you smell that?" he asks.

Now that he's mentioned it, I do. The air is full of salt. Before I died, Raum said he smelled salt water, but just like then it doesn't make any sense. We are weeks away from the coast. "Is this what you smelled before?" I ask.

"Yes," he says softly. He cranes his head up, stepping forward as he does so. "I smell him, too."

"What's wrong?" I ask when he doesn't move.

His lashes flutter as he scans the horizon, searching.

"The city," he starts and stops, his lips parting to reveal his sharp teeth that have elongated. "We need to find him quickly. The city thrives."

His words nourish the seed of fear that has taken root. The dark tendrils of it clasp my fast-beating heart. The kingdoms should have fallen by now. The return of the bees ensured that. That's what their return meant. Right?

"There's no way… Sebastian wouldn't run straight to demon city." I curse under my breath. I have not been impressed by such a magnitude of power since I left Michigan. There is only death and ruin behind those walls. The stir of memories it starts leaves me paralyzed.

"He would if he did not know any better," he says.

"He has to feel it."

Raum starts forward, finding new strength at being so close to his prey. A slight ringing bites into the back of my ears before I reluctantly start after him, taking up my place at his right side. I understand Raum's desperation to find Sebastian more quickly now. If another demon gets him before us, then Sebastian is lost—dead, marked, or possessed.

We *need* him.

I glance at Raum. The bond between us is where I draw the line. I will not be consumed by him.

The ground turns sopping wet. My boots suck and stick in the mud with obnoxious sounds that I know someone is going to hear.

I stop with Raum. Ahead of us, between the broken buildings, the ground looks like glass, a dark luminous mirror rippling under the stormy sky. It's shallow but the mass is unmistakable. It's water.

"Is that...?" I scan the definite line where land and water meet.

"Yes," he says, hushed.

The smell of the ocean coats the inside of my nose, opening my other senses. A fierce wind cuts through my clothes, slicing me to the bone. I shift Raum's weight against my aching shoulder. I can't support him much longer.

Raum's fingers brush the top of my thigh. When he turns to look at me, my worries give way to new confidence. The hard look in his eye is the only reassurance I need.

"Give me a knife," I say. I know he has one on him somewhere. "If we get separated, I'll need it in case one of them finds me."

"I'm not letting you out of my sight," he says. We hold eyes a moment longer before he concedes and hands me a blade from the pack. "Your mark will keep you safe."

I pull the blade sharply from his hand. "That worked so well last time," I snap.

Anxiety grips me despite my mantra of keeping a cool head. If we don't find Sebastian, we might not have a chance to face whatever *it* is, whatever is on the other side of that wall. I have a lot of faith when it comes to Raum's power, but I don't think it'll be enough should we be ambushed. This feels very much like a trap.

The knife is light with a short handle and a long, thin, flimsy blade. It's a skinning knife. I don't want to know how he came across it. It won't do well if I find need to use it.

We stop as we reach a crumbled gas station connected to an auto repair shop. The water gathers at the soles of our boots. We have to be careful to stay out of any demon's sight as well as Sebastian's. If he sees either of us, he will shoot. Deep in my bones, I know he won't miss his mark a second time.

Wait—

"You said he cut you. Is he out of ammunition?" I ask.

"Yes," Raum says quietly. "I doubt he will have found anything else. As far as I know, he only has a knife."

"What kind?"

Raum describes the blade to be approximately fifteen inches altogether with a thick antler handle. "The blade is long with similar lines like the one you carried."

"Damascus steel. Sounds like a bowie knife or maybe a short bolo." I glare at Raum. "It sounds like one of mine."

He shrugs. "I lost those."

"Did you?" As soon as I ask the question, I scoff. It doesn't matter. Sebastian is at least armed with one weapon more efficient than my own. He's probably had time to scavenge for others if the demons hadn't already cleared the ghost town. "Is this really all you have?" I turn the knife in my hand.

"Yes," he says.

Fuck.

We tread carefully. Raum has no trouble being soundless, but I have to make a conscious effort to walk heel to toe. Rubble and shards of metal scatter the streets beneath the water that make my path uneven.

Ahead, the dark wall glares back menacingly. How long before someone sees us?

I draw strength from Raum when he lends me his hand over crumpled bricks. I can practically taste Sebastian's blood on my tongue. I'd heard him cry out once before. I'd give anything to hear that sound again. There's something thrilling about the sound a man makes when he is afraid. It'll be sweeter once Raum's fangs are in him.

Raum throws his arm out in front of me, interrupting my train of thought. We're close. Is that a heartbeat I hear? The thrum of blood pounds in my ears, making my mouth wet. I crouch low and slip across the threshold of a cinderblock building.

The water is deeper in here, its murky red swirl coming up to my ankles. I allow my eyes to adjust to the change of light. It takes a moment for the shadows to clear, but papers float over the floor near an old telephone line and other office supplies. I signal to the cord for Raum to pull it free. He might need it to hold Sebastian. I hold up another finger to wait.

A tingling sensation runs down my spine as I work my way through the building. Sebastian escaped me once; he will not be as fortunate a second time. The longer I go without finding him, though, the more frustrated I become. Did we just miss him?

Stairs run up to another floor at the back of the building. Raum slinks toward their base, cocking his head to listen. I move past him, already knowing that he senses what we are looking for.

I test the weight of the first step. Like the others, the metal is rusted and broken. When it holds, I take the next and the next, testing each spot for weakness that might give off any sound. I crouch just under the top step and listen. Still nothing.

The air is stale. It's not your typical smell of mold, but something similar and much fouler. Sebastian can't have been here long, and if he is, he won't be able to stand it much longer. The burn of the air brings tears to my eyes. Raum's shadow slinks past me, melding into the blackness that blankets the room.

I take the shadows on the other side. Every hair on my body is erect with anticipation. He's close. I can feel him. I can smell the sweat on his skin—

"Sebastian," I whisper at the slightest bit of sound behind me.

Cool steel presses under my chin. A new sheen of sweat runs down the length of my spine. I tuck my knife against my arm, hiding it in case he hasn't seen it already. I'm quick, but I've never fought Sebastian, nor have I seen him in hand-to-hand combat. I suspect he is more skilled than I am considering he is ex-military.

The blade trembles against my neck.

"You're not real," I think he says.

I step back, pressing against his chest before turning. His blade doesn't follow, and he allows me to face him. I can't see him clearly, but I know it's him. I'd know the smell of him anywhere. Teak and sweat and fear.

Something pops between us and there's a loud hiss like an angry snake. The red light of the flare casts a demonic glow across his face, twisting his features into the monster he is about to become.

How weary he looks. His unshaven face, normally round and boyish despite his age, is gaunt by lack of food and rough weather. He looks older, the lines around his mouth more persistent, as well as the ones above his brow.

I turn the knife in my hand, pressing it against my palm as I slide it up his chest. The blade won't kill him, but if I nick him in the right spot, I can wound him for Raum to grab him.

"Leah," Sebastian breathes. "I killed you." All color drains from his sun-tanned face.

My name on his tongue does something to me. It's like a light turns on inside my head. Relief at seeing him makes a smile flutter over my lips. Then I remember why I'm here and absolute horror grips me.

His eyes flick across my face, and he takes a step back.

"Run," I say.

Sebastian's reflexes are rattlesnake quick. The blade flashes in front of my eyes when I stumble back. I throw my arm up as he follows me, letting the blade slice into my skin instead of my face. His face is twisted with rage, and he slashes again.

Behind him, Raum leaches from the shadows, seeping into the red glow like paint spilling. The light makes his eyes look like fire, hungry and burning. He is violent when he strikes.

Raum jerks the phone cord around Sebastian's neck, winding it around until the veins in his prey's neck expand. Sebastian's body goes rigid before he tries to stab Raum. He throws his knife back, hacking away at the shadows. With a fierce growl, Raum jerks the man away from me. The flare clatters to the ground.

I want to help, but for the first time, I don't know who I should save. I adjust my grip on the knife and shuffle forward, looking for any sort of opening.

Sebastian grunts and Raum lets out a vicious roar before he collapses, his knees cracking against the hard floor.

No.

Sebastian finds space and twists, freeing himself of the cord, and kicks Raum in the gut. Blinding rage shoots through me, narrowing my sight. He will not take him from me.

I fall onto Sebastian like a wild animal. I wrap my arms around his waist as I crash into him, pushing him into Raum. The demon's fingers slip into his waist band while his other hand grasps onto his shirt, pulling Sebastian down while I push from the other side.

Sebastian's blade sheaths into the corner of Raum's neck. Crimson paint spurts from the wound when he pulls it free, angling the blade down for another bite. Before he can find his mark, I thrust my knife under his shoulder blade with a wet crunch and climb higher, forcing his arms to fall out from beneath him. Raum twists with us, coiling around Sebastian like a snake, and fastens his mouth to his neck, puncturing the weak flesh with a satisfying pop.

A blood-curdling scream erupts through the air before Raum snatches Sebastian into the shadows.

Where did they go? I grab the flare, waving it through the darkness.

The burn of light sweeps across the ground, casting an eerie glow over their hulking forms. He holds the man firmly beneath him, so they are chest to chest. Sebastian's shirt has ridden up from the struggle, his back arches under the demon's white-knuckled grip wrapped around his wrists. Raum's mouth is no longer fastened over his neck like I expected it to be. Instead, his lips are pressed firmly to Sebastian's.

I don't know how demons possess their victims. With James, he had been consumed in the blink of an eye. There was no other demon in the room that I saw. One minute James's eyes were green and the next they were unforgiving black.

The circumstances were different, but they're exactly the same. I can feel the subtle change as Raum transfers from one body to the next through our bond. A scream wells in the back of Sebastian's throat, so much weaker than the first. He no longer struggles to push Raum's body off him. He pulls the demon's face closer, lacing his fingers between the hair and feathers at the back of his neck.

Confliction wars inside of me. The incessant ringing suddenly stops and the haze, though not physically there, lifts from my eyes. What am I doing?

I slam a fist into Raum's temple. A sharp pain erupts in the side of my head. I cringe and do it again.

"Raum!" I twist my grip on the knife. If I cut or stab him now, I could inadvertently hurt Sebastian. What have I done? I can't do this.

"Take me! Stop!" The words are forced from my throat. The back of my eyes sting like hot embers. I can't do this.

There is a slight break in their lips as Raum looks up at me. A twisted sneer turns the corner of his mouth up that makes my intestines curl. Beneath him, Sebastian tips his head back. His once brown eyes are surrounded by black clouds.

"Raum, stop!" I plead. "Please, take me."

He grins as he presses his lips back over Sebastian's. A thick smog seeps from the corners of his mouth that I couldn't see before. It passes between them like the plague Raum is. I hit him again, so hard that I stumble back as the shock of it rings through my own skull.

The body that was Raum's slumps forward. The wall chafes my back when I slide down to my butt. I clench the flare tighter, afraid of what will happen if I let them out of my sight. I force myself to watch it all, every jerk, every flex of their muscles. I did this, so I have to watch it.

Sebastian— Raum pushes the body that had been his to the side. Sebastian's body ripples and stretches as it adjusts to the intruder. It isn't until Sebastian's face starts to shift that I look away. I crawl toward Raum's old body on trembling limbs.

Whoever the man was is long dead. I hold my hand to his nose to be sure, and then press them against his neck. His features remain the same, stuck in Raum's image, but his sharp eyes are clear and amber. I touch his face gently, as a wave of guilt overcomes me.

A guttural moan stands every hair on my body upright. I lean over the body protectively before turning back. Sebastian is twice as big as he was when I knew him, the sleeves of his shirt are pulled tight, and his jeans have ridden up to his calves. When his eyes open, they are jet black.

"Sebastian," I whisper. I know he is gone even when I say his name.

Sebastian used to have a nice smile, one that could comfort you in the worst situation. It is nothing like that now. It twists at the corners and widens, altering to the laugh lines that belong to Raum.

"It's just me," Raum says.

I swallow thickly. I look between him and the body below me. I press my hand into the man's chest as I try to steady myself. Tears blur my vision, making it harder to see even if the flare wasn't dying. My hands skim down to his pants. I unfasten them before removing his boots.

Raum strips as I hold out the clothes. His fingers brush the top of my knuckles, releasing a stifled sob from my throat. He brushes his lips over each curve, in a caress, before pulling away to dress.

"Thank you."

I don't know whether he thanks me for the clothing or for helping murder the last person I cared about.

I stand and press myself against the farthest wall I can find in the dark. It doesn't take long for Raum to find me. His wicked presence washes over me like a downfall of water. From head to toe, I feel him rove over me, calling to me until I step forward against his chest and wrap my arms around him.

"You are free," he says, leaning back so he can press his new face against mine.

He runs his hands across my cheeks, through my hair, caressing me with the touch of an intimate lover as if he is experiencing me for the first time. I suppose in his new body he is. Do I feel different under Sebastian's skin?

I press into his hands, hating how I yearn for his touch.

"No, I'm not," I say softly.

A flash of white in the darkness is the only way I know he is smiling. "I promised it to you."

"You only told me so because you knew I would stay."

After James had been possessed, I abandoned him, not knowing that he was still a prisoner in his own body. Can I really leave Sebastian the same way? I don't love him, but I care for him, much like I know he does, or did, for me.

Raum's laugh is forbidden and dangerous. It's not until he speaks that my blood runs cold. What I can see of the world shifts, and I fall against his chest.

"Oh, Leah," he says with Sebastian's voice.

IV

Someone shakes me roughly from my sleep, throwing me from the darkness with a gasp. I reach for them, winding my fingers around strong biceps. Fragments of Sebastian's struggle come back to me, and I let go of Raum only to have him haul me back.

"Quiet," he hisses.

I stop struggling long enough to feel the presence of another demon. Demons, I correct myself. Wickedness stalks close. They don't appear to be inside yet, but somewhere preying outside the building. I press closer to Raum, holding my breath. Did they hear Sebastian's scream?

I look Raum over, but I can't tell whether Sebastian is still present or not. Perhaps I imagined his voice. The body looks like both of them now, man and monster. I've seen this before and I'll be damned if I go through it again.

Tears spring to my eyes. Raum looks back at me with fiery intensity. He shakes his head. "No," he mouths.

After several long minutes tick by, Raum softens against me. He presses his lips against my ear, whispering quietly so there isn't a chance anyone else will hear him. "Stay close." I open my mouth to say something, and he nips my ear. "Your voice will carry. I'll not let anything happen to you." He slides his nose against the side of my face and kisses me. It feels wrong, dirty.

I nod, ignoring the flicker that passes through his eyes. Raum or Sebastian?

There is no sign of the body Raum possessed before. I assume he ate it. It makes my skin crawl that he can discard something that had once been his so easily. At least there is no blood to draw the demons to us. The wound on my arm has already healed and, by the dampness of it, Raum has licked it clean.

The sky has lightened behind the thick cotton ball clouds. It would be easier to move under the cover of night, but staying longer puts us at risk of being found. Arm against arm, we move through the shadows, loping down the stairs and outside until we are retreating from the rubble and the ominous black wall.

The pressure of eyes bares against my back. Sweat holds my shirt tightly around my body. Raum grabs my arm, halting me in my tracks before I can jump. On impulse, I reach for my knife. The weight of Sebastian's larger blade meets my palm. Did Raum strap this to me? He straightens to his full height and takes a half step forward, so I am partially behind him.

The demons are closing in on us. Their power surrounds us from all angles. They've found us.

The first one to appear is a female with soil brown skin and bleach blonde braids that taper to her waist. Leather adorns her body, including wraps that run from her wrists to her elbows. The tops of her shoulders and sleeves are protected by what look to be scales. A nasty double-edged sword extends from her taut grip. It isn't unheard of that demons will take a female body, though it's rare. A man's body is better suited to accommodate their forms, but if the woman is exceptionally beautiful, like this one, they will take it. In the beginning, they weren't picky; they took what they could get. Once the demons gained total control, they became more selective with their hosts.

Two more demons flank either side of us and, by the prickle against the back of my neck, I count a fourth. By the flush and flawlessness of their skin, they are well fed. I might have bet against them had they looked a little more worn, but it appears whatever food they have in their fortress has kept them sustained.

"Who are you that comes to Pethaino?" the female asks. She looks Raum over slowly, her eyes taking in every single detail of him. Once she reaches his feet, she looks back to his face. Her eyes narrow.

"I have only come to retrieve something that belongs to me." Raum makes no motion, but I suspect he somehow signals to me because the female's eyes flick in my direction. Their assessment is not as thorough, and she turns quickly back to Raum. "Now that I have it, I mean to leave. It was by no disrespect that I came into your lands. If you will allow me to pass, I will bring no trouble to you and your king."

An air of deference creeps through his voice. Raum, mild? What is this? He might as well be showing them his throat.

"You may leave once the king has granted it," the female says. She looks at me once more then back to Raum, her lashes lowering then raising up as she gives him another once over. Does she really think she can take him?

Raum's lip curls. "Who is king?"

The demon lifts her chin a bit higher, and when she speaks it is with pride. "Orias of Eurynomos, King of Pethaino, the land where those who enter come to die." Her eyes narrow and her fist tightens on the hilt of her blade.

I sway against Raum. We'll never make it inside the gates alive.

A reassuring caress runs down my body like smooth hands. Raum flashes the female a broad smile and laughs. It barks out and then softens into the beautiful music demons make when they're happy.

"Tell Orias," he hisses the name, "that Raum of Eurynomos is outside his gates."

The female's brows furrow, her mouth presses together tightly. One of the male demons gives her a questionable look but no one moves. Raum's boldness comes back swiftly at their delay.

"I suspect you are not from the same court and that is the reason why you are unfamiliar with my name. I assure you, you will be in more trouble with me than Orias if you continue to delay. Fetch him. I'll wait." Raum wraps his hand around my neck. His touch of possession brings me the comfort I need to steady myself.

The female's stare hardens, but she nods to one of the demons. He takes off soundlessly, moving so fast the only thing I see of him is a black blur. "Your arrogance will cost you," she says.

Raum sneers. "As will your ignorance."

Tense silence surrounds us, pulling me closer to the edge. I turn slowly, looking over my shoulder to confirm that there is another demon at our backs. His body is that of an Asian man. He wears vambraces with daggers around his forearms and holds a curved sword in one hand with a hook on the end. He might have the smaller weapons, but they are some of the cruelest things I've ever seen.

Raum presses his lips against my ear, dropping his voice like before. "Orias served under me. There is nothing to fear. He will let us pass without trouble."

"Stop talking," the female snaps.

Anger flares inside my chest and I give her a sharp look. Her sword twitches, and she takes a half step forward only to stop abruptly when the demon she sent away materializes at her side. He glances at us before speaking softly to her.

An expression I can't name darts across her face, but like any good lady, she composes herself quickly. "My king will see you," she says smugly. "On the condition that you bring him an offering."

Raum's anger flares again. I clench my jaw to suppress a remark that will surely unleash the female's deadly hand. The way she holds her sword and keeps looking at me, she would like nothing more than to cut me down. I wince under the pressure of Raum's fingers as he tightens his grip.

"Myself," he says thinly.

The female looks at me again, but she doesn't say anything. I'm just as confused as she is. Why wouldn't he offer me?

The female leads with another male at her side while the other two walk behind us. Flashbacks of the last time we were in the company of this many demons screams red alert. I draw focus back to Raum's touch. He will keep me safe. Nothing like that will ever happen again, though I still can't remember the entirety of that night. Not how we were attacked, but why.

A horrible smell burns my nostrils as we draw closer to the wall. I pull the front of my shirt up, but it does nothing to suppress the smell of decay and rot. Between that, the heat and stench of the demons, and Raum's touch, I feel like I'm going to be sick. The weight of it all is overwhelming.

Towering iron gates swing inward as we approach. I jerk my head down as soon as I see what they're really made of. Bodies have been cast into the doors like they're a piece of artwork, each face contorted and broken, molded perfectly into an image of agony.

Try as I might, I can't disappear against Raum. His grip softens and his countenance falls void to all expression as the city opens to us.

The buildings are cast in the same black color that shines like onyx. The streets are dirt and stone, but clean. Everything is pristine and glistening despite its hideous appearance. I expected everything to be filthy, but in its own way Pethaino is as regal as any human kingdom I've seen in photos.

The path to the square is empty; dead trees with black vines line the walkway. As the trail widens, poles jut up from the ground, hundreds of them. They are decorated with both human and demonic heads. Or what I assume to be demons—I've never seen anything like it. I'd caught glimpses of their true face, leathery skin, and flashes of elongated maws. But none that were ever fully formed. The beasts look something between a wolf and wild boar with black leathery skin. Inside the gaping mouths are pointed teeth, and some have tusks curving up alongside the snout.

I think I speak for both of us when I say I'm scared. Raum's nostrils flare with uncertainty. Demons don't kill their own. They certainly don't flaunt it if they must.

Beyond the heads is a castle made of—

I stop dead in my tracks. "I'm not going in there." The female turns to look at us. I shake my head. I don't care what she thinks. "Raum, no. Do what you will to me, but don't make me go in there."

He frowns, looking between the castle and me. A low growl leaves his throat when the female opens up her mouth to speak. She shuts it quickly.

"Trust me," he whispers.

"It is swords and bones," I hiss.

And gore. The castle is a monstrosity crafted at the hands of pure evil. Marquette had been Leyak's playground. He made a small kingdom of his own in the little town of Michigan, but it was nothing like this. Every time I learned or saw something new from a demon it had always been more perverted than the last. It's no wonder this place still stands. There isn't a chance goodness could ever make it inside and, if it did, it'd suffocate before it had a chance to do any work.

I tear my eyes away. What I do notice, before my sole focus becomes the ground, is that every edge is sharp and pointed. Blades and sharpened bones thrust out on all ends, making the fortress look like a menacing rose bush. I have no doubt the dark coloring that makes the castle glisten is actually blood.

"Do you always let her speak out of turn?" the female growls.

"When it pleases me."

Raum gives the back of my neck a hard squeeze and pushes me forward.

I keep my eyes downward, watching my boots pass back and forth over marbled floors. Things move along the walls, but I'm not brave enough to see what they are. Their shadows scuttle in and out of my peripheral like spiders.

The air of the room we enter is much warmer than outside. The floor has shifted from black to charcoal stones. Heavy doors groan shut behind us, sealing in the hot air that causes a sweat to break out along my flesh.

"Thank you, Onna."

I look up at the baritone voice and follow it to who can only be Orias.

The demon reminds me of an Egyptian god. Like most demons, he doesn't wear jewelry; the dark bronze over his russet skin is the only adornment he needs. He is tall with a tapered waist and long, black hair that lies loose across his back in elegant waves with two braids over his chest. Aside from a sheer gold skirt, he is entirely bare, revealing muscles so well defined I wouldn't believe they were real if he wasn't standing in front of me.

He walks toward us. The hem of his wrap swaying against the ground gives the effect that he is floating. Raum meets him halfway. Both are tense and ready to fire faster than a hairpin trigger and then, they embrace. Orias is the first to smile, and he wraps his big arms around my demon. Raum presses his face into the crook of his neck.

"Raum," Orias says and pulls back. "I wondered if you would ever come to earth. My friend, brother," he corrects with a laugh. "It has been too long."

Raum smiles softly. "The days pass slowly here."

"Over a million years in Tartarus, was it?" He tsks. "Raum!" He says his name with such reverence, his voice drips with adoration. Orias glances at his guards, who have spread themselves along the back wall. "I hope Onna treated you fairly," he says.

"As best as she knew how. She is unaware of who I am," Raum says slowly.

Orias's upper lip curls. "Onna, you should recognize a king when you see one. Though your status was a bit of a secret," he says more quietly to Raum.

The female shifts slightly, as if she is unsure if she should continue to stand or kneel. In the end, she bends at the waist. "Forgive me, my lords."

I allow myself a brief glance around the room. It is round, surrounded by vast open windows. A high-back throne made of skulls sits at the head of the room. Rib bones fan out in the shape of a halo on the back. Above are weaponized rafters, spikes pointing downward. Seating sits behind them, just under the dome roof. My gaze drifts back to the demons where I find Orias is looking at me intently.

Hell's fury leaps into his eyes, and I lower my gaze. I find my knees stiffly, dropping to one and then the other. I'm sure he'd like me to sprawl out in front of him with my forehead to the ground, but that is something I won't do. There is still a little bit of defiance in me that I intend to keep.

"What is this?" Orias asks.

"Ozien," Raum says, using the demonic word for mine. "Or, Leah."

"Pretty thing," Orias says thinly. "But is this your offering? I have more than enough humans."

The familiar rise of Raum's temper lights within my chest. For the first time, his thoughts flow through me. He doesn't think he should have to offer Orias anything. Orias should be the one kneeling, offering his throat. The sweet flow of Sebastian's blood cuts across Raum's tongue in my own mouth when he bites down. I dig my nails into the hard floor as another wave of anger hits me.

"Would I not be better suited for you?" Raum purrs.

Orias's brow quirks before another wide smile splits across his face. He laughs. "Onna, take her to what is to be Raum's quarters." The weight of his eyes leaving me is such a relief that I let out a sigh. "I would never allow you into my service, though sitting at my side would be something to consider," Orias says quietly.

"There is an idea," Raum says. He gives a warning glance to Onna. "Let her kneel a bit longer. She's so pretty on her knees." Despite the heat that comes to my face, I thank him with a quick glance. He does not want me out of his sight.

"She is." Orias drops his voice. "I'll not deny you, but I would speak with you privately first. Just the two of us." His throat swells as a burst of air leaves it, making his words come out in a hiss.

Raum gives a curt nod. His upper lip moves as he runs his tongue over his teeth.

Onna jerks me to my feet roughly. I didn't even hear her come up. I let out a gasp and Raum turns sharply toward us.

"If I find any mark on her that has not been done by my own hand, I will kill you." Onna's gaze drifts to her king, but Raum's sharp command snaps her attention back to him. "Don't look at him, look at me," he growls.

Raum might have ruled before, but it is clear he doesn't now by the look on Orias's face. Either way, the king allows it to happen, though the tone of his voice is strained to retain some composure. "You heard him," he says. He tells Raum that I will be kept safe and sound.

The female bows stiffly, softening her grip. All I've wanted is to be away from Raum. Except, as Onna leads me out of the room, it is the last thing I could have ever wished for. This place is not safe. Every molecule in the air screams death, my death. I crane my head back to find Raum's gaze moving off me and refocusing on Orias.

Look at me, I say through the bond. I beg him to look at me, but he doesn't. Raum just smiles at the demon king.

V

Onna drags me through the castle with a grip that had hardened as soon as the doors closed behind us. Her long black nails scrape against my skin, threatening to break it if I try to flee. She doesn't have to worry about me running. I have no idea where I would go, much less if I would make it very far before a monster attacked me. I don't like my chances against anyone living inside Pethaino's walls.

The last thing I want is for my head to end up on one of the spikes. I touch my free hand to my collarbone on impulse. I know I'm only imagining it, but I can feel the cool kiss of steel against it.

The interior of the castle reflects much of the outside, built up with bones and blades. A string of fleshy lighting runs at the top of the molding. It looks like… entrails. As much as I want to look away, I cannot shy away from every bad thing that presents itself. I force myself to take in every detail of the halls. There might be need of the internal map I draw.

I hope we won't stay here too long. I doubt seeing an old friend will deter Raum from his path to Babel. He has been so persistent with his quest that we cannot waste time.

Onna shoves the butt of her sword in my back, sending me sprawling through a door. "Clumsy thing," she says as my knees make a loud smack on the floor. "You should be more careful."

I glower at her. Raum can only protect me so much, and not at all if we are parted.

"Enjoy your freedom while it lasts," she hisses.

If being Raum's companion is freedom then I fear what might become of me if we do extend our stay.

"When can I expect Raum?" I stand, keeping my face cool to hide the pain that is now radiating from my knees.

Her fist tightens over the hilt of her sword. A distinct tattoo covers her right hand. Five rings circle beneath each knuckle, save for the thumb and pinky that have some sort of rune on them. Triangles frame her knuckles with tiny dots within, and more lines stretch up her hand—which remind me of the outline of a fan—and end in various bands around her wrist that disappear beneath the sleeve of her armor.

"Whenever Orias releases him. Your master might let you speak freely, but in Pethaino it will cost you your tongue." She spits. A hefty wad of saliva splatters across the top of my boots.

"Wait!" I call as she grabs the handle. The door slams shut in my face before I can get any other word out.

A latch turns on the other side and then there is silence. I pull on the handle, knowing full well she has locked me in. I've got to get out of here. No. I'll wait for Raum and then we'll go. Everything is going to be alright. It will.

I slam my fist against the door. Raum had offered me freedom and now we are both prisoners.

A warm glow of fire comes from a dividing wall behind me. I pad around it to find two lounge-worthy couches and a fur rug facing the flames. Beyond all of that is a bed, big enough for at least ten people. Like the throne room, there are floor-to-ceiling windows along the back wall covered with black drapes that flutter in the wind.

Though the room is rich, it is more human than the rest of the castle. At least Orias and his people do not sleep in their murder. Still, there is no comfort in the space when I know what horrors lie outside of it.

Other than the cleanliness, another good thing about the space is that it has running water. To the left of the main room is a washroom dimly lit with the flickering light of maybe candles. I can't tell where the light actually comes from. The room is shaped like a cave with jagged stone walls. Water pours down from the top and filters over a small pool in the middle of the room.

I search the bedroom for something I can use as a weapon before bathing. It is better to be safe than sorry. Behind Hell's gates or not, I will not pass on an opportunity to wash.

I set a letter opener on a rocky shelf and strip. I stand under the fall and tip my head back. The water moves softly across my skin, wrapping and draping itself around my curves. I watch the transparent tendrils cut through the grime. It's warm. I could close my eyes and pretend to be somewhere safe, back in the compound before it burned. Before the blood.

I rub my palms over my face, digging crust out from my eyes and blowing the rest of the grime from my nose. It feels good to be clean. I could stay in here forever if this was a safe place.

A clear image slides into my head of Raum reclining on a leather couch and a woman with shaking hands holding a blade to his throat. I take a step forward as she slices the silver line up, stroking away the scruff on his chin. Her nostrils flare as she wipes the straight razor across a towel and attempts to steady her hand to do it again. I'm only vaguely aware that I am still in the pool, well away from Raum, because at this moment, I am seeing everything through his eyes. His stare frightens her, and that excites him. Her thin neck would be so easy to break. It's so close to his face when she leans forward, making sure she's gotten every hair, that I can hear her pulse.

On the last swipe of the blade, Raum snatches her wrist. A little squeak leaves her lips.

Behind her is Orias. He runs his long fingers through her muted straight hair. I try to look past him, but it's hard when Raum is so focused on the woman in front of him and the way Orias's fingers bring chills to her skin. There is movement in the background. Soft gasps and moans fill the room.

I take a step back to grip the edge of the pool's ledge and, somehow, it settles me deeper in Raum's conscience.

Orias pushes the woman forward so she is forced into Raum's lap. "Do you remember the old times?" he asks. The way he smiles is hopeful, wanting. I can smell the lust on him. It fills the air. Heated and metallic like freshly spilled blood.

"It has been a long time." Raum lets his gaze slide back to the woman.

My teeth ache, my whole body strains to tear into her. But before I can, before Raum can, Orias slides a broken talon down her neck, severing her carotid artery and spraying blood across Raum's freshly shaven face and chest.

Raum moans.

Orias pushes the woman to the side with a hard shove. Her body hits the ground without a sound. The king leans forward, pressing his weight on either side of Raum so they are barely touching. His need throbs against Raum's thigh, meeting his own.

Raum tilts his face up, his eyes slowly taking in Orias's long muscular build. When their eyes meet, every bit of my demon's blood flames. Orias bends his arms so he can move lower and lick the blood from Raum's face. Raum's appetite flares, and he grabs Orias by the chin, forcing a wicked smile out of the darker male as he pulls him down for a kiss.

Orias tastes like sweet fruit, but when Raum bites into the tongue he forces in his mouth, it is like fine wine. A sound, too animal to be human or demon, tears from the back of Orias's throat. He shifts forward and tries to straddle his prize, but Raum is faster. He pulls the king forward and slams his back into the flat of the lounge. He ignores the way Orias's claws slice his skin open, doesn't flinch when he sinks his teeth into his chest, his neck, and, once again, his mouth.

Raum's quick hand slides under Orias's wrap to his cock. It is when he touches him that Orias falls back, his blood-stained mouth gasping.

"Eager," Raum purrs.

"Impatient," he says. "You have made me wait long enough."

Raum brushes his lips across the demon's, but he doesn't kiss him. "What is waiting a little longer?"

Red flames spark behind Orias's eyes. His perfect, beautiful face twists into fury. He grabs the waistband of Raum's pants with one hand and the back of his head with the other, forcing their mouths together. His hands are as deft as Raum's, and he has his pants open and pushed down before Raum can stop him.

They are a force of power and rippling muscle. As much as Orias tries to gain the upper hand, Raum forces him down again with a shove against his shoulder and a firm hand pushing back on one of Orias's thighs.

Raum pushes me out with a very physical shove that makes my foot slip and nearly drops me under the water. I sputter, catching myself as the lower half of my face dips beneath the surface.

He has never done that before.

Shame, jealousy, but, most of all, desire runs through me. I don't know how long I stand there trying to gather my thoughts. They switch from anger to burning need and back again. I wash for a second time, trying to rid myself of the images he forced into my head.

What the fuck?

The bastard let me see through his eyes.

I pull myself from the water so quick that I almost don't register the heat that has crept into the air. In the next room is the presence of a demon. Its power ebbs softly, calling the shadows to it. I step around the corner slowly, peeking around the edge like a child trying to hide.

Raum is sprawled out on one of the sofas, sparkling clean. The vision was true. He's shaved Sebastian's face, revealing a stubborn chin. A black covering, similar to Orias's gold, sits low on his waist instead of the fitted jeans he had been in before. A long robe lies open across his shoulders, revealing soft skin, completely free of Orias's bites.

Between Sebastian's muddied traits and Raum's own, the demon is strikingly beautiful. A blank look covers his face like a mask the longer he stares into the fire. I take a half step forward, and he looks up.

The drum of my heart pounds through my ears, quickening when his eyes lower from my face. A sudden flick of heat curls between my legs and a sharp pull moves my feet toward him. He slides the robe away as I come to a stop before him and rises, slipping it across the back of my shoulders. Need and hunger run through me, sounding as loud as the bells going off inside my head.

"Were you trying to make me jealous?"

He grins. "Did it work?"

I lick my lips. "Should I be?"

His eyes, already glassy, glaze over. "Would it matter if I said I saved myself for you?"

A guttural sound sticks in the back of my throat and I am reaching for him.

In a swift motion, Raum scoops me up and carries me to the bed. I dig my nails into his shoulders when he sets me back. The quiet pop of his skin giving way to my nails is what makes me let him go. He slides us farther up, kicking one of my knees out as he does so.

There is no trace of the man he stole from, only the sharp features of a fallen angel. It's just Raum. There is no one else except Raum, beautifully wicked. Sinfully mine. All mine.

Warmth spreads throughout my entire body when he kisses me. It consumes me. Against any will of my own, I press against him, aligning our bodies together. When he breaks away and moves to my neck, I'm left gasping. I grab his face and pull it back to mine so I can kiss him again. Raum's lips turn up. He kisses back so hard that my lips part and he takes it as an opportunity to grab my lower lip between his sharp teeth.

Pain has never felt more satisfying than when it is inflicted by him. He makes it all worthwhile. Every bite and bruise sends a blushing wave through me. It pulls me deeper into his eternal darkness. I wrap around him as his power embraces me.

Relief floods through me as he enters me. He releases my lip to let out a quiet exhale as he slides in slowly, savoring me. I press my cheek against the side of his neck. He stills once he fills me entirely and lets out a low hum that reverberates against my face.

His lips press into the curve of my neck, parting slowly. Everything is so slow, so careful. I don't know what comes over me. I've never been one to initiate things between Raum and me. I might not have started it this time either, but I encourage him by grabbing his ass and pulling him against me.

Raum's bite is sharp and fast. I choke on my own breath, gasping as he withdraws and then violently slams into me. He reaches down and grabs my ass with both hands and lifts my hips up, allowing him to fuck me deeper. He ignores the sounds I make, perhaps mistaking them for noises of pleasure. Or maybe he doesn't care that he is hurting me.

I hold onto him tighter.

The pressure of his mouth withdraws and a steady flow of warmth spreads under my shoulder. The idea of laying in my own blood used to sicken me, frighten me even. Now, it is one of those things that leaves me breathless.

"Look at me," he growls.

I open my eyes I've narrowed shut. His lips are bright red with my essence. He flashes a sinister smile, knowing full well what I'm going to do before I do. His face swoops down to meet my kiss.

Raum comes, sending a painful jolt through me as he forces himself deeper than he should be able. I moan against his mouth, tighten my legs around his hips and find release in the pain he gives me.

I know what we've done is wrong, but I don't know why. The only thing I do know is that it feels right to be lying against him with my leg fit between his. The flow of his breath is a gentle lullaby that coaxes me to fall asleep where, for the first time in a long time, I don't have nightmares. I just dream.

I don't know what wakes me, but I sit up with a start. A low fire shines light across Raum bent over at the end of the bed. His fingers are white and tangled in his hair. I lean toward him. His taut back glistens with sweat.

"Raum." I brush his shoulder.

"Don't touch me," he snaps. He surges up from the bed so violently the headboard smacks against the wall.

My hand still hovers in the air where he had been moments ago. My fingers tremble.

"Sebastian," I whisper.

I thought he was gone. Dead.

He keeps his back to me as he leans against the mantle of the fireplace. Drops of sweat drop to the floor under his feet. Every muscle in his body shudders uncontrollably, spasming one after the other. I jump from the bed, disentangling myself from the sheets.

"Sebastian, look at me." I reach for him again, and he grabs my hand. I wince, making a little sound when he squeezes too hard. "Please."

He grabs my forearm with his other hand and slams me against the wall with enough force that my head throbs from the impact. It's Sebastian glaring at me, but he is struggling to maintain control. Even in his black eyes, I can see the war raging inside of him.

Sebastian presses against me and then, slowly, he slides down my body. The trail of his sweat along his hairline makes my stomach glisten. I tense as his hands slide down to cup the back of my calves. He squeezes hard. A shudder runs through his body and then he becomes utterly still. Tears splash between my toes when he starts to sob.

I stoop down and wrap my arms around him. It breaks my heart when he questions me. I don't have the voice to tell him because I too start to cry.

"Why? Why did you do this to me?"

Because I didn't want it to be me. The words are on the edge of my lips. I kiss the top of his head. "I'm sorry," I say instead. "I'm so sorry, Sebastian. Just stay with me."

He wraps his arms around my waist.

"After everything I did for you," he chokes.

I take more of him in my arms. "I know." I deserve whatever ill will befalls me in the future. If I died and

Raum brought me back ten times over, letting me live thousands of lives, it would never be enough time to repent for what I had done to Sebastian's family, and now him.

"I could kill you," he says.

I tense but I don't let him go. Instead, I hold onto him tighter. I shift so I am sitting on my bum, my legs partially wrapped around him. There are worse things to be afraid of than Sebastian. He slides his arm up around my back and leans into me.

We hold each other in our awkward half-kneeling, half-sprawled position for a long time before he finally composes himself.

"Sebastian?" I ask uncertainly.

"Still here," he croaks.

"Where is he?"

He shakes his head. "I don't know. He just stopped pushing all of the sudden."

I give a wry smile. Perhaps Raum is giving us space. Surely it isn't because Sebastian is strong enough to hold him off.

"Then let's take advantage of it." I pull Sebastian to his feet, drawing him to the bed. He pulls against me, and I run a smooth hand along his arm. "Just sit with me. Please?"

After a few seconds, he nods. He sits at the corner with his feet on the ground, staring listlessly toward the fire.

"Do you know where we are? Have you been aware of anything?" I want to ask him what happened after Onna took me away, but I'm more frightened if he knows what Raum and I did. How could I have forgotten about him when it is his face Raum contorts? His body.

I can't believe he is actually here. James was never able to break free for more than a few seconds. At least fifteen minutes has come and gone.

Raum is allowing this.

Sebastian nods. "Mostly. I can see and hear everything." He swallows thickly. "I can feel everything he does, the way he moves, his emotions. I feel all of it." He throws his head into his hands. "It feels like my head is on fire."

Which means Raum is more than likely listening to all of this, feeling this. I look at my palm on his knee. As if he hears my thoughts, Sebastian places his hand over mine. "I can feel the bond."

He still hasn't answered the question haunting me. I pause. "Everything?"

Sebastian's eyes snap up to mine. The tender-hearted man is replaced by one full of rage. "Yes. Could you not hear me screaming when he took you?"

A cold ache sweeps through my chest. Guilt is a powerful force, and when it takes me, it takes my breath with it. I pull my hand away and sit up a little straighter. If I had heard Sebastian, I ignored it. I didn't, though. The only thing I heard, could even think of, was Raum. Raum. Always Raum.

"Sebastian, I–" There is nothing I can say that will excuse what I've done.

He lies back against the bed, exhausted. His body shudders as the chill of his sweat starts to sink in. After a few moments, he says, "I hate you, Leah. I hate what he has made you. Is this how it's always been? That you're not even capable of doing anything outside of him?"

"I don't know–"

"You used me. And what's worse is that I know it won't be the last time this happens." He spits the last word out like it has a bitter taste.

"Sebastian, I begged him to take me instead," I say, exasperated. As if I have any right to defend my actions.

"You begged him only after it was too late to stop him. He would never take you when he had the opportunity to do this to me." He shakes his head before closing his eyes. "I hate you," he says again.

He holds up his hand when I try to speak. "But I… don't blame you. You don't have any control, and when you do…" He trails off, swallowing. His lashes flutter when he opens his eyes again.

"What is it?" I want to reach out to him to comfort him in some way, but I'm afraid if I touch him again, he'll hurt me. I wouldn't fight him if he did.

"I understand," he says thickly.

I shake my head. "You couldn't possibly understand what it's like. I don't know when it is me and when it isn't–"

"I killed Anna," he interjects.

I press my hand to my lips to stifle a gasp. Sebastian must hear it, though, because he winces. A ripple runs down his back, making his muscles tense.

"I think the demon that bit me was still a part of me. I felt hungry all the time. I couldn't feel him like I do Raum, but I wasn't myself. All I could think about was blood and Anna— Anna was so weak. I don't know how she lasted as long as she did, but I couldn't take it anymore. The sound of her breath growing fainter, looking at her— I just couldn't stand the sight of her. What was worse was the smell of her blood and how good it smelled. I wanted to hurt her," he growls.

Can demons actually do that? Tuck a piece of themselves away into a host? Is Eblis still a part of Sebastian even though Raum has possessed him?

"I saw her," I say quietly.

Sebastian rolls onto his stomach to look at me. "I don't know why I did it. I didn't even know what I was doing until she was already dead. I can't forgive you for everything you've done, but I understand what it's like to be hijacked. Even when he isn't manipulating you, he still has control."

I fidget with a seam on the bedspread. I can't believe this is what everything has boiled down to. Humans hurting each other with no path to forgiveness and yet we find a way to accept it anyway. I search the contours of Sebastian's face. If acceptance is what it takes to keep him, then I'll take it. I don't want to lose him. I think something inside of me will truly be broken if I do.

"Do you think he's still in you?"

Sebastian shakes his head. "Like I said, I couldn't actually feel him. I just feel Raum now. It's cramped in here."

I wouldn't wish this on my worst enemy and I had helped do it to someone I cared about.

"What happened to Devon?" I ask.

"She ran," he says hoarsely. "She was scouting when I killed Anna. When she saw what I did she just... ran."

My hips sink back as I slump forward. I open my mouth to bring it up and stop. He probably already knows. I doubt Raum would keep something like that from him. And if he doesn't, who am I to be the one to break it to him? He has the right to know. He knew Devon longer than I had, though I suspect us girls had been closer.

"She didn't make it," I say.

The line in Sebastian's jaw ticks. He clears his throat.

Sebastian slides up on the bed, allowing himself to get more comfortable. We lay side by side, staring back at each other. I wish I could say something to make everything alright. I miss the warm brown of his eyes, how kind they used to be. I know it is still Sebastian's body, but already his features have grown harder than when Raum first took him.

"I'm sorry," I say.

"I know you are."

"I'm not going to leave you," I say.

"Not while we're stuck here," he says bitterly. I wince. Sebastian's countenance shifts as his lids lower. "I can't tell if you mean me or him."

A sharp pain splinters across my heart. "You," I whisper. "I won't leave you, Sebastian. I did this to you." I lick my lips, trying to think of anything to say that might make the situation better. "I didn't think we would ever find you. I thought we might die before we did. If I had known you were still in there..."

Sebastian reaches toward me with a wry smile. "He wouldn't have let that happen. He would have jumped into you and found me anyway. You're strong, Leah, but Raum is stronger. There's nothing you could have done to stop him… from any of it."

I watch the rise and fall of Sebastian's chest, wondering how long it will be before that very demon bursts forth. I said I wouldn't leave Sebastian, but can I really go through this again? Can I watch a man lose himself a piece at a time as he is devoured from the inside out? If I stay, Raum will use me to break him.

"It's good to see you," Sebastian says.

I blink, coming out of my daze. "If the circumstances were different, I'd feel the same."

He doesn't say anything. I watch his hand move closer until his fingertips trace the top of my knuckles. He pulls back and then touches me again as if he is trying to test if I'm real or not. What is going to happen to us?

"He's coming back," he says suddenly.

I lace my fingers with his. "You can fight him. This is your body, not his, Sebastian. Do you hear me?"

Sebastian twists our fingers together. "I should tell you–"

Sebastian's whole body goes rigid and he breaks out into a sweat. The shallow breath in his lungs becomes ragged and strained. He groans my name, his eyes wide as he tries his best to focus on me.

"Stay with me," I say and sit up.

A deep arch curves his spine and then his body convulses. Thick veins stick out of his arms and throat, straining to burst from the thin layer of skin. He throws his head into my chest. I wrap my arms around him as man and monster struggle. Who is going to surface? Involuntarily, tears leak down my face as I tighten my hold, willing Sebastian to stay.

Warm lips skim across my collarbone. I run my fingers through his hair and kiss the top of his head. They've stopped fighting. I sigh as he wraps his arm around me, pulling me closer. The press of his lips becomes more insistent. They creep up to the side of my neck. A sharp pinch touches the hollow of my throat.

Raum.

I disentangle myself as he chuckles.

"Stop," he hisses.

I shudder, chills sprouting along my skin.

"Do you not want him?" The brush of his nose against my throat catches my breath.

"I don't want *you*," I snap.

Raum tsks and presses his face against my cheek. His fingers work their way across my back.

"Raum," I say thickly.

Raum slides his hand to the front of my shoulder and pushes me on my back. His dark eyes envelop me, sending pools of heat to the top of my cheeks. "The last time you said my name like that, I marked you," he says coolly. "Do not be upset with me, Leah. Revel in me."

"You knew what Leyak did to me, and you did it yourself." I hate the way my voice trembles. "You used me."

"As much as you used Sebastian," he sneers.

I've always known that a demon can't be trusted, not even Raum. Yet I never expected him to control me in such a way. Influence me, maybe. But he knew that I would never give into him willingly while Sebastian was still present. He took the knowledge from me, wiping the man from my memory long enough that I would succumb to him. He must have.

I shove against him and his muscles tighten, constricting like the snake he is.

"I am not Leyak and neither is he James," Raum growls. Steam comes from his lips when he speaks. "They are both dead, and you belong to me. As does this body and the man inside of it."

"Do you hear yourself? You're exactly like Leyak," I choke. "You're the devil himself."

Raum growls a warning. "Do not fight me. I promise you that this body will not be shared for much longer. Very soon, it will just be us again." Raum's tongue flicks across my ear and he hisses. "Just us, Ozien."

God help me.

VI

Cold. It slides into my warm veins, creeping and crawling its way toward my heart like a spider. Thin tendrils fan out over my limbs, smothering me with its weight. It's not until the cold touches my lips that I realize I'm not dreaming. I open my eyes, but that is the only thing I can do. Whatever *thing* was in my nightmare has followed me into the real world and holds me down. Except I can't see anything either. There's nothing but empty air above me.

My fingers twitch as I try to reach for Raum. The rise and fall of his chest brushes against my side. I can't move.

The cold retreats from my lips and, suddenly, I can breathe easier. I try to call for Raum but only a white puff of fog escapes.

Whatever is holding me isn't physically here. Not that I can tell, at least, and ghosts aren't real. Once someone dies, they're dead. They don't go straight to Heaven or Hell. Even if they did, according to Raum, Heaven no longer exists.

Leyak told me that the dead fall into a type of sleep. Being as it were, there is no rest for those who die. The demons have done a fine job in culling us so that there isn't a chance we will find peace once we're dead. I believe him. After all, when I died, there was nothing.

Another reason I know ghosts don't exist is because Leyak taunted James and me in the way that ghosts are said to do. I didn't know that hauntings were a sign of a demon intrusion at the time. Slamming doors, footsteps, hurling dishes—they were all pranks Leyak played before possessing my boyfriend.

I crane my head forward the best I can before it starts to hurt. Whatever has me is strong. I scan the room, straining my eyes past the edge of the bed, over the fireplace and sitting area, the cavern that leads to the waterfall.

My heart skips a beat.

There, across the floor, in the shadows of the cave, is a ghastly face. Gray peeling skin and hollow eyes with a mouth gaping in a silent scream. Fear. Panic. Run! I grip something beside me as the mouth widens further to reveal rotting gums. A scream of my own rises in the back of my throat when the face whips back in a curl of smoke.

Raum slides his hand over mine that has latched onto his thigh. I look down long enough to pull my nails from his skin, but by the time I look back, the monstrosity that was lurking is gone.

The weight peels away from my body and I lurch forward. "What was that?" I gasp.

"A wraith," Raum says quietly.

Too quiet. I press into his chest as he sits up behind me.

"What?"

"A spy." Raum slides away, more eager to search the shadows than I am.

I palm the kukri Raum must have slipped by my bedside during the night. Whatever that thing was, I hardly think a blade will hurt it, but I feel safer with the weight in my hand.

"It is gone," he says, reemerging. "It seems Orias is the jealous type, too."

I twist the hilt in my hand. This isn't a time to jest. "What's a wraith?"

"What is left of a human soul after it has perished and a demon latches onto it. A ghost."

"Ghosts aren't real," I say. Chills spread across my arms.

Raum shrugs. "Not really, but a wraith is as close to one as you can get. They are not the person they were when they died, rather mindless spirits that only last a few minutes before evaporating."

"Why would Orias send a spy? Doesn't he trust you?"

"I do not know what is going through Orias's mind. If he is the one that sent the wraith, I am insulted, but I cannot accuse him blindly." He throws a dark look across my body.

Heat touches the top of my cheeks and I look around until I can find the robe and dress. "Because of the courtyard?"

Raum nods.

"What were those things, next to the human heads? Are those demons?"

"Yes," he says after a long pause.

It's hard to imagine Raum looking like one of those beasts when he is so beautiful. I know he is a monster; I've seen his fingers turn into talons, seen the fire within his eyes as real as any flame. Even though he is a mockery of Sebastian's image, he is still striking. That's not to say Sebastian wasn't attractive on his own.

"What do you think they did?"

"I do not know. It is why I do not want to approach him about the wraith, though it is unsettling."

I scoff. "I didn't think anything unsettled you."

He looks around the room, slowly inspecting everything. If Raum is afraid, I don't catch it. The only fear I feel, I think is my own. "What happened after Onna took me away?"

The corner of Raum's mouth twitches. "He wants to know what brought me to Pethaino and why the only company I keep is a woman."

The twitch in his mouth isn't one of amusement by the hollow tone of his voice.

"Sebastian said–"

"Sebastian is not here," he snaps.

I dismiss the pang that pierces my chest.

"Burns."

"What?"

"He wanted you to know that Pethaino was Burns." He gives me a pointed look. "That is what he tried to tell you."

The name sounds familiar but, for the life of me, I can't remember why. "What does that have to do with anything?"

Raum shrugs. "Whatever he meant by it, I have already erased it," he says coolly.

I find it highly unlikely that, with the way things played out, Raum was able to erase Sebastian overnight. It would be foolish to keep my hopes up. Even more foolish to believe anything that comes out of Raum's mouth. Better to be indifferent and try to pull Sebastian out of him later.

"What?" I didn't catch what he mumbled under his breath.

"It has been a long time since I have seen another from my court."

"What do you mean?" I ask.

"There are five kingdoms in Tartarus; each has its own court," he says.

Whenever I've imagined Hell, I've always thought it to be run by a red devil with horns and a pitchfork, not five kingdoms. Is it all fire and brimstone? I wonder if the demons are trying to turn Earth into another inferno.

Isn't Tartarus another version of Hell? Are they the same?

"The way you make yourselves out to be royalty is appalling."

"We are royalty."

"Just because you wear a crown doesn't make you a king," I say bitterly.

"The only crown I wear are my feathers." He takes another glance across the ceiling. "You did well in front of him last night." His lids fall as he grazes over me.

"It's not the first time I've been in front of a demon *king*." I scoff.

"You've never shown me respect," he says irritably.

I roll my eyes. "I didn't know your status, not that it would have changed anything. I knew out there," I nod toward the windows, "I maybe had a chance. In here, I don't. Besides, it is not respect. It's survival."

"You never had a chance, not after I found you." He turns away. "Do not worry too much. Our time here is brief."

That offers me little reassurance. I can't forget everything I saw last night and that, somehow, I feel we are now trapped. Sunlight filters through the dense clouds, shedding muddied light into the room. I hardly think a bit of sunshine will be enough to burn the darkness from this place.

A band of gold cuts across Raum's face, highlighting an eerie shadow behind his eyes. His nostrils flare and his head whips around so quickly the pop of his vertebrae snapping echoes across the room.

"Cover yourself," he hisses.

Raum turns for the door, not bothering to dress himself. He runs a hand over his mouth, leaving a red smudge across his lips and chin. I tie my sash tight across my stomach just as he swings the door open.

Onna's long braids spill across her shoulders as she bows. The mock gesture makes my lips curl. It's as clear as day that she doesn't respect Raum as a king, and if she does, he is not *her* king. I can see it in the stiffness of her spine, the way she comes up too quick like she's done a bend and snap. The audacity.

"What is this?" Raum growls.

A smirk tugs at my lips until I realize it's not Onna he is addressing. My mouth falls with my heart to my stomach as the familiar face turns toward my intake of breath.

I know why the true name of the city is so familiar to me. I recognize the demon behind Onna with the sharp face and the cruel jet-black eyes that should be brown. The twisted line of his mouth is natural, not one that has been shaped by a demon.

But the man I recognize him to be is dead.

Liam came from Burns. He showed me the brand that covered the mark on the inside of his arm, a token left by the demon that tried to bind him. How did he make it back here if Raum killed him?

"Orias requests your presence," Onna says, interrupting the name on my lips. Her eyes graze Raum, taking their time to wind their way up his naked body. She is nothing if not appreciative.

"He could not come himself?" There is a playfulness in his voice he only gets when he is being coy. I'd be peeved if I wasn't so focused on Liam, who has also not taken his eyes from me since I recognized him.

Onna looks at the space between them. Her shoulders straighten. "No, but he would see you at once."

Raum holds her eyes a bit longer before nodding. A smirk plays at the corner of his mouth. "He will have to wait a little longer. There is something I have to finish." The last of his words come off as a purr, sounding sultrier than animal. A growl to mask the anger burning inside his chest.

I finger the fabric over my chest to steady myself.

Onna's upper lip curls. "Is it so important?"

"Onna," Liam whispers, hisses. His voice is different, smooth, and deep. He slides a hand over her shoulder and gives it a little squeeze. "Orias will not miss a few minutes." It's not until then that he finally looks away from me and directs his gaze to Raum. "Do be quick."

A flash of Onna's teeth lengthening flashes before Raum slams the door in her face.

He holds up a hand before I can speak. I stay at his heels as he crosses the room and tosses folded clothes at me from the floor. All the questions I have are starting to ache in the back of my throat.

"Hide a smaller blade beneath your clothes," he instructs as he starts to dress.

I have one leg into a pair of pants when he tosses a bag to me from his pocket. But the bag—my bag—is too large to have fit there in the first place. As soon as I'm dressed, I fish out my karambit and slide the sheath between my skin and waistband. It's not ideal if I must use it, but giving me a weapon of any kind will show too much favor, and that is something we can't risk.

The pressure eases in the room and with it comes my voice. "I thought you killed him," I say.

"I did."

"Then what is he doing here?"

"It is not him," Raum snaps.

"Who else could it be?" I thrust my hand through the leather sleeve of my jacket. "Liam is from Burns. That's why Sebastian recognized it. What is this place? Really?"

Raum attaches the kukri at his hip. He doesn't need a weapon, but if I do, it'll be another he can toss to me quickly. There is something profound in the gesture that makes the dread of Pethaino sink even deeper.

"Let us find out."

No pleasantries are exchanged when we meet our escorts outside the door. Onna's rage is palpable, but whatever Liam might have said to her keeps her tongue behind her teeth. Chills run down my spine as Liam's imposter takes up the rear.

Raum is right. Whoever the man was before isn't Liam. He has a distinctive scar across his brow that Liam never had. Demons don't scar. Aside from that and the black eyes, they're identical. Twins perhaps. Liam said he killed the demon that tried to mark him, but what if he failed? Is it really the body of his brother walking behind me, or a demon so obsessed he kept the face of the one that got away?

A giant spiral staircase rises out of the shadows of the castle, shining like oil in the inky blackness. I lose track of Onna as we follow her up, her skin and armor so dark she blends right in. I slide a tight grip up the railing as I search for her. There are enemies everywhere, but it bothers me more when I cannot see them. Light glints from a small crack in the wall, highlighting her blonde hair well above us.

At the end of a small walkway is a steel door with a carved snake eating its tail. Onna places her hand in the center of the circle, her long fingers splayed. She hisses. The sound is like a melody that moves through the air as a dark song, first light and then the sound grows deeper. The ouroboros turns, the fangs clamping tighter over its tail.

There is nothing on this floor other than the door. I glance at the bare walls, windowless. The source of light comes from an invisible source. A ripple runs through the pale light, shifting it to red as a loud crack shocks the air. The door opens, letting a blue haze spill across the floor.

The stench of the city hurdles into our small space like a rocket. I wretch behind my hand and turn away.

How does the smell of Pethaino get worse the longer we are here? The potency of it is enough to choke a horse. The taste of rot makes my eyes water.

Light stretches to the end of a hallway with an arched doorway. At the end of it stands Orias. I follow Raum hesitantly when the king turns his hand out to us, motioning Raum to come forward.

I have a distinct feeling of the walls closing in on us as soon as we step in Orias's presence. Liam follows me, his chest close enough that I can feel his heat against my back. Are they leading us to our deaths? Raum's mental touch catches my thoughts before they can run away from me. Another strong wind wraps around us, only this time it is laced with salt. I recognize the smell. It's impossible.

Raum stops as soon as he reaches Orias's side. What is it? I crane my head, but I can't see anything around their broad figures. There's a shallow wall, but what's over it?

"I wanted to surprise you," Orias says.

"What have you done?" Raum brings voice to my own question. He steps forward slowly, his body taut with controlled energy. I sense a trap, but as far as I can tell, Orias and our escorts are at ease. There are no other guards with us.

"Last night you said you sought Babel." Orias extends his hand toward a shallow wall. "I am bringing Babel to us."

Adrenaline floods my system. The heat I felt at my back spreads through every inch of my body, gathering beads of sweat across my brow. It feels like my heart is about to explode. If this cursed place didn't have its claws in us before, it does now.

I force a place between the two demons.

Outside the high walls of Pethaino is water. The sand and stone of the desert has been covered by black waters that give way to pink-tinged waves. It is the ocean, but like everything else, it has been polluted by the touch of demons. Farther down, closer to the walls, I can finally see where the smell of the city comes from.

We are not so high up that I can't make out that the mounds lining the shore are sharks and whales. Smaller sea life is scattered between the bodies, crushed under the weight of the larger animals.

Before the plagues, I'd been going to school to work with these creatures, to be a voice that might save them. It was for nothing. Humans hack away at the carcasses. They are mortal; a demon would never do slave's work. They cut the fins from the sharks and toss them into broad carts that someone else hauls away. The whales and porpoises are stripped of their gray hides.

The bees' return had been a cruel trick.

"What have you done?" I reiterate Raum's question.

A dark presence presses on either side of me. Their arms brushing against mine, pinning me between their power. The murky pools of the king's eyes are full of laughter when he looks at me, yet his smile remains cruel.

"The water was poison to us. Their blood purifies it and gives us the power to shift the tides." Orias looks over me to Raum. "Are you pleased?"

I close my eyes repeatedly, wishing this nightmare to be over. Birds circle overhead, their cries mocking me. They're all crows. Their hideous caws rise into one voice and let out a blood-curdling cry. One lands among hundreds and begins to tear savagely at the hide of a shark.

This is not what life is supposed to be. None of this should have happened, yet we had all the warning signs. What did we do to deserve this?

The world tilts. I lean forward, pressing myself between the banister and Raum. The smell is stronger now that I can see where it comes from. The taste of stale blood and salt burn the back of my tongue. This isn't happening. The demons are supposed to be dying. The bees came back.

A low growl rumbles in Raum's chest. "You have done this on your own."

"Pethaino shares power. It is why we are one of the last kingdoms that still stands. You said all others were falling." Orias nods toward the water. "Not us. Once Babel is within reach, our power will be limitless."

"How long until you have it?" Raum asks thinly.

Raum didn't expect anyone else to go after Babel. There is no one more ambitious than him. Or so he thought. Orias is no longer the young guard that served beneath Raum. He is older, wiser, and more powerful. His entire existence is an omen.

The thoughts fade from my mind as soon as Orias touches me. He plucks a strand of my hair from my shoulder and turns it between his thumb and index.

"Soon, but sooner if you would lend your hand." That sounds like more of a question. Orias looks up at Raum with a hopeful gaze.

Raum smirks. "That is something to consider." He isn't taking the bait. The only thing he bites is the outside of his tongue. I can taste the metallic flow of blood in my mouth.

The upturn of his lip falters when he notices Orias's hand in my hair and how the other has made its way to my shoulder. I forgive Raum for everything as Orias pulls me back into his chest. The demon king leans down. His long hair tickles the side of my face when he turns toward me.

He groans on an inhale. "Surely this is not worth more than the city you seek," he says.

Raum runs his tongue across his teeth, extending his lip. He flashes Orias a dangerous smile. "Nothing is worth more than Babel. Not even you, brother. Choose your threats wisely."

Orias laughs and squeezes my shoulder. He releases me quickly and sidesteps, slinging an arm over Raum's shoulders. "You have not changed a bit."

Raum looks down at his hand, but he doesn't return the touch.

Orias sucks the back of his teeth and steps away from Raum. "Think of what we could do together," he says, his voice lighter than the darkness in his eyes. "It is only through unity and the utmost care that we can do this," he waves his hand to the horizon, "lest we flood Pethaino or Babel itself." He thrusts his chin out in the direction of the workers below. "Legion!" His voice is powerful enough that it takes no more than two seconds for every head to turn and look up at the tower.

Orias raises his hand toward the ocean. When he speaks, it is with the voice of many. Throughout the kingdom I can feel the voices coming forward, strengthening the vibration that hums in Orias's command. Onna's rises behind his, adding strength to the growing power in the air.

The words are unfamiliar to me, but their meaning is clear. The waters shift with a thunderous roar. On the horizon forms a great mountain; it rises higher the closer it draws to Pethaino.

A dagger pierces both sides of my skull. That is what the sound feels like as it crashes against me. I fall to my knees and clamp my hands over my head. The closer the wave draws, the more intense the pain. I fall on my face as wetness spreads beneath my palms.

I've never been one for prayer. I never thought about God until after Sin and, even then, it was not often. Raum told me once that God no longer existed. Call it human nature or desperation, I pray. I cry out in anguish so fierce that not even Raum can protect me from it.

A jolt rips through the tower. As the last of the tremors subsides, so does the pain in my head. I roll on my side. Raum's gaze is transfixed by the water on the horizon. Onna wears a satisfied smirk on her face, though she too looks straight ahead. Liam's imposter has moved closer to me, his stance broad, protective.

I sit forward, leaning against Raum's leg. Invisible hands move over my body, searching, caressing. I brush them away but there is nothing there. Raum glances down at me as I struggle to my feet with an unreadable countenance.

I know my ears are bleeding before I see the blood on my fingers.

"You have exceeded any expectations I might have had for you." Raum looks at Orias with true appreciation.

The shoreline has receded, giving way to another foot of ocean. The carcasses along the beach and rubble are piled on top of each other now. Some of the workers have been pulled into the surf. Their arms thrash as they try to swim back to the shore.

"It has always been my desire to please you," Orias says slowly. He looks at Raum under his long-curled lashes. There is something mischievous about him, like a cat playing with a mouse.

Raum looks him over then back toward the water. "First threats, now flatteries." His brow arches but he smirks, easing the tension that has been building between them.

"I'd like both of you to join me over the next few days. I trust your judgment, Raum, and I'd like your opinions on this kingdom I have built," Orias says.

It is important to know that no demon can be trusted. What throws my guard up is that Orias wants me to accompany wherever it is Raum goes. While Raum is entitled to drag me wherever he pleases, it is a surprise Orias would extend any sort of courtesy to me.

Raum tips his head. "It would be an honor."

He is up to something. Surely, Raum hasn't become stupid.

"Clean her up. You can follow me as soon as she is presentable," Orias says. He reaches out and swipes a string of blood from the side of my face.

I look back as Raum leads me through the other side of the threshold. Orias rubs my blood between his fingertips before sticking them into his mouth. He sucks them clean, tonguing the ruby smear. I look away as his eyes come up to meet mine, but I see the way he looks at me. There is hunger in Orias's eyes.

VII

Our tour of the city leads us back through the courtyard of heads. They're even more gruesome in the brighter light. Most of the eyes have been pecked clean, while others, the fresher ones, are bloated and white. Something wet drops on the top of my head. I brush the blood off quickly, not wanting to offend Orias by getting dirty.

Pethaino is more expansive than I originally thought. If I had to guess, it is about the same size of Boise. It is demon-made after all; the crude walls and monstrous buildings are in no way of human design, though previous buildings lay scattered throughout. Spikes line the interior of the walls that have smaller thorny points protruding from them. There is no way to climb the wall without tearing yourself apart. Remains of people who tried are wedged within the tight spaces.

Unlike a normal city or kingdom, Pethaino is not made up of homes or markets. Instead, there are torture chambers. Everything from medieval torture devices to modern man techniques flood my senses. I've never smelled so much blood before. The rich metallic smell goes straight to my head.

One of the more gruesome sights is a woman bent over a stock, her back cracked open and ribs splayed out like wings. A faint moan leaves her lips. I look away. How is she still alive? Someone laughs, and I look back to see two male demons touching her crudely. Marked and suffering, that's the only way she could survive.

"This is everything America should have been," Orias says. "Fotia was like this, Tan's kingdom in Africa, until they started to fall." Orias tsks as he leads us farther down the strip. "They continue to hold power there, but they have weakened. Once we claim Babel, we can aid them. We can restore our power across the whole world."

"You never struck me as one to share," Raum teases.

"I am willing to do anything if it means restoring order," Orias says.

Raum nods in agreement. He takes everything in, his eyes roving over every dirty weapon and carcass that we pass. I hate the look of excitement on his face, the way his nostrils flare to get a better scent of death.

The more gruesome the sight becomes, the calmer I feel. Intrigued even. I don't even consider what's happening until I see a young man strung up. I pause and look up at the dangling feet. Raum has me under his influence, I realize. He must be doing something, or I'm going into shock. I feel like I'm on autopilot as I reach up and brush the toes of the boy.

I know that this is horrible and that a normal reaction would be to scream and sob, but I feel nothing. The back of my neck tingles and I pull my hand away.

Orias has stopped walking. There is a curious look on his face, his lips plump and parted to make a little "o".

"I wish you wouldn't impress yourself on her," Orias says. "I would like to hear her scream."

Raum takes a couple more steps before turning to us. The change in the air is so drastic that my eyes burn. Tears well up in my eyes as the surge of my own emotions assault me. I feel Raum looking at me, can even feel Orias still staring at me, but the only thing I see is a man that's been torn in half just over Orias's shoulder.

It's not real, I tell myself. *Don't cry. It's not real. Don't cry.*

Don't. Scream.

I tear my eyes away from the man and stare directly into Orias's empty black orbs. I can feel the body of the child hanging somewhere beside me, but I ignore that, too. I must.

"Will you not mourn for your own kind?" Orias taunts.

The only thing that comes out of my mouth is the breath I've been holding. It bursts from my lips and moves the hair beside his face as he bends down. A wave of strength runs through me.

"There is nothing left to mourn," I say. They're only bodies, empty shells.

Orias watches my mouth when I speak. "You're exactly right." He grabs my lower lip between his thumb and knuckles and gives it a gentle pull. "I bet you look so pretty on the inside."

I jerk my face away at the flash of an image of my skin being flayed. Leyak could project impressions on me the same way. There is something vulgar and sexual in the way he looks at me when the image pulls away. I don't doubt that Orias would enjoy hurting me.

"Dagon," he barks, making me flinch. "I think she'd enjoy the aviary." The mere suggestion that I might enjoy anything he proposes makes me more fearful. "There is something I want to show Raum without her eyes." It's a command and suggestion at once.

The imposter's sudden grip on my elbow startles me. A moment of panic strikes a chord within me as the two kings and their escort turn away. Raum's back stiffens, but he doesn't reprimand Dagon touching me or comment on the way Orias has addressed him.

The unfamiliar heat of the demon brushes against me as Dagon draws closer. A strange part of me wants to turn around and throw my arms around his neck.

"You know me," Dagon says once the others are out of earshot.

I turn slowly. "Liam?" I know it's not him, but what's the harm in asking?

The stern countenance falters. Recognition, maybe, passes through what I imagine were once brown eyes.

"He was my brother—William's brother," Dagon corrects quickly.

I follow his gaze to the demons who have long disappeared from view.

"Twins?" I choke.

He nods.

So, Liam really is dead. I knew it to be true, but seeing Dagon gave me a sliver of hope that maybe, just maybe, Raum had spared him.

"Is he alive?"

"No," I say softly, turning back to him. "That's why we were so angry to see you." Angry? I meant to say surprised, but it had been anger I felt seeing his face. I realize it's not just his heat I'm feeling but that same fury boiling in my blood.

Dagon takes a step back to look me up and down. After a few heartbeats, he exhales and begins to circle me. I turn with him, not wanting to leave my back unguarded. He stalks me, his shoulders hunched, chin lowered, and turns so his throat is exposed. I've seen animals do the same thing when in submission.

"How far did he make it?"

"Boise," I say hesitantly. What game is he playing?

"Was it quick?"

"What does it matter? One less human the better."

Dagon whips his head around, his body following, and gravitates toward me, almost as if he floats over the ground to close the distance between us. On reflex, I prepare for some sort of blow and widen my stance. My fingers twitch for the blade hidden beneath my shirt.

"I am the one that helped him escape," he hisses. I gag at his rank breath and turn my face away. "I bit him to save him."

"Your venom damns us," I snap.

"I gave him freedom–"

"And it drove him mad. I knew him for a very short time and even I could see it. I don't know what you did that kept his eyes clear or so he wasn't bonded to you, but you damned him all the same." It takes everything in me to keep my palm pressed against my thigh. I can't reach for my blade; I can't hurt him as much as I would like to.

Dagon grabs my elbow sharply. "Let me show you the mercy I gave him." He snaps his pointed teeth in my face.

"He said he killed you." I jerk my arm back, but his grip doesn't budge.

"That is what I told them to say." He hauls me forward, pushing me in front of him so I can't stop.

What reminds me of a massive bird cage sits just around the bend Orias and Raum disappeared to. What makes the aviary so striking, and in fact beautiful, is the stained glass between the iron bars that make up the structure. Flashes of gold, blue, and even pink are some of the vibrant colors glinting in the rainbow. We stop just in front of a red door with a smiling angel that bears a bright halo around its upturned face.

I look at Dagon hesitantly. "Let the child of God enter first," he says and lets me go.

I take a step back, two down the twenty we walked to get here. This isn't right. This place doesn't belong here and. though I've yet to decide if I believe in God or not, something about it feels blasphemous. I have no desire to set foot inside.

"They're watching," Dagon prompts.

I have felt eyes on me the entire time I've been here, but maybe he means something else. I call Raum's name silently, but if he hears me, there is no response.

The door is cool beneath my hands. It swings delicately on pristine brass hinges to a sight that I find, truthfully, stunning. Angels fill the space beneath a ceiling painted with blue skies and stark white clouds. Each one different than the next. Some have two white wings, while others have four or even six of different patterns and colors. Their skin is like porcelain. Even those of darker complexions are ashen and pale.

And then the truth sets in.

The mouths that are open in what I thought to be song are silent screams. The wings all different, some too small to suspend the much larger bodies. They've been sewn crudely into their backs.

"God says those in His image hold power over the stars, those fallen and still shining bright as day. So, we gave them wings that they might soar higher than the eagles," Dagon says.

He brushes his shoulder against mine when I go to turn away, pointing. "There, you see the one with osprey wings, the one with the long blonde hair? That's our sister. The rest are everyone who fought back and tried to escape. These are the bravest."

There is no mistaking the fair woman is related to Liam and his brother with her light brown eyes and strong jawline. Her dirty blonde hair ripples out behind her, held up by some invisible breeze. Four powerful wings extending from her back make her look almost elegant, but her legs are pulled up like she is jumping away from something.

"This is what I spared Liam from becoming."

I have no doubt Liam fought for his life in this place. There was a natural cruelty to him that refused to be broken. How Dagon convinced him to be bitten is still beyond me.

This is one of the more disturbing installations I've come across. Flashes of the zoo in Boise come to mind but this—this takes the cake. No words come to my tongue when I open my mouth to respond. It's ungodly, evil.

"I'm not so sure what we have been doing is the right thing."

I blink out of my daze and turn to Dagon. "What did you say?"

"Some of us are looking for forgiveness," he whispers.

I can't tell if this is just another trick or if he is being serious. "What game is this?"

Dagon leans casually into a banister to face me. "This isn't a game. Merely a battle that is a part of a war that has waged for eons. Since my fall from Heaven, I have believed to be on the right side of that war, that God wronged us. Having been amongst you and sharing a life with a human has swayed me."

"Swayed you." I glance around the room again. Are there cameras? Surely there is a spy lurking.

"It's just us. No one comes here. Orias built this as a mockery to the Enemy, but it scares even the wisest of us. Most of us proclaim to be more powerful than God, yet no one will set foot in a place built to be a church, blasphemous or not."

"You would have me believe that you're what... sorry for all of this?" I motion to the angels.

"I am," he says seriously. "Though I don't speak for my brothers."

I regard Dagon coolly. "What do you want?" I'm not that much of a fool to believe there isn't some catch to his moment of honesty.

His mouth makes the same twitch Liam's would whenever he was being smug about something. "That all depends on your relationship with Raum."

"I wouldn't call being marked a relationship," I retort.

"Do you trust him?"

"Make your point."

"I recognize his name from Tartarus—Hell," he says with a scowl. "And there he had a particular interest in hurting women. Nothing you can imagine compares to Raum's torments and yet here you stand, unblemished save for wherever he has made his mark. He mutilated them before extending their suffering for days, sometimes weeks." His lids flutter as my heart quickens. "Orias served beneath Raum as part of his personal guard, but they were closer than that. They would often visit my court, never one without the other. They were inseparable."

A creeping feeling inches its way down my spine. The threat in his words is unmistakable. Raum and Orias together is no good thing.

"Relax. I'm not going to bite you," he says, mistaken that my horror is toward him. He cocks his head and grimaces, catching the pun. "Consider me your ally."

I want to crawl out of my skin, but I force myself back into the opposite railing as a sign I'm willing to listen.

"Orias is trying to show Raum that he is a suitable hand, or warrior, that has surpassed what he was before. But that little act on the landing has caused Pethaino more damage than he will ever admit."

I have so many questions. A flash of the vision Raum forced into my mind strikes me. So they had been lovers. Is Raum going to sacrifice me, and is that why he has kept me? A million thoughts assault me. I take a deep breath to refocus.

"I thought he was bringing Babel closer."

"Two months ago, the waters began to rise on their own. We have been watching it closely. At first, we tried to hold it off but quickly realized, if we wanted to bring the western lands closer, we would have to make the sacrifice of the tides. Orias's demonstration has only escalated that timeline. He will drown us before he admits to his pride, and we cannot turn the entire sea red. Raum's presence will surely drown us."

"To sacrifice a whole kingdom to impress him is absurd." They're supposed to be calculating, not rash. Orias has been meticulous with the details of his kingdom. The aviary itself being something fine and unique. I allow another glance to the ceiling, purposefully looking past their sister. What was once Burns is now an entire fortress. Out of all the places to have chosen, a small town in the middle of nowhere is a strange place to raise a kingdom. It doesn't make any sense.

"He would kill us if it meant giving any of it up to Raum. He was both elated and terrified when he heard who it was at the gates.

"So, what I *want* is to know why he keeps you. Either you are both lying and you're unmarked," his eyes trace the outline of my body, "or you're incredibly important to him, meaning you'd be important to anyone, especially Orias. Raum has kept you alive for a reason, and Orias intends to find out why."

"I have wondered the same thing from the day he found me," I say.

"He has requested an audience with you."

"Raum will never allow it."

Dagon shrugs. "He will have you regardless."

I shake my head. "I'm not important. I can't tell you why Raum keeps me other than he is possessed by his own obsession in torturing me."

Dagon steps from the banister, moving through the air like an apparition, too slow and yet oddly graceful. He looks down on me, his black orbs absorbing too much detail. It feels like he is looking inside of me. "Deep down, I don't think you believe that. If anything has frightened you today, I hope it is that. You'd better find out your worth before Orias does. Raum has it and he is already using it against you. Orias seeks to do the same," he warns.

The air clears as he leans away, and I inhale heavily. I stare at his arm when he opens the door, motioning for me to follow through to another exit. I take a few more breaths to gather myself. Dagon's heat does little to comfort the stark chills still standing against my skin.

"Allies, you said?" I look back at him as he comes up behind me, his weight resting on the door as he leans his arm above me.

"I will do whatever I can for you so long as you are in Pethaino."

VIII

The thunderous rumble of hooves sounds through the air as we exit. Raum and Onna are led by Orias on three large geldings, with a fourth in tow. "They've found Corsen north of the border."

Dagon goes stiff beside me, but he covers it up with an even quicker nod. "Do we already have men out there?"

Orias nods. "No; we will see to this ourselves. I don't want the entire city knowing. Let's keep this quiet." He turns the ebony horse sharply when Onna tosses Dagon the reins.

Raum circles around on his blood bay, extending his arm to me. I slip my foot in the stirrup he has left free for me and take hold of his hand so he can swing me up behind him. "Are you alright?" he asks quietly.

I wrap my arms around his waist and give a little squeeze. Yes.

Dagon's face gives no signs of whatever it is he may be thinking. Is Corsen like him or is he someone else? Someone we should all be worried about.

My embrace around Raum tightens as we near the gate. The doors swing wide, and as soon as there is enough clearance, Orias takes off. Having never ridden in my life, I let out a sound of surprise as our horse bucks before powering behind the others. I press my face firmly into Raum's back as my hair is whipped back from my face. The cold air bites into my skin.

Light shines on the path we ride as we distance ourselves from Pethaino, its darkness hanging low like an ominous cloud. The glimmer of red-tinged water ripples about a mile ahead. My stomach turns involuntarily. The heap of corpses is worse than it was from the tower.

"What's going on?"

Raum shifts his weight slightly, turning his head back. "Orias believes Corsen to be a traitor. According to him, he is one of many that have chosen to repent for their sins."

That would explain Dagon's hesitancy. Why would Corsen risk coming back if he knew he'd be killed?

"The demons in the courtyard," I say.

"My thoughts exactly."

A breeze kicks up the thick odor of decay that brings bile to the back of my throat. It burns the inside of my nose. The open bellies of the whales are full of carrion birds and flies. Isopods crawl beneath the skin in a hurry to hide as we approach.

Our horses slow to a trot to better maneuver the carnage. Their hooves pick carefully across the sand. Onna's dark gray slips in something, stumbling forward when Orias holds up his fist, bringing us all to a halt.

We stand in silence, the only sounds the swish of a tail and waves sliding across the sand and bodies. Back home, the waves on the lake water sounded like the wind in the trees. It was peaceful, comforting. This is just noise.

"We'll go on foot from here. Split up and be wary." Orias directs his attention to Raum. "Any of us can take him, but he was a throne before. He's fast."

Raum nods. "Do you want us to kill him?"

"I'd like a few words."

This is probably the most collected I've seen Orias. The wild flit of his eyes has steadied. He isn't overly dramatic with his gestures as he had been. There's an eerie calmness to him that I find unsettling. Something doesn't feel right.

Orias looks at me when he dismounts. That façade breaks for a moment, so brief, to flash me a condescending glare that strikes me square in the chest.

I swallow a flutter of fear and hold his eyes. I could get in a lot of trouble for this, but I don't care. I'm tired of appearing weak to them.

He smiles. "Might want to keep her close."

The urge to throw a knife into his face makes my hand twitch. It's not that he thinks I'm incapable, or maybe he does, but he is threatening me. Dagon's words ring in the back of my head: *He will have you regardless.*

Dagon waits a moment until Orias and Onna start out. He pulls a bow from the back of his saddle. "He's bigger than any throne I've ever seen," he comments. He looks up at us, holding my gaze a second longer. He taps the bow against his thigh and nods.

"What's a throne?" I ask when he turns away.

Raum grabs my arm and pulls me to the side, swinging me to the ground. The horse turns its head, biting at the bit over the suddenness of it.

"A demon. They are small, known to be very fast. He will have chakrams," he dismounts, "if he has kept true to his nature here on Earth. Do not let him get close to you with them if he does. Which blade are you most comfortable with?"

I lick my lips. "I still have the karambit. Raum–"

"I will not let anything happen to you." He leans forward. I glance to see if anyone is watching, but I know they're already gone, already hunting. "Keep low and quiet. And do not dare leave my sight." He gives the back of my neck a comforting squeeze.

It takes everything in me not to bolt as we creep through the decay. It's been hard enough to keep myself from vomiting, but once we are actually in it, I find it hard to control. My feet sink into blubber and are soaked with the bloody water. A part of me feels calm, though, my senses focused on hunting a demon. Ha, demon hunter. I didn't think I would be able to add that to my resume. Sure, I've killed a couple, but only when I've had to. I've never been stupid enough to go out of my way in search for one.

I pause behind Raum, listening but still unable to hear anything other than the slosh of the water. The birds have flown off somewhere down the shore, the flies buzz nothing more than a soft hum. I do a double take when one darts by my face, half expecting to see a flash of gold.

The red water seeps into our clothes. Already, it has spread to the knee of my pants, making them tight and uncomfortable. Raum's hesitation brings something to my attention.

"In the tower, Orias said the water was poison to them. What did he mean?"

Raum grunts. "The same way honey weakens us."

When a wave curls around his knees, he pays no mind to it. I'd imagine he would be a little bit more wary based on his experience with honey, but it doesn't seem to slow him down. I'd been there to sustain him, after all. And here I am again if he needs it. His eyes are fixed on anything in front of him. The quietness stretches out as we stalk deeper into the remains.

"Why do you think the bees have such an impact? Or this slaughter?"

"They do not. Now be quiet. If Corsen has not heard you by now, he certainly will if you continue."

It really isn't the best time to be discussing this, but I know Corsen isn't the real reason we aren't going to talk about it. This is a conversation better to be had with Sebastian. I drop beside Raum's shoulder, looking at the side of his face. Will he let him out again?

"Smell that?"

I lift my head. A shudder runs through me as the first wave of rot sweeps through my senses, but beneath all of that is sulfur.

I press my hand on the hide of *something* and peek over the top. Nothing.

"I want you to go left," Raum says.

"What happened to not leaving your sight?" I hiss, still scanning the slopes of gray and black for any sign of life. Demons aren't stupid; Corsen isn't going to make this easy.

"I will have my eye on you. I want to see how right Orias is about Corsen's love for humans."

He is smirking when I look at him. I scoff. "You want to use me as bait."

"If Orias is who he says he is, then he will try to protect you."

"And if not?"

"Then stay clear of his blades until I can subdue him."

Dagon has only partly convinced me he means his repentance. The courtyard is proof enough that some sort of rebellion is taking place. That, or Orias is paranoid. Both are equally believable. There is a madness to the king that just thinking about him sends chills across my arms.

All of this feels particularly too convenient. I want to tell Raum of Dagon's confession as a sort of warning. But the secret feels too important to reveal just yet, and I slink off as instructed.

When I look back, none of the demons are to be seen. Bloodied, gouging eyes stare back at me from another animal that has been picked apart. I don't know about the demons, but I'm not going to be able to find Corsen if I am to maneuver through this grotesque design of a maze. Raum is close, I can feel him, and if he wants to use me as bait then bait is what I will have to be.

I walk until I find a whale that is more intact than the others, though not by much. Its stark rib bones make for a decent ladder as I haul myself up. The height advantage allows me to see past Pethaino's looming shadow to the first break of the waves. On the air is a clean breeze. It's just a whiff but it gives me a sense of relief.

Something buzzes past my head, small and dark. I wave the fly away, turning slowly to get an idea of where everyone is. Every cell in my body screams to drop down and hide. Where are all the people we saw harvesting from the tower? It's deathly quiet.

The fly swoops toward my face again, but this time when I swat it, I see a flash of gold. My breath catches. I turn on my heel, looking for the bright stripes of hope.

A demon, far bigger than any monster or man I have ever seen, is barreling toward me. In both hands, he holds two rings. One of them he throws beyond me and the other slashes dangerously close to slicing my face open before I fall back, my feet slipping out from beneath me, the first ring whizzing overhead. I land on the open carcass, the ribs sending a pounding blow to the center of my back that makes my teeth rattle. I roll, falling into the muck and God knows what else.

The demon, with his pale skin and too white face, is hot on my heels, darting in front of me before I can take more than two steps. He snatches the flying ring out of the air as it whistles back to him.

"Are you the little bitch that got away?" he snarls. "They'll see the bodies. They'll know." He tightens his grip on those nasty looking rings—chakrams Raum called them. They are a little larger than a flying disk with a sharp edge all the way around. The edge doesn't cut into his hand.

Corsen's shaved head has a scar down the right side, disappearing somewhere behind his ear. On his arms are other scars that would make more sense if they were tattoos. They look like wings. Sweat and blood stain his ivory skin. The muscles in his shoulders are abnormally shaped, bulging too close to his neck. The rest of him is like that, too, distended and bulky. He's massive.

All of this is a split second of sizing him up. I can't take him. A single blow will knock me unconscious, if not kill me. If I get my knife anywhere in his skin, it would be a graze. I tighten my fist that is covered in gore and sling it forward, hoping that whatever is left in my grasp will make it into his eyes, and run.

The first line of blinding pain slices into my shoulder blades. The blow should send me to my knees, but I keep running. He cannot catch me. I look haphazardly to my right, willing Raum to come to my rescue. Where is Orias?

It's hard to run when your feet are being dragged down by water. A cluster of fish slide in a silver waterfall beneath my boots and then I'm slipping farther into the water again. I bring my knees as high as I can to fight the resistance, finding a new sense of speed when a slight clearing presents itself.

The clear water bursts as I crash into it.

By clear, I mean it isn't red. It's murky with sand and debris but it's not bloodied like the water behind us. God, let me be right.

The little voice in my head screams at me to run.

I face Corsen, whose breath had been on the back of my neck moments ago.

His eyes are so fixated on me that he doesn't see the trap I've led him to. Smoke flares up from beneath his boots when he meets the water. He recoils violently, retreating to a tail that creates part of the barrier. The water drips from him like acid. It hisses as it eats into his skin. He kicks his foot, then the other, in an attempt to be rid of it.

"Clever bitch." His lips curl back to reveal his elongated canines.

"Come get me," I challenge, my voice shaking. I'm out of breath, but I'm also scared shitless. There's nothing stopping him from slinging one of those rings into my body.

Corsen eyes the distance between us. "I don't need an invitation." He palms both rings, his lids flashing up, then down, judging the space between us.

Come on. I take a step to the side. The sand is slanted beneath my boot. I slide a little farther before I can't feel the ground. It can't be a real drop-off the way the carcasses are piled around us, but maybe a divot in the ground that can get me lower.

The demon throws his arms forward, releasing one chakram and then the other. I drop, but the decline is not as low as I expected it to be. The water only rushes to my stomach. The first blade whizzes over my head. The second stops short of my face. Someone else catches it a breath from my nose. Pain, worse than when the blade first cut me, winds its way up my legs. White smoke coils across my body and up Raum's thighs. It grips my hips like a vise, digging its searing talons into my skin, trying to bring me down.

"Raum!" I grit.

He throws the ring so hard that, when it lands in Corsen's chest, he flies back. The weight of his body hitting the other side of the bloodied water makes everything ripple.

Sheer panic envelops me, but before I can grab Raum, he is hauling me out of the water so fast I can hardly stand. How is *he* standing? My legs go numb; even if I wanted to, I couldn't run next to him.

God, it hurts!

Raum's fingers are spread so wide that it's not until we fall apart that I feel them pulling out of the wound in my shoulders. The suction they make skitters a cold sweat across my skin. I lean against him, looking to make sure Corsen is not coming for round two.

Dagon mounts a gray whale and releases an arrow in the demon's throat when he tries to stand. Corsen stumbles forward, his hand fluttering over his bleeding chest. The ring is buried so deep that only a quarter of it remains outside of his body. Another arrow is released from Dagon's bow, fitting snuggly against the first.

She's mine.

I catch Raum as he suddenly stumbles into me, pushing us both to the ground. Dagon turns at the sound, his eyes darting past us to the tidal pool. I nod.

Raum grabs me by the back of the neck, twisting my head awkwardly so he can bring it to his lips. Before I have the chance to deny him, he sinks his fangs into my jugular. Blood bursts across my tongue in hot spurts. Its lush essence eases my thirst. It glides down the back of my throat with ease. I could drink this forever, this sweet taste. It is only something this sweet that can quench my hunger, this pain.

Raum tears away from me. The flavor evaporates, leaving my mouth dry and stale in its place. He holds my head close to his, his palm over the side of my face, tangled in my hair. The strangled breath in his lungs evening out slowly.

"Forgive me," he says quietly. He stands slowly, pulling me against his side. I press my hand into the wound. The pain wavers from red to white hot but it doesn't slow me down.

"Did you get enough?" I ask, shaking.

"Yes," he says. My blood makes his voice thicker.

"Good."

For once, I am too fast for Raum and he can't stop me. It'll take him a few more seconds before he can stand. It'll take that long for my blood to heal the damage the water caused.

"Help me pull him into the water," I say to Dagon.

Corsen has torn the arrows from his throat. He fights to pull the ring from his chest, but he's struggling. Even on his knees, he cannot get the leverage he needs. His breath is shallow.

The tightness in my chest bursts and I pull my karambit free, ripping it from beneath my shirt and the sheath in two fluid motions. Like a tiger's claw, I hook it into his hand and pull, severing the extensor tendons. They snap like one rubber band after the other, locking his fist in place. The second of horror on his face allows me the time to do the same to his other hand.

"He's going to heal quickly," Dagon grunts as he grabs him by the shoulders.

"I'm going to rip you apart and fuck you while you bleed, you filthy bitch." Corsen's skin ripples, shimmering to ash to scales of black as he rages. He kicks madly, pulls his arms, but his hands don't budge. I slip the knife under his chin and pull his head back by his forehead.

Absolute fury overwhelms me, and it takes everything not to slice his throat then and there. If I kill him, I'll have both Raum and Orias's wrath hailed down on me. This won't be lethal.

I twist the hilt and thrust the blade through his chin, and the curvature exits the other side and cuts into the roof of his mouth. His scream is like music to my ears. I hook my arm under his and, with Dagon's help, pull him back into the water, knowing full well that by pulling him with the blade it is slicing his jaw in two.

I jerk the karambit free, blade against bone, and shove Corsen face down in the water before jumping free of his reach. Smoke and silver spray fly into the air as he screams.

IX

The world tilts when Corsen screams. My heart races and I get a wave of giddiness that makes me lightheaded. I press my hand into Raum's thigh to steady myself when he stands beside me. His heat eases its way into me, slowing my breath and shaking hands.

But it doesn't stop the excitement building. Is this the same thrill they get when they kill us?

I've never seen one of them suffer.

"It won't kill him," Dagon says softly.

Is that anguish in his voice? I look at him accusingly.

"No," Raum answers. "Tell me, where is Orias?" He looks coolly across me to Liam's twin. His face is flushed with my blood, his lips still painted red with it.

"Here!"

Orias's voice is like the sound of a whip cracking. I jump at the sharpness of it. Malice drips from the single word. Has he been watching us this whole time? Why hadn't he come sooner? This is his man, after all.

The excitement I felt is doused by the cold water of his presence.

"What a show," he says, his eyes lighting up like little fires. "I could not intervene with such a delightful scene. I wish you had not thrown him in. Pull him out," he commands, looking at me.

I'll be damned if I'm getting in that water again, albeit it's probably the safest place for me—but Corsen can still drown me.

A low growl edges its way up the back of my throat. I swallow it down and cut a warning look of my own at Raum as he glowers.

"You have forgotten yourself," he says.

If Corsen were not still screaming in agony, I think you could have heard a pin drop, because I swear the wind and waves stop. Everything stops. Though no one has moved, it looks like someone has just slapped Orias across the face.

Raum continues. "We are your guests. If you seek to harm her, I will rip your head from your shoulders."

Onna—I'd nearly forgotten her, for she moves like she is Orias's shadow—touches the hilt of her sword. I tighten my grip on my knife I've yet to let go. I take a slow breath, readying myself for the trigger that is about to be pulled.

Orias stares at Raum and bursts out laughing. "You have become more cynical in this land."

"Do not mock me," Raum says. "What is mine belongs to me. Ozien."

"Et ozien. I jest, brother, nothing more," Orias replies. He tips his head down. A sly smile creeps across his face as he looks at Raum beneath long lashes. "Dagon," he commands.

Dagon leaves momentarily to return with a lariat. He twists the loop over his head, turning his wrist and releasing it, where it lands over Corsen's head and pulls tight against his throat. The veins and tendons of the demon's neck bulge as he is pulled free of the acidic water. His whole face turns purple and the eerie sheen to his skin flashes once more.

All the while, the tension builds between the four of us, waiting for someone to strike so the rest can follow.

Orias turns away abruptly, directing his attention to the writhing demon who is hardly recognizable now that his body has been burned. His skin sloughs off like jelly. It falls to the ground and in globs, making a soft *plop w*henever it does.

Onna's eyes cut into me as she passes to take the other side of Corsen. Her hand remains steady on the hilt at her side.

"You're a hard man to find," Orias says.

"You have lost your head," Corsen forces out, his speech slightly slurred by the wound I've given him. He heaves, sucking in the air like his life depends on it. His hands still clench the chakram. They're shaking.

"Why do you say that?"

"You don't need to know if I am innocent or not. You have decided you will kill me regardless. You are *no* king. You are not even a tyrant. You are the mud on someone's boots you'll never be able to fill." Corsen rips the chakram from his chest and rushes forward. His body slams into an invisible wall, splaying his arms against the air, yet there is no sound when his chakram hits the force and debris scatters around us. "Coward," he seethes. "I am not the snake you should be worried about. You're in a nest of them, and one is going to strike soon." He shakes his head, slinging more skin into the air. Beneath the black crisps is pink, new skin.

"Who are they?" Orias asks coolly.

"Look around you!" Corsen motions to all of us. He points to me specifically. "You accuse me of repentance yet this one stands among you."

"Her soul belongs to me," Raum says. A wicked glint falls against his eyes as the shadows in the sky change. "There is no one left in existence to restore her salvation."

"You are as much of a fool as Orias if you believe that."

The amount of anger he has kept harnessed finally unfurls itself in the form of smoke. It's a wonder traces hadn't shown earlier. One more thing and Raum is going to snap.

A flutter of hope brushes its wings inside my chest. There's still a chance for things to turn around. The bees hadn't just been a fleeting sign and Dagon isn't lying. I don't believe Corsen is either. I risk a glance at the doppelganger, my heart surging that finally there is someone on my side. His countenance is grave. His fingers are poised at the edge of his bow, ready to spin it off his shoulder.

"If not you, then who was it that freed the humans?" Orias presses. His anger has revealed itself, coiling around his dark arms like snakes.

The chakram drops from Corsen's hand. He flexes his fingers, opening and closing his hands. The bands I cut are whole and stark white. "Who was it that gave you my name?" He looks between Onna and Dagon. "This rise of repentance did not start with the humans. I was close to finding out who before you sent your dogs after me."

Orias is thoughtful. He does not blink, nor does his body waver. He is staring at Corsen, but it's as if he sees through him.

"Your madness has caused a stir in the kingdom that I cannot excuse. Do you understand this?" Orias finally says.

"My madness! Take a walk in your own courtyard, you–" Corsen is abruptly cut off.

His eyes go wide and his mouth is left gaping. He shakes his head and clasps his hands tightly on either side. He takes a stumbling step back to the pool. He teeters on his heels, his knees bent and shaking. It's as he crouches lower that I finally hear the ringing. Instinctively, I cover my ears, not wanting to repeat this morning's experience. The intensity doesn't touch me. It doesn't touch any of us except Corsen. His body drops to the ground and seizes, every limb going rigid until he starts to shake uncontrollably. That's when he falls into the water. This time, his whole body bursts apart, scattering pieces of him in every direction like he's fallen on an explosive.

I jump when something hits me in the chest. No way the water did that. Silver curls of smoke wind up from what is left of Corsen's body.

"People will wonder about this," Onna states. Her spindly fingers relax, her shoulders evening out now that there's not an immediate threat.

"Let them. There is no room in Pethaino for the mad. Raving or honest."

"He's right," Raum says. "Men like Corsen are going to be problems regardless of their cause."

"He was desperate," I say. They all look at me. When no one interjects or hisses, I take it as a sign to continue. "He would have started a revolt that would have overthrown Orias. At least with Corsen gone, Pethaino is safe a little longer." I don't know what makes me say any of this. It's an observation, but something about it feels plain wrong. A little longer. Why had I said that? I've felt unease since we got here, but maybe there's something bigger at work that I've yet to realize and this is just my conscious trying to warn me.

This place makes me feel sick. I know Raum is the only one that can potentially read my mind, but it feels like someone else's thoughts are running through my head.

A fly… a bee buzzes past the tidal pool. It's so small, but the color is undeniable. I start after it before giving any of them a second thought. My feet carry me nimbly across the carcasses. The bee makes a straight path then abruptly turns to the right, toward the ocean. I stop in my tracks. The bee vanishes. It doesn't turn in any particular direction; there's no *poof* of smoke it's gone up in. It's just gone. Instead, there are bodies. Human bodies.

There's so many of them that they're buried beneath the surface of the water. The few that are on top float in the surf, red waves curling between their torn limbs.

The hair on the back of my neck prickles and I turn around. They followed me.

Dagon walks past me, surveying the scene. He bends down and pulls a young woman from the waves. Her eyes flutter. "He left a few," he says.

Orias's full lips are pressed into a thin line. "Find what you can."

"Even I did not hear them," Raum says. He looks at me questioningly, waiting.

"I just–" I can't tell him about the bee. I can already tell he is angry with me, for who knows what, and talking about them will only irritate him further. "I had a feeling," I say.

We'll talk later, his look says. Raum runs his hand across the back of my neck and gives it a firm squeeze.

By the time we head back to the fortress, we have rounded up twenty-two humans. I hate the way they look at me. They hate me. They think I'm on the demons' side. I want to tell them it's not true, but there's no denying what it looks like when I pull one from the water and push him toward the rest of the herd—group. My stomach turns.

There were a few people I had met that sided with the demons. Very few. Even murderers and rapists were said to have feared them and their ways. Those who didn't followed at their heels like dogs. It never ended well for them, though. They were always tossed aside, tortured in some unfathomable way before meeting their end. Demons don't care about anyone but themselves. We are all expendable.

I look across at Raum. The closer we get to Babel, the closer my time comes. I wish I knew what he had planned for me. How is he going to kill me? Why, out of everyone else he could have picked, did he choose me?

On the horizon is a mountain ridge I didn't notice previously. With the shift of the lands and tides, I shouldn't be surprised to see it. I wonder if Babel waits on the other side.

Once the humans have been corralled, we take to the horses to ride back. Raum lets me mount up first and then seats himself behind me. He adjusts my body for me, pulling me closer into his chest. I feel less exposed with his arms around me, his rein hand resting lightly over the top of my thigh while his other is wrapped snuggly around my waist.

The dark shroud of Pethaino settles over our party when the gates close behind us, locking us inside once more. Protecting us from what? Even if the tides are changing for humanity's fate, no one would dare test the strength of this place.

It's Dagon who orders two demons in strapping leather to take the humans to the pit. It sounds like a terrible place. I imagine they will be tossed in some sort of dark hole. I look at him pleadingly when he turns around, but he does not meet my gaze.

"Let this be the last of our troubles," he says to Orias.

Orias grunts as he dismounts and passes the reins to a human man who stands by, ready to take the horses away.

I lean forward with Raum, letting him dismount first. He passes the horse off just the same and then holds his hand out to me like the good gentleman he is not. I narrow my eyes.

"Don't patronize me."

Raum's facade breaks and he smiles. It's charming but just as dangerous as the one he gives when he is angry. This is all a big joke to him. He is toying with me in front of everyone. It should be the last thing he does under the circumstances, but even demons get bored and like to play with fire.

I swing my leg across, ignoring him entirely, when his hands grip my waist and he lifts me the rest of the way. Heat creeps up my neck when he digs his fingers into my hipbone. I slap his hand. The boldness of his public attention unnerves me.

"Raum said that he let you act freely," Orias says.

I pause in my removing of my captor's hands. It's only then that Raum lets me go, laughing. When he doesn't answer for me, I tip my head. "I am of better use to him with a clear head."

I don't like his directness toward me either. Maybe that's why Raum is being so blatant. As if he needs to prove I am his. Not that he will let anyone forget it for a second.

Orias looks at me thoughtfully, his inky eyes softening slightly. "While I have known Raum to fight and defeat many wars on his own, it was quite the sight to see you intervene in today's skirmish on his behalf. I do not favor your kind. It is my desire to see that every last one of you is wiped from the face of all creation. But we must honor those that serve us, however brief it may be."

So, he had been watching us. He saw me go after Corsen when Raum couldn't stand. Heat blooms over my face. I'd been afraid Orias would look on him with weakness and instead he is commending me for my strength. I'm ashamed of myself for going after Corsen to protect Raum. There wasn't anyone else in my mind when I dug my blade into his jaw.

What the fuck is going on, though? Demons don't *honor* us. They degrade us, use us. I don't like where this is going.

"If it would please your master, I want to give you something." He reaches into the satchel at his hip. It's beaded together with amethyst. He withdraws a pewter chain, the links shaped like scales or plated honeycombs, with a circular ring in the front and a latch to hold it in place. A collar. "It will allow you freedom in Pethaino."

Freedom is such a loose word with them. I watch it dangle between his hands numbly. Wearing that will be worse than bearing a mark. Everyone will know that I am a pet.

That's what you are.

"It would please me," Raum says.

I fight a scowl. They have both gone mad.

He will have you regardless.

I've made many mistakes in my time with demons. They're always one step ahead. They like to play games because the match is always one they will win.

Whatever game Orias is playing is dangerous. The subtle threats he has made to Raum, teasing with a sharpened point. Raum isn't stupid, so I know he is aware of what his old friend does, but part of me wonders if he isn't giving him too much grace. Even his threats to the king were mild. If this was Leyak, he would be dead by now.

It's no secret that Orias is displeased by Raum's relationship with me. Whether he believes I'm a pet or not doesn't matter. Raum's eyes are on me. Not him.

Well, he certainly has his attention now.

I step forward hesitantly and pull my hair to the side when Orias unclasps the chain. I turn my back and meet Raum's eyes, heart pounding. The wet pools of his gaze are stormy. I won't be wearing this long once we are out of Orias's sight. I have a feeling Raum is going to wring my neck to get it off. My fingers ache in anticipation as I imagine doing the same to Orias until those little fires in his eyes blow out.

"Be careful not to stray too far from your master," Orias whispers. He pulls my hair from my grasp, letting it fall across my shoulders. The threat sends a chill down my spine. I get the sense that this collar is not for protection, but a target.

X

We eat with Orias and his kingdom that evening. Meats galore are brought in by naked men with flowers woven in their hair, set out like a true feast and garnished with fruits for pops of color. Demons only bother with blood and ash. There isn't anything the vegetarian options can offer them. When a plate is set down in front of me, Raum swaps it for another and places two apples beside it.

I'm not naïve; I know most of the meat is human. I'm thankful that Raum makes sure I don't have to stomach any of it. I know he would never.

Two women are the center piece of the table. They hold fast to each other, their eyes darting wildly to the monsters around them. Like the men, they are in nothing but their fair skin. One has copper curls while the other has straight blonde hair. Blood shows up best on white skin, Leyak told me once. "Look at how beautiful it is," he would say to me. He would hold his fingers in front of my face and paint my blood on his. He loved the contrast.

Unable to stomach the rest of the memory, I set my fork down.

Raum laughs at something Orias has said. It's such a beautiful sound, I can't help but swoon when he flashes a smile with blunt human teeth. His black shirt is high collared with peacock-colored feathers down the sleeves. It reminds me of the scars I saw on Corsen's arm. Surprisingly, the leather pants he wears suit him even better, fitting him tightly across his muscular thighs. One of which sits warmly beneath my palm.

I hate how beautiful he is, with his raven hair braided back and smooth golden skin. Sebastian's image is a distant memory. Everything about the man next to me is monster.

"I must ask," Orias says, his voice lowering but not so quiet that I can't hear him. "Why have you kept her? I remember the days well when we would bathe in their blood after a night of torment."

I nearly choke on the wine I've just downed. I grip my glass tighter so it won't shake as I set it down. Raum said he didn't like to share. Or did he only mean that with me? I don't meet either of their eyes when I feel them inspecting me.

"Her scream is... unique," Raum says. "And her blood, I must confess, is the sweetest I have ever tasted."

"And you have not grown tired of her."

It's not a question. Orias sets his chin on his hand when he leans forward on the table.

Raum grabs my hand still resting against him and gives me a gentle pull. As if I'm in a trance, I let him. I move out of my seat and onto his lap, my face fully flushed and flaming red. He moves his leg so I am straddling one of his.

"I have never had one like her. She does not break as the others did. When she does scream, it is an agonizing sweetness. Surely, it must be the way our voices are to them. It gives me great pleasure to torment her."

Oh, I know it does, you bastard.

He caresses my neck fondly, tracing the mark of his bite that he hasn't allowed to heal. It's tender to touch, but I grit my teeth instead of flinching.

"May I?" Orias asks. He holds out his hand, but it's not me he is asking permission from.

Every muscle in my body goes rigid. Raum chuckles when he takes my wrist. I hold it close to my chest, but he is stronger and pulls my arm out to the king.

"The more you resist, the more it will hurt," he whispers against my ear.

Orias holds my gaze with his cat eyes when he takes my wrist. I hardly notice when Raum moves my hair back. I watch, horrified, as his lips part to reveal his fangs. His teeth are first to rest on my skin and his lips follow when he pierces me. Raum's mouth follows suit on my neck, reopening the wound.

It does hurt. It is agonizingly painful until their tongues stroke the blood free and then it is unbearably blissful. My eyes threaten to close, but I'm still held under Orias's hypnotic stare. I'm afraid if I close them, he will relieve me of my hand. As if reading my mind, he sinks his fangs a little deeper and I let out a strangled gasp.

Raum withdraws and Orias detaches from me just the same. Blood runs down his lower lip. A red drop falls somewhere to the floor. He is still looking at me with his wicked, wicked eyes.

"How sweet indeed," he says.

Raum chuckles and nuzzles the side of my neck, burrowing his nose into his bite.

Twice he has embarrassed me like this. Twice he has put me on show for his own amusement. The first time had been done to show Leyak that I no longer belonged to him and, no matter what he did, he would never have me again. At least then he hadn't let any of them feed on me.

Foggy-headed, I clasp my wrist to my chest. "May I leave?" I hate how thick with tears my voice sounds. I can't let them see me cry.

Raum runs his fingers through my hair. He looks past me, toward the women on the table, one of which is being called over by a particular group of fair-haired demons.

"You may. Don't think our fun has ended for the night, though."

I hate him. I would cut his head from his neck if I could.

I don't see Orias give a command, but he must because Dagon is standing behind Raum's chair, waiting.

"Don't look so forlorn, little bird. You have been blessed," Orias mocks. His angular eyes hold mine a little bit longer before he turns his attention to the loud clash of dinner plates.

The redhead has either slipped or been pushed from her position and is laying sprawled across the table. The room roars in laughter. Raum won't look at me when I turn my heated glare on him. The most attention he gives me is the wave of his hand, if it's even directed to me at all.

It's not until my fist curls that his eyes cut to me. I dare you, they convey.

I let out a heated breath and turn on my heel, following Dagon out of the hall. I flex my fingers, wriggling the urge to slap Raum into the abyss.

Dagon touches my elbow when we are alone outside Raum's chamber doors. I flinch at his touch, and he withdraws his hand quickly.

"I only mean to see how you fair," he says softly.

I'm angry at him. I'm angry at Raum, Orias, Onna—all of them! I whirl on him. "How do you think? You have never been used as bait. You have never been used at the expense of someone's amusement. You have never been used at all! You took what didn't belong to you." I poke him hard in his chest. "All your kind does is take and devour. How dare you ask me how I fair!"

He slaps my hand away before I can push him. He shoves me against the door, throwing me into the next room, and slams the door shut behind him. I have a thought to stop my ranting but I can't bite my tongue. Even when he stalks toward me, pushing me deeper into the room, I stand tall.

"I want to help you," he says thinly.

"You *want m*e to believe that you are on my side and yet you sent all of those people to their prison. Their death. You do not care about them, and you certainly do not care about me. What have you done that has helped my people's cause?"

Dagon looks taken aback. He blinks, looking too stunned to say anything at first.

"Some things must be done quietly and in secret. It pains me no less than it does you to keep them in chains. I have sacrificed my place in Heaven and now Tartarus. I have sacrificed much at the risk of losing everything."

At that, Dagon turns on his heel and leaves. His own fury is palpable, and I truly believe if he stayed he would have slapped me. I can see it in the way he clenches his fist and hear it in the bang of the door when it latches shut behind him.

His words unnerve me. I want so badly to believe him, but experience has taught me that every word from a demon's mouth is a lie. The ones with the softest voices and kindest eyes are often the cruelest.

I can't sit still. I pace the room until, finally, I am overwhelmed and drop to my knees and scream. The sound is ripped from me when I burst into tears. I let every bit of rage and regret unfurl until there are no tears left to shed. The weight of Orias's necklace hits me and I rip it free, breaking the skin on the back of my neck. I hurl it across the room.

When I do manage to collect my head, I wander to the bath. I don't even bother taking my clothes off until I am halfway in.

I scrub my skin until my skin is bright red. And then I scrub some more. I dig my fingers against the bite on my wrist, willing it to go away. When I rinse it in the water, it is gone. That's impossible. I touch the smooth flesh.

"I'm sorry," Raum says.

I jump and instinctively drop lower in the water. As if he hasn't seen everything else before. It's not that I didn't hear him; I didn't even feel him come into the room.

"You can save the act," I say.

The top of his shirt has come undone, and his hair is askew like he has just rolled out of bed or been in some sort of tussle. His bloody fingers dance down the rest of the buttons of his shirt. I wonder if it was the redhead or the blonde he tore into.

My stomach turns.

"I am sorry that I hurt you."

"Which time?"

"All of them," he says softly.

I look down at the water when he starts to unbutton his pants. I don't look up again until I see the ripples in the water when he enters. I don't want him anywhere near me, but I don't move away when he draws closer.

He takes both of my hands, turning my wrists up. He kisses the one Orias bit. It's in that moment the fire that had been building within me explodes. I slap him. The sound is like a clap of thunder within the stone walls and his head snaps to the side. A bright red imprint of my hand welts immediately against his cheek.

"Don't you ever do that to me again. You might think that you own me and that allows you to do what you want with me, but I will not stand for it. Once was enough, but I will not be passed to your friend like a piece of meat."

Raum shoves me back so hard that when the rough edge of the ledge hits my back I gasp. "You do belong to me and I can do whatever I want to and with you. You do not have a voice, you have no will, you have *nothing* unless it comes from me." The darkness of the room draws closer to us. The temperature of the water increases dangerously, tinging my skin scarlet. His anger is terrifying, yet I can't stop myself. I have restrained myself too long and I'll be damned if I am snuffed out again.

"What are you going to do if I defy you? Kill me?" I hope my gaze is steady. I hope he sees how angry I am instead of how scared I am at my core. "I have suffered you before and I will brave it again."

The little bit of restraint he has left is evaporating, and with it my anger grows. I don't have my knives, but I will break my nails off into his skin if it comes to it.

"I can make you suffer still," he growls.

"Then do it."

Raum spins me around so fast it knocks the breath from my chest. He grabs me by the hair and pulls my head back until my neck pops. In one motion, he enters me and bites me with a powerful blow that makes me scream. My voice keens higher when he locks his jaw. His teeth slide through flesh and muscle, stopping just short of the bone I know he is about to graze.

He doesn't give me the chance to catch my breath. He rips his teeth free, spraying blood into the air. "Is this what you want? Do you want to feel the pleasure I get from bringing you pain?"

I try to press myself away from the wall, but every thrust is a painful hammer that keeps me trapped. He pushes my head down on the ground and his other into my back as he shoves me away from him. I face him, not giving him enough time or space to retreat. Before I can hit him again, he has my hand, with his other circling around my throat.

His nose is curled with disgust and then the veil drops. The revulsion is replaced with open scrutiny.

His chest heaves as he runs his thumb beneath my chin. "You make me hurt you when I do not want to."

I tremble like a leaf beneath him. The blow of air that escapes my lips shudders twice as hard when he tips his face down to mine. He breathes me in as he trails his nose across my cheek.

The soft touch of his lips is against my ear through the curtain of my hair when he speaks. "I came to apologize, and you insist on angering me. Why will you not take my kindness?" His hands slide down my arm and shoulder until both are cupped around my waist.

"Because I hate you," I breathe. Blood runs down my chest, tinging the water between us scarlet. The wound closes as soon as I notice it.

Raum's smile is sinfully inviting as his lips hover over mine. "Show me how much."

I hate him. I fucking hate him.

I grab him by the face and press my lips tightly to his. My fingers tangle in his hair and pull him closer to me. I want to devour him. I want him to hurt as I do. I want to take everything from him the way it has all been stripped from me. I bite into his lip until it is his blood in my mouth. Hot as fire, it burns its way down my throat. I dig harder, my nails piercing his scalp.

A stifled moan escapes him. His broad hands slip up the back of my thighs and grip my ass to lift me to the ledge where he follows me on hands and knees. Seeing him crawl to me is something I never thought I would witness. His eyes look wickedly black when he holds my gaze as his lips make a trail from my foot to the inside of my thigh. He kisses between my legs, softly at first, like a caress. And then harder, his lips parting for his tongue to fill me up.

He's right. This is better.

I tense when he slips his fingers inside of me. When the talons don't tear me apart, I allow myself to breathe. He curls his fingers up along my inner ridge and places his mouth over me again. My breath hitches. I shut my eyes to the building pressure as his tongue quickens and the force of his fingers hardens. All at once, I slam my fists into the ground and tighten my legs around his head. I scream as I come.

He doesn't stop. He pulls the sound from me as long as he can, working his fingers in and out of me, dragging out my orgasm wave after wave.

My fingers find their way back into his hair. They wind farther down until I can latch around his feathers. I give a firm pull that earns me a painful hiss. Good. I pull again so hard I think some have come free in my grasp, but I don't let go.

"You little devil," he says against my skin. I lose myself in his eyes when he looks up at me. Whoever I was before is slowly being devoured by the creature between my thighs, and there is nothing I can do to stop it.

"Let me tear you apart," I say.

He rises, his shadow blocking out all light behind him. He slides into me quickly, his own need getting the best of him. My nails leave red trails down the length of his back. Loose feathers fall from my grasp. Piece by piece, I break him.

Despite how exhausted I am, Raum falls asleep before I do, with my fingers running through his hair and his song humming in the back of my throat. His head is resting on my chest and his arm is draped across my waist. He looks so innocent, so much like a quiet man.

I run my fingers over the marks I've given him. I wonder if it is some form of repentance that he lets them stay. Stranger still that he let me mark him at all.

Dagon was right about one thing. Raum keeps me for a reason, and I need to figure out what that is and soon. Does Orias know? Has Raum told him? He's never been one to share, yet he offered my wrist to Orias after threatening him again and again when the king stepped out of line. Dagon said they were close, so I wonder if they have only been jesting.

Raum said our time here would be brief. I'm going to hold him to that. If I can't, I will find my own way.

XI

Stay here until I return.

I crumple the note and toss it over my shoulder. The bed is still warm from his heat, so he can't have left too long ago. Perhaps he thinks after last night he has culled me back into submission.

At least he had the decency to pull my clothes and knife from the pool. The clothes have been laid out to dry beside a stack of an outfit that has yet to be soiled. For someone who doesn't want me breaking the rules, I'm surprised to see he left my knives out so carelessly.

It's a test.

Fuck the test. I take my kukri and change into my new clothes. The first garment is a long black dress, or tunic, with slits up to my thighs. Iridescent feathers are sewn across the chest and fan out onto the back that makes it look as if I have wings. I slip on leather pants that lace together at the sides and tall boots left beside the hearth.

I find Orias's necklace discarded beneath the bed.

The design must be some sort of joke. The irony that the links look like honeycomb is priceless. I fiddle with the chain before hooking it around my neck.

Though it doesn't physically burn me, there's something about the metal that irritates my skin.

I gently test the door handle. It doesn't budge. I pull on it harder, slamming the flat of my palm against the door twice in frustration. I take a couple of steps back, to survey the rest of the room. I cross to the window and peer over the edge. It's three stories from the ground. I can probably drop the last story without injuring myself too badly. Raum is unlikely to tend to my self-inflicted injuries when he instructed me to stay put. At least he healed me from the rest of last night's damage.

I risk free climbing my way down. Throwing sheets out the window will draw too much attention. I'll worry how to get back in later.

There's not much sound in Pethaino save for a few caws from the crows somewhere outside the walls. The ground is wet, damp with the water that has started to creep in from the outside. I'm going to leave tracks and there isn't much I can do about hiding them.

While Orias claimed I could move freely, I stick to the shadows. I don't want anyone looking twice my way if I can help it. I have no idea where I'm going. I have no idea if Orias writes his thoughts down or maps out his plans. Leyak never did; he swore on his sharp mind. While I expect Orias might claim the same were he questioned, he's a bit more of a loose cannon than Leyak was.

Guards patrol the battlements, their attention focused on what's outside the wall. I pause when one stops above my head. Please don't look down. It takes everything in me not to run. I'll never get used to their presence and the distinct instinct to fly when they are near.

I suspect Orias's quarters will be somewhere near the Hall. No particular reason other than he likes being the center of attention, so it would make sense to stay as close to it as possible.

The stark red door of the aviary catches my eye. I shouldn't go back, but I can't stop my feet from carrying me forward. I argue that it is off course and a waste of time. Dread spreads like poison beneath my hand as I push through the door.

There are more angels hanging from the ceiling than before. I recognize a few faces from the beach. There are no cords that hold them, but I wonder if there is a way to get any of them down.

Don't do it.

"Let's just see," I say to myself.

The iron walls make it easier to climb, and I'm able to secure myself to one of the rafters by wrapping my legs tight around it. I shimmy forward, looking desperately until I see her blonde hair. Liam's sister floats beneath me, her arms outstretched, reaching for something. The blonde strands flow like they are stuck in a current of water. I reach out gently and touch her.

She's warm.

I snatch my hand back, my stomach curling in horror. She is very much alive.

I wave my hand above her, looking for the invisible strings that may hold her, but there is nothing. I don't know anything about breaking spells and curses if that is what grasps them.

There has to be a way to get them down.

"Can you hear me? Can you speak?"

Of course not. If they could then I'd be able to hear the screams they so clearly cry.

Dagon will know how to cut them down, though. He is the one that put them here.

The thought is shut down immediately. Another wave of terror hits me as someone enters the room. I wrap both arms around the banister to keep from falling and looking desperately for the demon. I know it's somewhere close–

Fuck.

Orias moves to the middle of the room. He is dressed in a delicate sheer robe that shows the contours of his body. His head is decorated in wild twists that make it appear as if he has horns curling behind his head.

He flinches, his shoulders turning in. The movement makes him appear smaller than he really is.

I feel it, too.

It's not the same as when a demon is close, but the power is just as strong. It reverberates from the stained glass, humming soundlessly through the air in a way that makes my blood sing in my ears. I crane my head back, moving as slowly as possible to not draw attention to myself. It'll be sheer luck if he doesn't see me.

The demon, I think it's a demon, is unlike any I have ever seen before. He has burnished red hair that has been cut and braided into a Mohawk. He is adorned with bronze chain-link armor that fits snugly over his black clothes. His arms are sleeveless. I squint. Is that? Yes; he shares the same black hand tattoo as Onna. It encircles his fingers just like hers, and a more intricate pattern races up to the top of his shoulder. But what's more is that he also has the same outline of wings that Corsen had scorched into his pale skin. Even though his skin is ivory, there is still a gold shine that shares the gleam of his armor. I lean forward as much as I dare. I can't see his face to get a better description of him.

Two pewter hilts are sheathed on both hips. Save for the two, albeit small, blades, I can see no other weapons.

I've never seen one with so much color. Of course I've seen them with red hair, but this… this one looks as if he could be a flame, not just mimic it. It's in his being.

Orias looks up, and I hold my breath. His gaze skims everywhere but my direction. "This is a shameful place."

"You are the one that created it," the red head says.

"Its power was meant to be mine," Orias grits. He runs a hand down his smooth chest and turns his attention back to the demon. "Yet somehow it has become a haven for your people and a torment for mine."

"Why have you summoned me?" the red demon demands. His voice rings with the same power hanging in the air.

Orias flashes his infamous smile. "I have found the key to Babel."

The demon turns his head to the side, a very subtle tilt. "There is no key."

Orias claps his hands together and laughs. "Of course there is. Why else did you seek me out?"

"You are the closest to reaching the land."

"You need my help to control the gatekeeper. He is more inclined to listen to me than he would you. We will have Babel within days."

The fiery demon turns on his heel, circling beneath me where I can still not see his face. I breathe slowly. It stirs Liam's sister's hair. "What is this key?" he asks, moving farther away. He is lost behind another woman who blocks my view, and the only things I can see are his hands clasped behind his back.

"So you can steal it out from under me? I am no fool."

His hand curls into a fist. "If we are to be allies, there needs to be trust between us."

Orias takes a step back, sliding his foot across the floor as if he means to dance. "I trust us to work together until the other is no longer of benefit." He turns again, stopping beneath my hiding spot. "Enter our gates in six days."

"In six days, your kingdom will be under water," the demon growls. "Do you have the key or not?"

Orias holds up a finger when the fiery demon steps closer. He doesn't move, but a wave of nausea sweeps through the air. Fear. I can smell it in the sweat that breaks out over Orias's body.

"In six days, Babel will be here and we have everything we need to access it." Orias takes a step back, regaining the space the demon closed between them. It looks as if he is about to keep the information to himself until he forces the words out. "It would do you well to know that Raum is here, too."

The demon moves back into view as he follows Orias. He is just as tall as the king, but he makes the darker demon look small in his shadow. "What?"

Orias tips his head, a toothy smile flashing quickly. "He arrived a few days ago. I was as surprised as you are now. But we have had conversation, and with the tides shifting so quickly…"

"Do you believe Raum will help you gain Babel?" The demon's question is condescending, his laugh mocking.

At that, Orias's eyes light up. "Of course," he says. "I served him well before and he has seen all I can do. Besides, he will not have much of a choice. He can either help us or be forced outside the gates to drown."

The demon leans back on his heels and chuckles. With a shake of his head, he steps back, almost in disbelief. "You will need to find a way to restrain him."

Orias smiles again. "That has already been arranged."

There is a shift in the air where the fiery demon stands. Smoke and embers burst through the air in a vertical line. He takes a step back and places a hand on one of his hilts. "Were you there when he succeeded the throne?"

"I was," the king answers slowly. His lids flutter when he looks past the demon, as if searching for something, or someone. "I helped him to it."

The demon nods and something like a mocking laugh escapes him. "Then *you* would do well to know that he cannot be trusted. If you are wrong about this, I will not assist you when Pethaino falls." He steps through the seam. It closes behind him in a single wisp of black smoke.

Orias lets out a deep breath, his body shaking. He holds out his hand, inspecting the tremors. He closes his fist and takes another broad look across the ceiling.

This time his eyes pass in my direction, but it is so quick that he does not hesitate. He doesn't see me and he leaves through the red door.

I hang onto my hiding place for a long while. There is a likely chance Orias saw me and is waiting outside. When it appears no one is going to rush in and grab me, I make my way down. "I'll get you down," I tell Liam's sister. I'll find a way to save her and everyone else before we leave this horrible place. Right now, though, I need to find Raum.

I wait even longer once I am on the ground. I peer through the painted glass until I'm sure the coast is clear.

Whatever help Orias thinks he will lend, Raum isn't going to give him. The cost of Babel is too high for him to risk sharing it with someone else. Which means Orias is going to betray Raum.

XII

Onna and Dagon fall into step behind Orias, Onna closer to his shoulder as she tips her head to say something. He waves his hand at her. "Where is he?" I hear him ask.

I look ahead to see if there is anyone else before jogging to another building to get a little closer.

"They're both gone," Onna says. "I have Ipos and Keir looking for them."

"When you find them, bring them to me. Raum and I have much to discuss."

I assume that means they are looking for me, too. Let them think I am with Raum instead of spying. I wonder what Orias's intentions really were when he gave me the collar. What will he do if he catches me out here on my own?

"He will help us," Dagon says, not quite a question.

"He will." He turns his other hand out to him, holding his fingers slightly in the air. "A little bit longer and this world will fall. We are so close."

Other words are exchanged, but they are lost under the pounding of my heart. What he is saying isn't true. It can't be. We are so close to things turning around. I can feel it. The demons are *dying*. There has been more proof of their loss than anything else.

Yet Pethaino is strong. There is no denying that this monstrosity of a fortress thrives with an intense hunger.

Raum will never give up whatever it is Orias thinks he has. That's the only relief I allow myself as I follow them a few more paces before turning around the side of an old barn with stockades stained in old blood. I press my hand against my chest in an attempt to slow how fast my heart is beating. Hopefully, none of them could hear it.

I slip through a sliding door and peek through one of the windows.

Only Orias and Onna make their way through the city. I move hesitantly forward, looking for any sign of Dagon. I need to get back to the room before it is discovered I've been tailing them.

A warm hand slides around the front of my body, another pushes into my shoulder, and all at once they spin me around, slamming my back to the weathered wood. There is no kindness in Dagon's eyes.

"You're not very good at hiding," he says.

It's hard to relax when you have a blade running up your side. He caresses the line of my body with the tip, starting at the top of my thigh and stopping at my ribs. He twists his wrist to angle the blade where, if he were to slide it forward, it would puncture my heart.

"What are you doing?"

Dagon smirks; the arrogant curve of his mouth is something he and Liam have in common. "Putting on a show."

I look past him, expecting to see an audience, but the three demons passing behind him don't pay attention to us, their focus on wherever they are heading.

"This isn't funny, Dagon."

"It's not meant to be," he purrs.

I shove against Dagon, and he slams me back by throwing his free arm across my chest, under my throat.

"Careful. Leah is our guest." I go rigid beneath Dagon at the sound of Orias's voice. His eyes smolder when his gaze drops to the collar. "It pleases me that you still wear it."

"Didn't you tell her to stay close to her master?" Dagon digs the blade a little deeper, so I feel the point, before stepping off to the side for Orias to approach.

My eyes narrow. Point taken. I shouldn't have been out alone and now I've been caught where Orias can do who knows what to me.

Onna scans the area before leaning casually against the corner of the barn's entrance. Her braids lay loose over her shoulders instead of the ponytail she normally keeps them in. She turns her hand out, absentmindedly inspecting her nails.

The intensity in which Orias looks at me is disheartening. The casual tone of his voice is a facade because, by the look in his eyes, he still wants to rip me apart.

I am thankful for the shield of Dagon's body.

"Raum rarely lets me out of his sight. I wanted to see Pethaino for myself. I have never seen a kingdom quite like yours. Please don't tell him." I'm not afraid of what Raum might do to me. Providing Orias doesn't know I was actually spying on him, I think Raum will be very interested in what I have to say.

"Does he beat you?"

The question catches me off guard. "And more," I say, trying to gauge him.

Orias's lids lower as he looks at me from head to toe. Dagon steps to the side reluctantly when the king reaches for me. My shield gone, I am completely bare to Orias when he grabs my jaw.

"I think I will tell him then. I'd love to hear this scream of yours that has him so infatuated." He runs a talon across the underside of my throat. "Would you scream for me?" He slides the talon up to the edge of my chin.

A tremor runs along the ground, eating its way through my boots into my legs. Rusted blades clatter from the barn's wall to the ground. The three demons stand erect all at once, their eyes flashing to the sky. As soon as Orias's eyes leave me, I throw my entire weight into him to throw him off balance. He turns to catch me, but the tremor increases and he overreaches, only the sweep of air from his hand grazing me.

Onna sticks out her leg as I move to dart past her and sends me sprawling. I claw at the ground, gaining purchase, and hoist myself up before any of them have a chance to grab me.

"Run!" Orias's deep voice rings out. "Run, Leah! I'll see you soon!"

I don't stop until the barn is out of sight and I am forced to my knees when the ground makes a thunderous rumble. Bare trees bend without wind and pebbles scuttle across the ground. The hairs stand up on my arm. I look behind me once to make sure they aren't in pursuit. When no one comes, I look to gain my bearings.

Even as my mind screams at me to flee, I am frozen, too terrified by whatever is about to happen as the tremor continues to intensify, shaking swords loose from the city walls with a loud clatter. A shout comes from the battlement when a crack splits up the side of the wall.

The explosion comes with a terrible screech. I fall forward onto my hands and curl up against the building next to me for a second to regain my balance. If I stay here, I'm likely to be impaled by a falling weapon. I stay low, moving as quick as I can. Two demons rush past me, but they are too busy shouting orders to pay any attention to my eyes. No one cares because they are running as I am, looking for safety.

It's minutes before the earthquake stops. I stumble into the bushes beneath my room. My stomach lurches violently. I crouch again, throwing my head between my knees until the nausea passes.

What the hell was that?

Orias hadn't behaved as if he had done it, but he didn't seem surprised either.

There is a thick haze that hangs in the air. Shadows dart back and forth as they scramble in preparation for another aftershock. I swallow hard when I hear them. I glance up at the window. I can make it in time.

It's harder to climb when your muscles are tense and shaking. I dig my fingers into the shallow grips the wall provides, willing every inch of me to keep moving no matter what. When my foot slips, I hold on even tighter, chipping my nail. Sweat breaks out over my brow and I grit my teeth, pushing with everything I have for the final climb.

I'm halfway through the window when the next quake hits. Someone grabs me beneath my arms and pulls me through. I yelp as I fall against their chest.

I let Raum's familiar scent envelop me and I throw my arms around him. He holds me close, caging himself around my body as the room shakes. Around us, the room falls apart. Glass shatters just behind me and I flinch in his arms.

I'm breathing hard when the quake stops. I don't let go, terrified that another one is going to rip through us again any moment.

"Are you okay?" Raum asks. He pulls back, taking my face between his big hands to look at me. One thumb brushes across my temple and the other across my cheek.

"Yes," I say breathlessly. "What's going on?"

"Where were you?" he asks, blatantly ignoring me.

I pull away, but only so he is no longer touching my face. Raum follows me to my feet, not letting the distance grow between us more than a few inches. "I was scouting."

"Scouting for what?" His eyes drop to my neck and narrow.

I touch the collar involuntarily. "I like it even less, but it has its advantages. Orias is up to something."

"Orias is my *friend.*" The word sounds awkward on his tongue. "He served me. There is nothing you need to uncover that I would not already know about."

I scoff. "Have you forgotten about the wraith?" He takes a step back and very subtly looks past me. He'll never admit that he is wrong. "What did you find?"

I glance out the window, nervous that the sheer mention of the wraith will bring another one swooping into the room.

"Orias has the key to Babel. I saw him speaking with another demon in the aviary about it." When he looks at me further, I roll my eyes. "I was hiding in the rafters above the angels."

Raum grunts. "It is impossible. Orias wouldn't know what the key was even if it was directly under his nose."

"And how would you know? You shouldn't trust him the way that you do."

Raum isn't looking at me now. Something has caught his eye through the window. I step in front of him, placing my hand on his chest. "You have it." It's not really a question. I look at him, dumbfounded.

"Why else do you think he needs me?" The corner of his mouth tugs up, but he moves past me. "He has not let up on us ruling together since I arrived."

I follow after him. The dust has settled across the rubble in the streets. Demons and men heave against the bigger stones in an attempt to move them closer to the wall and buildings they've fallen from. Raum leans over the sill so his long arms drape out the window. I can see he is contemplating something.

"Maybe he thinks you'll give it to him," I press.

The smug line of his mouth finally breaks when he laughs.

"Do you not see the way he looks at you? He believes you to be more than friends."

The smile falters but he doesn't say anything. A twang of jealousy courses through my body. I have no reason to be jealous. I only desire Raum because of his hold on me. Raum does not look at Orias the same way Orias looks at him. His eyes have rarely left me since we entered Pethaino. And still, it hurts me to see the flash of pain behind his eyes.

"Where were you this morning?"

He straightens, lifting his head to look farther out. "I flew past the city to read the land. It's moved since we got here."

A chill runs down my neck. I wonder how many times he has turned into a crow and I've never noticed it was him. I'll never forget the way his beautiful face turned jet black and morphed into a beak and feathers. I'll never forget the way the bullet felt striking my chest.

I blink the memory away, focusing desperately on the present.

"I was wondering if those were mountains." Raum looks back at me quizzically. "On the horizon after Corsen was killed," I press.

"That is a wave. With this new quake, it is going to continue to build in size before it hits."

The wave would have to be stories, massively tall to be seen in the distance like that. I've never even heard of a tsunami that size before. There won't be anything left of Pethaino when it hits.

"There is talk that the city is going to be under water soon."

Raum nods. "Orias has always been impatient. He is flaunting power he doesn't know how to wield, and it is going to cost him." He frowns again before turning away from the window to press his back against the wall. He looks torn, his brows furrowed, and a grim line is set into his mouth.

I take a deep breath. "Raum," I say softly, waiting for him to meet my eyes. "He remains loyal so long as he thinks he is in your favor. If you deny him this key, he is going to betray you."

He holds my eyes for a long moment. "I know."

"So, what are you going to do?"

"Whatever we may have been in the past has no weight on our present. I cannot help him. Power cannot be divided and wielded responsibly. With that sort of fire in Orias's hands, he will destroy everything."

Raum cocks his head, blinking slowly. It's as if he is seeing me for the first time. I look behind me to make sure there is nothing there, but when I look back, he is still staring. There is a flicker of hope that it's Sebastian looking at me instead of the demon. Looking more closely, I realize it's still Raum. Sebastian's features have faded, his jawline and cheekbones more defined with Raum's bone structure. A wave of guilt washes over me. I had used him again without a second thought. Only he hadn't resurfaced again. Perhaps he is dead, as Raum promised.

The demon smiles softly, his full lips parting to reveal his canines, pointed and hungry. I close the space between us, laying my hand against his chest.

"You have so many uses, my little spy," he says.

"Does this mean you have decided not to kill me once you are finished with me?" It's a dangerous question.

He takes my face in his hands and slides his fingers through my hair, turning my head to the side to expose my throat. He runs a thumb along the vein there.

"We will see."

XIII

A single flame sparks between Raum's fingers when he snaps them together. It licks the side of his index. When he turns his palm up, the flame spreads to his open fist, stretching out with flexed fingers. He turns out his other hand to do the same.

"What is the key?" I ask carefully.

He told me before that he intended to become a god once he took Babel. I can't let him do that. Taking the key is as close as I'll ever get to stopping him.

It has to be somewhere on his person. There's not a chance he would have it tucked away somewhere in the room. Though, it doesn't keep my gaze from searching. Perhaps it is glamoured and my mortal eyes can't see it.

"A relic," he says.

"What sort of relic?"

He cuts me a warning glare from his position by the fireplace. "One useless to humans." He turns his hands, letting the flames he has created lick up his arm.

"Well, if–"

"Enough," he snaps. He tosses his hands, sending the flames on his skin into the fire before him.

I fold my arms across my chest. "I give you information that Orias intends to screw you over and you continue to be dishonest with me."

His glare hardens. "It is in your best interest that you do not know."

Liar. He wouldn't keep it from me if it wasn't important.

"Do you care about me, even a little?"

"You know that I do."

"Then prove it."

"I do not have to." There's a silver lining to his voice that strikes a chord in me. Of course he cares about me. In his strange, twisted way, he is as entangled with me as I am with him. At least one of us was able to make that choice.

I turn on my heel to stalk across the room. In six days, Pethaino will be under water and I am not willing to wait around until that happens. There is nowhere for me to run, and I cannot act unless Raum wills it.

His quiet reserve unsettles me as he falls back into a trance the fire casts. He looks more withdrawn than ever. I know it's not just keeping secrets that has him in such a way. It's strange seeing him like this. It makes him seem too human.

I knew they were close, but seeing him so only confirms he and Orias were more.

Does Raum love Orias? Did he? When his sharp eyes meet mine, I dismiss it entirely. No, he isn't capable of such a thing, but perhaps he had been close to it once. I scratch at an old scar on my chest, brushing away the needling prick of jealousy.

Through the windows leaks an eerie song. It pulls me from my seat and straightens the hairs on my arm.

The note is high and clear pitched, soft like silk and slow moving. There is a definite sense of wrongness about the music, despite its beauty. It coils in the air, fading to a soft echo before picking up again in an even higher, stranger note.

Below the window, demons walk casually through the streets. Laughter, beautiful music of their own, mingles with the melody.

"What is that?"

"Siren's song. Though I doubt there are any here. More than likely it is a spell cast on one of the women to give her such a voice." He looks off in the distance, his head slightly cocked as he listens.

A chill runs through me. What other creatures of myth are real? The thought is dismissed when Raum continues.

"It is the night of Eirini. In Tartarus, it is one of the longest nights of the year, a night of peace." He takes a place beside me, looking down as the crowd makes their way in the direction of the Hall.

"It feels wicked." I scope beyond the walls, but the light of the sun has sunk so low that I can't make out much past the barrier of bodies and blades. "I wouldn't think there would be any need for peace in Hell."

He smirks. "It is not as you have heard. Every world has war and blood lust in common. But they also have tranquility and order. You are right that Tartarus is more hostile, but we are not savages." He gives me an arched look. I scoff and he smiles softly in return. "On this night, the only blood shed is in celebration, not of violence."

"Are demons not always violent?"

The look in his eye shifts as he cocks his head. "I am not always violent with you."

"Your kindness is a cruel thing." I dread the idea of what acts they might consider peaceful. If Raum's kindness is any inclination of this night, it is still enough to sicken me.

The intensity of his gaze does nothing to ease my concern. I focus on the fires lighting across the battlements and streets of Pethaino. Anything to keep me from looking back at him. If I look, that hypnotic stare will swallow me up and I'll be helpless once more.

"Here, you need to change." He extends a bundle of glittering cloth.

"I have no interest in however it is your kind celebrates this little holiday."

"None of that. Tonight is the best opportunity for us to leave without causing a stir."

Relief never tasted so sweet. I'd be more relaxed if it were not for the incessant music in the air. It heightens my urgency to run, to get out of here as quickly as we can. At least we would finally be able to put this horror behind us.

I slip on a similar outfit to the one I am already wearing. The tunic has a high neck and stiff shoulders made of glittering tulle. The bodice is a leather fit, the rolls of fabric cutting off at my thighs. I exchange my pants for a cleaner pair and re-lace my boots.

He hasn't taken his eyes off me. There's something lurking beneath the hunger that I can't place. It shakes the unease I'm struggling to bury.

When it comes time to retie my hair, Raum runs his fingers through the knots, untangling each piece with care. He braids a few strands back so it is out of my face but leaves the majority of it down the way he likes.

In the dark, Pethaino is more menacing. Whether ghosts are real or not doesn't erase the fact that the city is haunted. I'd call whatever stalks us a ghost. Perhaps what I see are only wraiths though. White and gray wisps float through alleys while others glide through closed doorways and bricked walls.

The haunting music of the woman's voice still moves languidly through the air, drumming up the suspense that any moment something is going to snatch my hand from the shadows.

Raum leads us through darker parts of the city, taking the long way until we come to the courtyard before the Hall. It strikes me then that our path has led us away from the gore, as much of it as we can avoid. I press my shoulder into Raum as we move quickly beneath the heads, noticing that his eyes are down but fiery. It is a special type of fear that whorls around him, one laced with contempt.

My eyes glaze over as a powerful fog clouds the rest of my senses. I wish it had smothered them entirely, but no amount of shock can stifle the heady scent of blood and where it comes from as we enter the Hall. Bodies, some less alive than others, are splayed before the dais, laying open with spread legs or gaping chests. Amongst them are demons with their faces buried in whatever part of a cadaver they can feast on.

The floor is open, the tables arranged around it like there is to be a dance. The outer ring is decorated with cotton white flowers in gilded vases of roses. Skirting on the edge, between the vases and tables, are black palms. Though not decayed by the look of their full plumage, they still stink of rot. Plants are not something I had expected to see.

One demon in particular catches my eye. He has the handsome face of a young man, soft wheat colored skin and short sandy blond hair. Deep dimples pierce his cheeks when he smiles at the human woman he is speaking with. He reaches for her, taking a strand of her dark hair between his fingers and bringing it to his face to sniff. The muscles in his back twitch and his lower half coils with anticipation.

My mouth goes dry. I look at his face again, thinking the shadows are playing tricks on me, and then back down to his body. From the torso up, he is a man; from the waist down is the body of a snake. Brown and black scales in a python's pattern lay wrapped around the woman's legs.

An invisible tether tugs at my throat. "Come," Raum says, breaking me out of the trance. I didn't realize I had stopped walking.

"What is he?" I take a hesitant step to follow Raum, but the demon—the creature—holds me captive.

"He is like the rest of us. Have you never seen one of us shift?"

I swallow. "Not like that," I say, shaking my head.

I let him take my hand, unable to take my eyes off the demon as he slithers on the table next to the woman, leering over her with a smile so charming it should be sinful.

There are more creatures like him, but Raum does not allow me to pause like before. Between them are humans, lounged in a petrified state. I catch glimpses of ivory horns on one demon and a bristled tale like a lion on the backside of another as we cross to the back of the Hall through a silvery black door.

As it closes behind us, the twisted magic of what I witnessed sets in and I have to lean forward to catch my breath. Raum lays his hand on the back of my neck, but there is little comfort in the weight of it when all I can imagine are the coils of a snake. I swat his hand away as I stand, taking a deep breath.

"I hate this place," I murmur.

Tudor arches rise out of the darkness as my eyes adjust to the dim light. It reeks of decay. The stench of rotten leaves and flesh taint the air. The pungent smell sits heavy on the back of my tongue. I fight the urge to gag behind the back of my hand.

The shadows reach out, long invisible tongues lick the side of my face, and I bolt forward. Raum catches my elbow and hauls me to his side. In the shield of his body and arm, the invisible things do not touch me. Whatever they are scurry along the walls, pausing once they're ahead of us to watch and running again when we get closer.

."I can't take this," I breathe.

Funny how it is more terrifying when you can't see the things that go bump in the night.

"What about a story?" Raum suggests.

I lick my lips, my eyes darting frantically for something to jump out at us. "Do not try to scare me further." I take another deep breath. "A good one, not a scary one."

He chuckles, the sweet music of his voice softening my building hysteria. A smooth caress follows the sound. It glides over the chills on my arms and settles the urge to run. "But it's so delicious when you are afraid."

I slap his chest lightly and he chuckles again. The simple ease that passes between us makes me scowl. It's what I need to clear my head. The pristine music of his voice fades while he contemplates.

"There once was a world full of darkness created before memory. It was cold with white-capped mountains and black desolation. Creatures of scale and fire roamed the land and creatures of lightning and flesh the sea. It was a cruel place meant to be forgotten.

"One day the sky opened, like a great storm cloud, and thousands of stars fell into the black earth. Their screams filled the expanse of the world. They burned their way into the soil, creating a giant pit of pain and torment. Out of this pit their screams rang as their light was stripped from them.

"The stars that were strong enough rose from the ashes, clawing to the surface before the pit could claim them. Those that did not escape were wrapped in chains of darkness where they would suffer for eternity. Never to know the touch of peace and warmth again.

"Though the stars had lost their shining light, a new one of fire and brimstone surfaced. It was a hungry flame that lit the land. Forests grew where there had been nothing and rivers burst free of the ocean. What had once been nothing became something beautiful. The sky was the most beautiful thing about the world. Light burned holes across the sky where the stars had burned through, creating galaxies and images you cannot fathom.

"But the beauty had to come from somewhere. Where the stars had been full of color with many wings and crowns, their skin became bloodless and slick as leather. Their straight smiles, pointed. The hunger for blood started almost immediately, became insatiable. And what was left of our burnt wings–"

Raum has gotten so caught up in his own story that he barely catches himself. I told him no scary stories and instead he gives me one of suffering. It's on the edge of his voice as if he relives it, his dark eyes wide with memory.

"Our wings," he says softly. "They became tatters, shards of bone that stuck from our backs. A cruel reminder of what we had lost."

I step in front of him, halting our pace by sliding my hand across his chest. The steady thrum of his heart pulses beneath my palm. I've never heard the story from one of them before. Angels fallen from grace and the creation of Hell.

I wish the bond worked both ways, so I could see inside his head. When I press, searching for the chord, there is nothing. "I'm sorry," I say. "I'm so sorry that happened to you."

He takes my hand gently from his chest and gives it a little squeeze. "Every choice comes with a sacrifice. Some with a price higher than others. I knew what it would cost me before I fell."

At the end of the hall are Dagon and the Asian demon I recognize to be Ipos. They stand erect with their hands clasped, chins up and eyes sharp. There is no signal between them when Ipos turns, slipping through the doors behind him.

Dagon looks between us, his obsidian stare settling on me briefly. Too long.

"Careful," Raum says. "You will not be getting this one." He knows, he knows who Dagon is and what he has done. Why wouldn't he if he can see into my head?

Dagon stiffens, but before he can open his mouth, Ipos reappears, opening the door wider for us to pass. I don't know what is going to happen to us in the next room with Raum's threat dangling in the air between us. What is to come of his refusal to Orias? What price must be paid? I take reassurance in Eirini and the soft touch of Dagon's fingers on the back of my hand as we cross over the threshold that, at least for tonight, nothing can hurt us.

XIV

I expected Orias's chambers to be as elaborate as he. They are dull with muted colors of black and gray. On the far side of the room are sheer curtains. There's a glint of black light that slides somewhere behind them. Another curl of wind billows the curtains apart to reveal a shining black wall, from the floor, disappearing somewhere into the heights of the ceiling. It looks like it would be a giant mirror, but from this angle, it reflects nothing in the room. Just darkness.

There is no bed or dresser. A fire burns down the side of another wall on the far side of the room in a waterfall of blue flames, and in front of it stands Orias. He is already facing us, his hands folded behind his back and his face lifted so the blue light highlights his perfect face. When he smiles, it almost looks as if he is glowing.

Raum looks around the room absentmindedly. He seems entirely disinterested in being here even though he is the one that invited himself. The rest of Orias's personal guard are silhouetted along the walls. The only one I am able to distinguish is Onna, due to her lighter hair standing out amongst the shadows.

"Have you considered my offer?" Orias asks.

My heart slams against my chest. I'm thankful I have my knife on me and that Raum isn't facing him alone. This is it.

"I will not help you," Raum says evenly.

Orias's smile falters and then drops entirely. There is a long pause, one of shock, before he speaks. "Why not?"

"Neither of us is naïve enough to believe we will divide the Power once it is within reach. Have you so easily forgotten the court of four kings? Look where that rule got them." He turns his eyes slowly back to Orias, as if it's a task to even look upon him. "When I get to Babel, I intend to take it all for myself."

The king blinks as he tries to gather himself. "Those kings were weak creatures we cannot compare ourselves to. You think so little of me to be your equal, but—"

"No," Raum says. "I hold you in high regard, Orias, but in this matter you have no place. This is something I must do alone."

Orias's beautiful face twists into a menacing snarl. His eyes fall on me, and I can instantly feel his rage. I should drop my eyes, but the power he holds me with demands I keep looking. It must take great self-control for him not to cross the room and rip me apart. I am certain he wishes he had done it before, when he had me alone. I think he would do it now if Raum were not beside me. It looks as if he considers it anyway as his nostrils flare.

"Why do you really keep her?" His voice is much more composed when he speaks.

Raum strokes the bite on my neck he has yet to heal. His fingers drop down to the invisible one on my shoulder. Though he had wiped away that mark, there is still a deep ache where his fangs touched bone. "She sustains me. You know as well as I that we cannot survive in this world without their blood. Or what other reason to harvest the humans? I hear you have them strung in the rafters until they are ripe and ready to be picked."

"Enough!" Orias gnashes his teeth together. I jump at the loud clack they make. "I am a *king*. I am *cyn*. I served you faithfully and now, when you are *my* guest, in *my* kingdom, you refuse to show me the same loyalty?"

The hiss that emits from the back of Raum's throat is so low I know I'm the only one that hears it.

All the guards have their hands ready at their swords, a silver flash as they catch the light, even Dagon. I wonder who he will protect if it comes to it. I can't imagine him giving up his secret so easily, not when there is still so much work to be done. Raum and I are outnumbered greatly, and I don't like the odds. I feel like the walls are closing in on us and they have very sharp and very big claws.

"It is not loyalty that I lack," Raum says. The cruelness I know so well trickles through. "Tread lightly, brother. Tartarus still holds more power than Earth and we are all bound to it. I more than you. I do not want to fight with you."

Because you will not win. I hear the unspoken words. I can see it in the shock in Orias's face.

He regains his composure quickly, though his rage still coils tightly around his body in smoky tendrils. "I think you would be surprised what would happen in a fight between us." The black of his eyes lights up with the light of hungry flames. "Tomorrow, you will leave. No assistance will be granted from Pethaino when the waters take you."

Relief and dread fill me. Who is to say Orias wouldn't shift the tides again and drown us as soon as we were outside of his gates? I look at Raum hesitantly, but his eyes are locked on the demon he was once so close with.

While I firmly believe nothing good can come from an alliance with Orias, I wish Raum could have lied about it in some way, bought us a little more time until we were safely out from under his claws instead of at his mercy.

Raum turns me with him as he walks away. Every part of me wants to scream. How can he be so confident when we are so exposed?

"Raum," Orias calls. The light pitch of his voice chills me. Raum's fingers tighten, but he stops to look back. "Join us tonight, for the sake of Eirini. There is going to be a feast. There will be far more blood than that little *bag t*o quench your thirst." He emphasizes the last word. It's not the first time I'd been called a blood bag for one of them. "Do me this honor."

Raum places his fist over his chest. The gesture I'm sure is meant to be respectful but there isn't an ounce of humility in him. "For Eirini."

The tension is so taut I don't know how we make it out without either of them at the other's throat. Raum's muscles are swollen with contained energy. The veins in his neck and arms stand out like they are about to burst.

"We should leave now," I hiss under my breath as the door shuts behind us. This time we do not have an escort. Orias has left us entirely alone and unguarded. I wish Dagon had been sent with us. At least I felt somewhat safe with him.

"No," Raum says. "If we leave now, it will appear as if we are running. We will go to his banquet tonight, and before the last hour of Eirini ends, we will leave."

I step in front of him, placing my hand on his chest. His wild heartbeat matches my own. "Please, Raum. I want to leave now."

He looks over my head before grabbing my hand and leading me to a dark corner of the castle closer to the Hall. Laughter rolls down the hallway.

I have a hard time seeing Raum in the low light, but I find his eyes glistening back at me. "We will leave tonight, but first we must do this. Orias is going to be a problem I must deal with in the future, and staying will soften the blow."

I shut my eyes to fight back the scream I want to release. It's not what I wanted to hear, but at least he is meeting me halfway.

"Promise me we will leave as soon as we can." I meet his eyes again in the darkness. His breath washes over my face as he bends down and presses his forehead against mine. Our noses brush and our faces tilt farther still until our lips are pressed together.

"Soon," he says.

***

Neither of us touch any of the food that comes our way. While my stomach rumbles, I refuse it in case someone has been instructed to poison us. I know I'll regret it later, but that's a bridge I'll cross when I get to it. I'm sure Raum would cut himself again if it came to it.

It's all for show that Raum keeps his place beside Orias on the golden throne. I stand between them like the good pet I am supposed to be. I had tried to stay as far away from Orias but, somehow, he had worked it so there was no other place for me to stand. I run my palms over the long tunic absentmindedly to keep anyone from noticing how bad I am shaking. From there, I run my fingers along the belt where my kukri is still strapped safely.

Breathe. We will be gone from here soon enough.

Dagon and Ipos stand readily behind Orias's throne. I search the crowd, but I do not see Onna. I don't like knowing she is about somewhere lurking and I have no way of knowing when or how she might strike.

I turn my attention back to Raum and Orias as I will my mind to focus elsewhere. I give a subtle glance at Dagon before I do. There is a grim line to his mouth that makes my stomach clench.

Side by side, Raum and Orias look like snakes. Their loose, dark hair like the hood of a cobra, framing their beautiful faces in shadow. The blue light of Pethaino casts a dull glow amidst the golden fire that lights the ceiling, casting rippling colors across their shining skin. For all the talk about being kings, neither of them wears a crown. Tonight, neither of them bares any skin but their face and arms. Where Orias has always been bare chested, he now wears a shirt made of chains so fine it could be thread. It makes a soft tinkling sound when the links hit together.

Raum, for once, is in dark red. The fabric might as well have been dipped in blood for its color. It brings out the red tones of his skin. His pants are the same black as before with a cargo pocket on one thigh that I hope has some sort of weapon in it. Just in case.

Orias looks down at everyone. His face evolves like a mask, the fake smile molded in place while the rest of his body remains taut. The only thing revealing his near slip of control is the crazed look in his eyes. Every sharp edge of him has grown soft except for those wild, black eyes. My heart skips a beat when he stands. I reach for Raum.

"How good it is to have wounded the Enemy!" he shouts. "And what timing it is to fall on Eirini!"

The crowd answers in unison, raising their fists into the air. The guttural sound of their cry reverberates across the room. Demons shove their shoulders into one another, flashing their dangerous smiles. I learned while in Leyak's company that by the Enemy, the demons mean God. But what a strange thing to say when God is supposed to be dead. Well, Raum has eluded that He no longer exists.

Orias holds up his hand to quiet the mass. I touch Raum gently; something doesn't feel right. It's a subtle shift in the air, like all the peace mentioned has been sucked out of it.

"There have been rumors moving through the city." He turns his palm out to Raum. "Raum is cyn of Eurynomos for those of you lesser and unfamiliar with his name. It has been a long time since any of us have been home, and word travels slowly. I think I speak for all of Pethaino when I say we are truly humbled by your presence." The wild look darkens when he looks at Raum. My heart beats faster and I dig my nails into Raum's shoulder. I am not sure if I am holding onto him for my own good or his. Raum feels like he is about to spring to his feet by the roil of his muscles.

"It is with great elation that I thank you—that we all thank you," Orias says, turning back to the crowd, "for the power you will lend us in changing the tides. Tomorrow, Legion, we will have Babel."

The roar of the crowd is not loud enough to drown out the angry growl beside me. It is not enough to stop even me from laying a hand on Orias. The fury that sweeps through me removes my hand from Raum to grasp Orias.

"Have you lost your mind?" I hiss.

Orias grabs my hand and jerks me against him as soon as I feel Raum come up behind me. "Careful, brother," he snarls, lips curling back so much his gums flash. "You did this. You deny me what is rightfully due to me for the years of service I gave you. It is I who am the king now and you the servant. Don't make me take this, too." He grabs my chin roughly and forces my head back so far, I catch a glimpse of Raum. Either my vision is obscured from the pain of this angle, or there is smoke sifting around his body.

Another eruption of clamor breaks through the crowd. Someone throws their fist into the air, and there, just behind it, is an arch of blood. And behind that is Onna.

I reach for the hilt of my kukri and push against Orias. He releases me, sending me stumbling back into Raum's protective grasp.

The crowd spreads to reveal Onna standing on the body of a fallen demon, her sword poised at her side with a fresh sheen of blood running down the edge. A burly demon bursts onto the floor with sword and shield in hand.

It's not the attack I thought was happening, but some sort of entertainment. The gladiators of the Fallen, it would appear. I unsnap the hook of my sheath in case I am in need of a quick draw.

"Take it into consideration it is because of your service that I do not humiliate you in front of your kingdom. Eirini is the only thing that keeps your head on your shoulders. As of this moment, you are my enemy."

Fuck this night of peace. Why doesn't Raum kill him? Isn't he strong enough? Or can he not take on a whole kingdom should they rise up to their fallen king?

Orias waves his hand dismissively. "Watch," he says and points.

I follow his finger back to Onna. I don't understand what is happening. I don't understand why Raum is still doing *nothing*.

I look between Onna's carnage and Orias, trying to piece together which one of them I should be watching.

Onna is incredible to watch. She moves with the grace of a dancer, the stroke of her sword like the turn of a page. Everything she does is soft but deadly. The elegant slice of iron into flesh is so fluid that I catch my breath. She creates a masterpiece out of a massacre—something I never thought could exist. Blood spilled out of celebration, not violence.

She terrifies me.

Her opponent is twice her size, height and width. The bulk of his biceps are bigger than her entire frame and yet she pushes against him as if he weighs nothing.

The flow of her sword is merciless as she hacks into the raised shield. The large battle axe he stepped onto the floor with was lost some time ago when she slit the wrist he now holds pressed to his chest.

I don't know how she does it. Onna moves too quickly for my eyes to keep up. In one moment, she is slicing her sword toward his throat and the next she is sliding between his legs and cutting into the thick meat of his inner thigh before she comes up behind his back, her sword following the length of his spine.

The animalistic roar that leaves the demon's throat sends chills across my spine.

Onna strolls back to the demon gripping his inner thigh, his shield forgotten. Her strides are prominent like she walks the runway. With a twist of her wrist, the blade curves into a pristine arch and, at the last moment, as it comes down, she takes the hilt with both hands and cuts the demon's head from his body in a single stroke.

"Who will face Sake-Onna?" Orias bellows.

A ripple surges through the crowd. Even Onna stands a little straighter, her dark skin cooling to a soft brown.

Movement behind me makes me go rigid. Ipos is lunging at me, and even as Dagon makes a move to stop him, he is not fast enough. Ipos slams his shoulder into me and I fall forward.

It feels like I hit every stone step before I finally slam into the floor at Onna's feet.

Above me, Raum makes a move to step forward then stops. His eyes turn sharply to Orias. He can't come to my rescue. It'll show his blatant favor toward me and I, after all, am supposed to be replaceable. A bloodbath is the only outcome if he comes for me. Raum should have listened to my pleas. Orias has laid a trap for us that we might not escape.

A chuckle fills the air when I find my feet. I reach for my kukri tentatively, surprised to find it still in its sheath.

Sake-Onna. Say her name.

The voice inside my head jolts me out of the daze of my fall. Reflexively, I tighten my grip on the handle and whirl back to look at Raum. Except it wasn't his voice inside my head I just heard. It was Sebastian's.

Distantly, Orias belts about a challenger, but I can't make out the words he says. Not when Sebastian is yelling at me.

There is a tremor in Raum's face and he twists his head violently, his teeth gnashing together. I take a step toward them only to have Onna step in my path. Her shadow swallows the light around us.

She laughs. "The fight is over before it has begun."

"Let her bleed slowly!" someone calls from the rafters. "To honor the Enemy," another mocks.

I pull my kukri free. If I am to die, it'll be because I fought until the end. I try to shake Sebastian's voice from my head and the way I saw him fighting to break through Raum. One thing at a time.

I take a couple of steps back, putting as much distance between us as I can. Onna watches me and smiles. She follows me, taking a wide birth as if she stalks me.

I know I won't be walking off this floor, but the words that come out of my mouth shock even me. "How poor Pethaino must think of you to offer me as your opponent."

Her upper lip curls. "We will see how much you have to say when your skull is crushed beneath my boot."

And just like that, she closes the space between us again.

She covers the hilt of her sword behind her palm and keeps the sheath hidden. I already know the length of her blade, though. Another couple of steps and her two-foot-long sword will be able to reach me. That's the problem with fighting with shorter blades. I'm going to have to get very close to her to do any sort of damage. The other problem is, if I have any chance of surviving, I should have chosen a better weapon.

The double-edged blade glistens as she tightens her grip and takes a slow step toward me. Now that I can see the fine details of her sword, it favors something of a katana with a sharp end and twisted hilt. It makes sense that she would use such a weapon for how quick she is.

I'll have a split second to try and hook her arm when she draws on me.

No sooner has the thought entered my mind that she does. I jump back when she brings it down, but I'm not fast enough. She thrusts the sword forward out of the arch and into the top of my hip. The sharp pain that tears through me grits my teeth. I stumble back and look between her and the wound.

It's superficial. She's playing with me.

When she approaches again, I'm ready. I step with her, keeping distance between us. I twist as she pulls a similar move, but this time, I hook her forearm with the curve in my blade and pull.

She follows, pushing her arm into the blade to throw me off balance. I slide my foot back to accommodate for her weight and pull again, slicing the blade deeper until it meets bone. With an angry grunt, Onna jerks her arm free and stabs the sword into my thigh. Twice. It's quick like a snakebite.

Burnt flesh fills the air beneath the hand she's clamped over her wound. I let a smile flutter over my face as red oozes between her fingers. A demon shedding blood is a sign of weakness.

Except Onna is anything but weak. She comes at me with a vengeance, her blade cutting and stabbing into me while I have barely enough time to defend myself. I get a lucky hit to her inner thigh that she returns by kicking me in the face.

I get an even luckier shot in a turn she makes that leaves her neck open. I thrust my palm into her shoulder blade, and with my other hand, I bring down the kukri where her throat meets her shoulder. It's not until I see her smile that I realize she has done it on purpose.

Onna lives and breathes to slaughter. It radiates from her. She cuts her sword through the air in a graceful arch and brings it down on me. I pull my blade up with barely enough time to block the blow. The force of it rattles my bones.

Onna slices again as I try to widen the space between us. She isn't going to give me the opportunity to steady myself. I lose count of how many times she brings her wrath down. Searing pain erupts under her blade, appearing in my back, torso, and, hell, everywhere. My blade is too small for hers. And I'm tiring quickly. Why isn't Raum helping me?

"You call this a challenge?" She thrusts her sword out as I stumble away. "What a lap dog you are. A true king would have a warrior at his side."

Blood flows from her attacks. I can't even stand upright anymore, and my shoulder is fucked, leaving my left arm useless. The fury that rakes through me numbs the pain as it splits apart like a dam.

"Drop your sword, Sake-Onna," I spit.

Fury ripples across her face. "You bitch," she snarls. She slings her blade at me, but it's clumsy. Her movement isn't as graceful as she has been and I'm able to dodge it without being cut. It slides across the floor, spinning to the feet of the crowd.

The playfulness she had exhibited evaporates entirely. She tackles me with slender fingers that change to talons in midair and sinks them into me. Her claws slash down my face, chest, and belly. Again and again. I pull my arm up to try and deflect her, but she cuts into that, too, relieving me of my kukri.

I twist as her hand closes around the side of my neck and her claws follow.

"Stop!"

Onna freezes, her touch pressing into my jugular.

The pain that attacks me is unbearable. I cry out as what she's done finally hits me. Blood crawls across my body, seeping through my clothes to spread across the ground. It's slow, like the onlooker requested, but I'm dying. I crane my head back toward the thrones. If anyone else had been looking at Raum, they would have noticed the same pain reflected in his eyes. Can he feel this? Why isn't he stopping it? I look at him pleadingly.

"Stop," Orias says again. He slams his hands on the skulls that make up the arms of his seat as he stands. "Do you concede, Leah?"

I can't speak so I blink, trying to clear the blood away in my eyes. *Yes.*

"Yes?" he snaps.

"Yyyy," I sound.

"It is Eirini," he tsks. "As a sign of good faith, I cannot allow her to die," he speaks loudly for the crowd. He looks down at Raum and then over to Dagon. "Take her to my quarters."

Raum shoots up out of his seat, moving in front of Dagon and successfully blocking his path to me. "You will not take what belongs to me," he growls.

Orias rounds on Raum so that they are nose to nose. "She lost. So, for tonight, she belongs to me. Besides, it's not like I can kill her."

Yet. The unspoken word is harrowingly loud.

Onna's hands change back, and she steps away when Dagon comes for me, shoving his way past Raum. He tells me to take a breath. I bite my lip to stifle a cry as he lifts me. It comes out as a muffled groan anyway.

I only catch a snippet of Orias speaking to Raum as Dagon carries me past. The level of his voice has quieted from the rest of the kingdom. I reach for Raum, a twitch of my finger.

"The laws here are the same as they are in Eurynomos. You offered yourself to me when you first came into Pethaino. I have decided to reject your offer and take her instead. Ah, ah, don't worry; I assure you Leah will be kept safe."

"You would dare hold us until morning," Raum seethes.

"The whole kingdom believes you to bring Babel to our lands. What is more precious to you?"

Rage trembles through Raum's muscles. If I were not so broken, I would leap from Dagon's arms and fall on Orias, ripping him to shreds.

"She is to be returned to me before dawn. Alive."

"Of course." Orias touches his chest in disbelief.

It's over. Whatever Raum was trying to hide from Orias is undone. Whatever escape we would have made has gone up in flames. And I, I am dead. Surely this is the true end because not even Raum will save me if it means giving up Babel.

I can't bear the expression on his face when he looks at me. Hatred, so pure and raw, reflects in his eyes, revealing the true monster he has always been.

Don't leave me, I beg. *Don't let them take me.*

But my voice doesn't come and darkness takes me mercilessly.

XV

Fire lashes across the front of my body. Too quickly, I touch a hand to my face, wincing, to the lacerations that start at my scalp and cut off just above my chin. My fingers tremble as I skim over the rest of my face. Marred. How badly, I'm too afraid to wonder. There are more urgent matters that need my attention than worrying over my appearance. One is that I'm alive. The second is that the one who spared me is in this room.

I touch the deepest cut on my face. Smooth.
What?
I trace over the lines I know were just there. I felt their trauma in my flesh. Nothing.

"Your skin is clean," Orias says. "It's a shame, really. He healed you before you left the floor. I wanted to dissect you while you were still so... open."

A cold hand with the grip of ice runs down my spine. Somehow, I'm standing up and not lying down like I originally thought. Wasn't I just on a couch? The space I'm in—a room maybe, but it's not a room—feels like a void, yet it is full of color. Rich fabrics hang from the invisible ceiling and lush pillows and cloth stack together like a nest, decorating the floor.

And since when are demons cold?

A shiver follows his fingertips as they glide away from my skin. My ripped tunic and pants have been traded for a skirt and cut-out tank top that exposes my shoulders and lower back. The material is dangerously thin, and I fear it'll fall apart if I move the wrong way.

"What is this place?" I ask when he steps next to me, surveying the room that looks much too intimate for us to be in together.

"It's whatever you want it to be." Orias waves his hand. The colors blend, forming paint strokes and drippings until the *room* looks like a wet canvas.

His mouth has a smug line to it. He has let the shadows fall over his face, and though I can't see his eyes, I imagine they're still quite mad. When he turns to face me, a sliver of them catches the light. Two black orbs glinting in the darkness. I swallow.

"Go on." He nods.

I look back to the paint. All of the places I've missed rush to mind, and the room shifts with my thoughts. A white bed with cotton sheets. A porch swing under a haunt blue ceiling. The next is the wall of books next to the big bay window—no. *Don't let him see that.* I can't let them see what they haven't tarnished yet.

Orias can see my struggle as the chair deflates and molds into... what is that? Bars of a cell?

"This is a safe place," he says. His cold hand, warmer now, touches my arm. "No tricks."

Never trust a liar.

Light cuts in through a skylight window. It slices through the books like a knife, causing pages to fly into the air. Within it is a hum that vibrates through the air, like the sound of a million wings. I flinch from the touch against my hand. Wheat. I take a step forward, following the field deeper as it expands. Boxes rise in their midst.

"A hive." Something in his voice draws my attention back to Orias. The light I've created washes over his face, exposing the fear behind the confusion he tries to mask it with. So, all of them are afraid of bees.

"Whatever I wanted."

"And I said no tricks." He holds up a finger. In this light, Orias looks more like a boy than a man, his smile full and charming. There's a dimple in his cheek I didn't notice before. How unfair it is that they are as beautiful as they are wicked.

"It's the last place I felt safe." I put my back to one of the hives. I can feel their wings' vibrations in the air. Real or not, it's comforting.

He nods.

"Is this where Raum found you?"

I shake my head. "This is where we killed everyone. I helped him murder who I thought were maybe the last people on earth. It was a massacre," I say distantly.

Orias's hand hovers over one of the hives before setting it on top. Hesitantly, he pushes it down, turning the white stand to smoking ash.

"And then he burned it," I say half to myself, remembering. It feels like only yesterday, not so long ago. I try to remember the days spent with Devon, the way her blue eyes shined whenever she watched me soak it all up. I close my eyes. Get out of my head. When I open them, Orias is staring intently.

"Why did you bring me here?"

What I really mean is, why am I not dead?

"To talk. In here, time moves differently. We can spend hours, days—years even—and the whole outside world won't change. I need more than a night with you."

Someone moves in the field behind him. I look past him, but it's just a shadow. I can't make out who it is supposed to be. They look too large to be Devon.

"You want something."

Orias points at me. "I want to know why Raum keeps you at his side."

"That makes two of us." It especially concerns me with the new knowledge of Raum's hatred for women.

"Tell me about yourself. Where you're from, your family, your friends. I want to know everything."

Another shadow moves in my peripheral and a chill runs down my spine. That one is supposed to be Mike. I can see the distinct outline of his beard, but he doesn't really have a face. Have their ghosts followed me?

"I'm from Michigan," I say slowly, turning my attention to Orias. "Near one of the Great Lakes. I was a student at the time of your arrival for marine biology. I'm an only child to parents who were lost to Sin. I had a few friends, a boyfriend. We hiked a lot and went swimming." I'm grasping at straws. I can't think of anything significant about my life that could be beneficial to him. "I used to have a dog." I lick my lips and glance at him.

Orias looks at me expectantly.

"Forgive me, but I don't know what you're looking for. I know Raum seeks pleasure in hurting women and he *does* hurt me, frequently, but I don't know why he has kept me alive other than to feed. I'm marked."

He looks at me for another heartbeat before looking over his shoulder to spy whatever has me spooked, but the apparition is gone. "Looking at you, you're of no significance. But if you've drawn Raum's eye—no, his mark—then you must be quite special," he says and nods to me. "Look up."

I look up into the harsh light, exposing my throat. His fingers, now warm, grip the edge of my jaw. The unmistakable intake of breath is followed by a string of demonic words. Orias's hands clasp the top of my shoulders, and he extends my body directly in front of his.

He's smiling. It's even wider than the grin he flashed before the fight. When he laughs, it is as sweet as silver bells.

"I thought my eyes deceived me there in the Hall."

What is there except a few freckles and a mole?

"I had thought you were some sort of key to Babel. Perhaps you still are, but..." Orias shakes his head and smiles again. "You're a weapon."

"A weapon?" I must have misheard him.

"In the old days, there was King Solomon, a mortal man, but he wielded powers shared between Heaven and Tartarus. With his seal and the true name of a demon, he had the ability to command us. The Fallen. Some said the seal was what you would call now the Star of David that he wore as a ring. But," he touches his finger to my chin again to look, "truthfully, it was a crescent burned into his skin beneath the ring." His finger follows the curve of freckles that cluster together.

"I'm not much of a weapon. I lost to Onna." Having a demon think you're important is worse than if they believe you're nothing.

"You used her name, and it worked. Didn't it?" Orias's jaw clenches. "You knew what you were doing."

"I–" I didn't. I did it to mock her and because Raum–Sebastian told me to. Of course it had been Sebastian because Raum would never let something so important slip. *This* is what he had been keeping from me. There was never any relic.

How did Sebastian gain access to that information? Do they share the same thoughts? I can't believe he is still alive. Fuck.

"It was in ignorance that I used it. Believe me, if I knew saying a demon's name gave me power over it, I would have been free of Raum a long time ago."

Orias sneers. "Do you really think Raum is his true name? He would not give that up to you. He's never given it to anyone." He waves his hand through the air and spins dramatically away. "Whether you are lying or not doesn't matter. You're better than I could have fathomed."

I jump back at the rush of fabric. A dress, a completely different outfit, has slipped over my head. A sheer dress with curling patterns that doesn't leave room for the imagination. Two very high splits run up to my hipbones. The front is plunging just as the back.

"Do all demons keep their names secret?" I ask tentatively, ignoring the way he has exposed me.

"You're referring to my use of Onna's true name." He pauses, his lids lowering as he grazes me with his stare. "There was a rumor that said Solomon's heir would have a hand in the new world and that it was a woman. Seeing you at Raum's side and that he wouldn't offer you made me suspicious that you were her. Onna gave me her name when she swore her loyalty to me. Our names are precious, but I needed to know if my guess was correct."

Having power to control demons doesn't do me any good if I'm still missing a key piece in manipulating them. Besides, is it true or is this just another way for Orias to toy with me? Perhaps using Onna's name had been a freak thing. And who the hell is Solomon?

What would it be like to really control a demon? If I had Raum's name, I could expel him from Sebastian. I could break his hold over me. I could send him back to Hell. I could send them all back…

The thought whispers through my mind and fades like an echo. It would take a long time to learn every demon's name. It would be impossible. I push the turmoil rising inside of me.

"Now that you have me, what do you intend to do with me?"

"To use you," he says matter-of-factly. "But I want to make a deal with you first."

That's not what I was expecting.

"I'm in no position to make a deal with anyone."

It is a moment of forgetting who I'm speaking to. An overwhelming wash of power hits me, and I stumble back as Orias crowds me. The hive I forgot was at my back topples over and a black cloud of bees swarm into the air. We both stop and watch as they turn into smoke when they hit the sunlight.

"Raum knows my thoughts before I do," I warn. "There has never been a time where he wasn't one step ahead of me. A deal means going behind his back and that isn't something I'm capable of."

The smoke trickles down from the sky and wraps around Orias's arm, coiling around like a cuff. "I want Raum dead. He was right that we cannot rule together. The power within his blood compares to the highest in Tartarus, to the seraphim. That sort of power can only lead to destruction.

"Babel is a holy city. The tower that marked its location was destroyed in the early ages of men and was believed to be a gateway to the Enemy's throne. Whoever holds Babel holds the power to Heaven. It opens the door to every realm after."

I try to keep up, but I'm having a hard time following. I don't know what seraphim are, but they sound bad. I can agree with him that I don't want Raum to reach Babel, but neither do I want any other demon to get there. Besides, God doesn't exist anymore. The information grips me like a vise.

"And you want me to help you... stop Raum? A mortal—"

"A mortal that has the ability to control *us*," he bites, snapping his teeth together. "Everyone knows the name of the Gatekeeper. Control him and you control Heaven and Tartarus."

I laugh. It's so sudden and sharp that I surprise myself. "I'm as good as dead whether I serve you or him. Were I to succeed in killing him, I'll be of no use to you once you have Babel. What could you possibly offer me that I can't refuse?"

Orias circles me, drawing closer to another hive. He pushes the box over but doesn't watch them disintegrate this time.

"Cool your tongue," he warns.

I tip my head in response. It's just all so asinine.

"I think it would be obvious that Raum suspects us both in wishing his death. He only expects one of us to succeed, though. He won't see you coming, not with my power behind you. He is one of the most powerful beings between eternities, but he is not immortal. None of us really are.

"I am offering you a shot, a real shot at killing him. In return, I will grant you immunity. Serve me and you can have anything you desire."

"A bite from you is still a collar," I say coolly. I touch my neck, but the collar Orias had given me before is gone. I suspect because there is no longer use for it. Orias is going to have to mark me in order to survive Raum's death. I've never even heard of a mark being transferred, but by the way he is speaking, I assume it's possible.

Orias flashes his brilliantly white teeth. "It would be a very lovely and very loose collar, better than the one I have already given you. This is no small thing that I am asking of you, and I would be a fool to waste an opportunity such as yourself."

"And if I refuse this deal?"

"You won't," he cuts me off.

The deep pools of his eyes envelop me. I lose myself in them, lose track of time. I have nothing to lose by trusting him. I don't know if I can take Orias's word to heart, but he is offering me an opportunity no one has ever given me. I'm already considering the possibilities that he would call me back to control some other demon for him. He sees me as a weapon in a war

I want no part of. I've seen and shed enough blood to last me ten lifetimes.

"Anything I want?"

Orias opens his hands. "Anything you want." His brow quirks and he looks up. "You could even stay here when it's all over. Create your own realty if you wanted. Bring back loved ones."

On command, something moves beyond his shoulder. Another ghost. A man walking through the field with dark hair and eyes that I know are green. I look back at Orias, willing the image to disappear. "It wouldn't be real."

Orias shrugs. "Is this not real?" He motions to the field and plucks the top of a wheat head from its stalk. "And you would be happy. You'll never truly be able to find it again in this world."

"At your side," I say hesitantly. Is standing beside a demon any better than behind them?

"I am giving you free will. Do this thing for me, kill Raum and the Gatekeeper, and you can have anything. You can have it all while you do it." He waves around us. "I am willing to pay a heavy price for the use of your gift."

I run my hand through my hair. The apparition that I know has green eyes is lurking somewhere in the field. I think I see it drop down behind one of the boxes, but I'm too afraid to look. Because if it's not who I think it is, it'll hurt that much more.

"How do I know this is not a trick?"

At that, the image of Devon appears, real and solid as I remember her, shining blue eyes and all. She shifts to my olive-skinned mother and then my fair-skinned father. After that are faces I do not know but recognize as demons of sorts, their beauty too pristine to be human. The being, or whatever it is, changes on a whim as people I have lost come to mind and then shift to whomever Orias commands with the flick of his hand.

"This is a sanctuary. It holds memories, places, and people who have been lost to all those who enter." He reaches out to stroke the side of a young man's freckled face with brown eyes flecked with gold. He motions for me to do the same.

I reach out a shaking hand as the image shifts back to Devon. When I touch her, her skin is solid. I recoil on instinct and the being disintegrates.

Orias brings my hand still hovering in the air just below his mouth and drops it suddenly to appear behind me.

"You have all the time in the world to think about it," he whispers against my ear.

"I–" He is gone. I spin around, but there is no door he has escaped through. Simply vanished. "Orias?" Silence is the only answer. It would be foolish to believe he left me alone but... I think of light, expanding the room until every shadow is forced to show its face. No demons are uncovered and no doors either. He's left me alone.

XVI

The ground catches me softly when my legs give way. I feel so heavy. I'm so tired of this place, of earth. The sharp scents of the garden and old books are comforting. Somewhere, a candle burns that smells like whiskey and oak. I lean my head back, into the soft back of the rocking chair that has a tear in the seat after curling up with my shoes too many times. I rest my hand on the table beside it, let it fall to the white pages of another book I didn't need to buy but wanted. The light changes behind my eyelids, from stark white to a warm glow. This room, with its peacock blue walls, has always had the best light.

"How did I get so lucky?"

I squint my eyes tighter together. It's not real.

"How am I so blessed?" I answer.

I feel him right in front of me. I know if I open my eyes, he'll be looking up at me, his sharp face open and eyes full of awe. He always looked at me like it was his first time seeing me. He always told me I was the most beautiful woman he'd ever seen.

"Because we were made for each other."

Warm green eyes, like the forest in a morning glow, are smiling back at me when I finally open my eyes.

His face—it's James. Not Leyak or any other monsters. It's James. *My James*. The sob that overtakes me flings me from the chair and into his arms.

"I've got you, baby," he says.

"Oh my god," I cry. I cling to him. The fabric of his shirt feels so real; the musk and sweat of him *is* real. His skin is warm and pumping full of blood. "Oh my god."

"I told you I'd never leave you."

I tangle my fingers through his hair with one hand and squeeze the back of his shirt tight.

"But you did. He took you from me."

He leans back, taking my face between his palms. "There is not a damn thing that could ever take me from you. Do you know why?"

He thumbs the tears from my eyes.

"Because I love you."

I rub my face into the crook of his neck. Inhaling his scent that has always driven me crazy. The rational part of my brain says this is a trick. How can it be when he is saying everything James would and did say to me? How can everything be so exact?

"What is this?" I should have inquired more of Orias when he was here.

"It's whatever we want it to be," James says.

"How is this possible, though? You're... dead."

It's the first time I've said that. Maybe it's the first time I've even acknowledged it. Before James had been possessed and just gone. But when I shot him, shot Leyak, I knew he was truly gone, and I would never ever get him back.

He smiles. "Just think of it as if I went to sleep. You woke me."

My fingers find their way into the crooks of his face, his hairline, the sharp edge of his jaw.

Mine.

"It's really you."

There is a strange yet beautiful light that sparks behind his eyes. "Yes."

A shaky exhale slips between my lips. Refusing Orias doesn't seem like an option anymore. There's a funny feeling that nudges me, but I brush it away before it can form a complete thought. Can I really have James? Will Orias uphold his end of the deal?

No. I'll have to ask for something else.

"What are you thinking so hard about?" James asks. His hands come to rest on my tensed knees. He pushes them apart so he can slide closer to me. The move is so innocent, but it sends a spark jolting through me.

"Do you know Orias? Do you know what has been happening since you died?"

He gives me an arched look. "I know nothing."

I let my hands fall between us and tip my face into his. He moves to kiss me, thinks better of it, and places his forehead to mine instead. He's always known when to and not to kiss me. Though I crave his kisses now.

I tell him everything.

From my time escaping Leyak all the way until a few moments ago where Orias offered me the deal. I feel out of breath by the time I finish. And tired. Three years of my life summed up in a single night.

His hands feel so warm on my thighs. I swallow thickly, forcing the horrors and tribulations down and focus on his warmth. I've longed for this sweet comfort he gives me now. Having him here means everything is going to be okay. It's going to get better.

The surprised laugh makes me jump. What's funny?

"Leah… I never imagined. I always knew you were something special."

I smile hesitantly. "I owe it all to you."

He shakes his head. "You escaped Leyak when I could not. You have killed… you've survived apparently one of the most powerful demons in Hell. And now you have another wanting to bargain with you. I doubt there is another one of us that can say the same. You're an amazing woman."

He doesn't understand how hard it's been. How terrifying living is. *Stop that. Of course he does. He was possessed.* That is one thing I never had the privilege of experiencing, and I pray that I never do.

A visible chill spreads along both my arms.

"So, will you do it?"

"Do what?" I look back at him.

"Accept his offer… this Orias."

My mouth twists as I try to find the right words. It's not that simple. I want to say yes but you can't trust a demon. They're all liars. Every single one. Once I allow Orias to bite me, I am at his disposal. And if I refuse, what is to keep him from forcing his mark on me?

It would be better to make the choice freely.

"I'll need something else from him," I say slowly.

"Am I not enough?" His voice is light and teasing.

I squeeze his hand. "You know that's not what I mean. If I let him bind me, I need to feel safe. I need *more.*"

I can tell he doesn't like that answer, but he also knows me well enough that arguing won't help. Once I've decided my mind on something, that's it. But he is right, too. He isn't enough, not this time. Real or fantasy, James is irrelevant to Orias. I need something that he values in exchange for my power.

That's it.

"What is it?"

"I need his name."

James turns his hand in mine as a frown line sets deep above his brow. "I don't think he'll be that trusting."

"He has to. He can't compel me, not with Raum's mark binding me. At least, I don't think he can. That's why he needs him dead. When he replaces the mark he'll control me, but not before. So, the only other option he has would be to kill me. That way, no one gets me." I hold up my finger. "Which Raum won't allow. He'll keep bringing me back until he gets whatever he wants." I lean closer to his face he has turned away from me. "What's wrong?"

"There has to be a way to do this without you bearing any of their marks." He keeps his eyes trained to the wall that has become far more interesting than me.

"His name," I say again. "With his mark holding me, and his name on my tongue, that's it. It's a fair trade."

He scoffs. "I don't think there is anything fair when it comes to demons."

"Maybe not. But it's worth a shot."

He gives my hand a gentle squeeze, but still, he won't look at me. It's funny. He was the one who took whatever risk necessary to keep us safe. It was me who was always hesitant, always cautious. Maybe that's why he was possessed and I wasn't. Maybe he delved into something he shouldn't and that's why he was taken.

I cringe inwardly and turn my head down, feeling guilty.

"It's alright."

"None of this is alright. It never has been. But what more can I lose?" I turn his hand in mine and trace the lines creased into his palm. I splay my hand out across his, looking at how small mine is in comparison. "Besides, if we come to terms, I won't have to lose you again."

I feel his eyes on me. I've always hated attention when it was too long on me. I've never minded it as much with James, though it took some getting used to. After all, it's not a bad thing when the man you're in love with looks at you. Especially with that adoring manner. Always looking, always appreciating me. The weight of his eyes unsettles me now, though. There's an intensity behind them that makes me nervous to meet his gaze.

"You'll do it then?" he asks.

Halfheartedly, I say, "Yes." I look up hesitantly, half expecting him to be looking back cruelly, but instead there is a soft smile, a pained one. And why wouldn't there be? There is nothing cruel about James. There never has been.

He laces his finger with mine. "Then I will stay here with you for as long as I can. I'll never go back to sleep." He smiles. It's contagious when he smiles like this, and I find myself doing it, too.

He kisses me. The soft press of his lips against mine unties the unease that has fallen over me. Every bad thing that has happened since we have been parted evaporates when my lips part to his. Sweet, like honey laced with the warm undertones of whiskey. The taste of him is just as I remember.

Breathlessly, I pull away. I run my tongue over my lower lip, savoring him.

"Are you really here?"

He looks thoughtful as he follows my tongue. Slowly, his eyes meet mine and then he traces the outline of my face, looking up to my hairline across the contours of my face, down to my chin before he meets my eyes. "I don't really know. It feels like I am." He runs a strand of my hair through his fingertips, "I can feel this," and pushes it back behind my ear. He leans in for another kiss. When our lips touch, a spark crackles between us. It's an invisible fire that blazes when we touch. "I can feel that," he says with a smile.

"I've missed this."

"I've missed you."

I take his face with both my hands and kiss him as the last word leaves his lips. God, I have missed him so much. The light sparks between us again and I am consumed by him. I dig my fingers into the back of his head, holding onto him desperately as I pull us closer. I need to be as close to him as I possibly can. He responds to my urgency, pulling me up from my seat, letting our mouths break enough for a breath of air.

The button of his jeans pops free beneath my quick fingers. He doesn't wait for me to finish pulling the zipper down before he pushes his pants over his hips. I pull my shirt off, breaking us apart for a second before we are pressed together again. In the process of trying to take my own pants off, I turn us around, pushing him back into the chair.

His green eyes are darker at this angle, devilish. I let him pull me down so I can straddle him. It's not until then that I slow myself.

"What?" He runs his hand along the back of my neck.

I duck my head, letting my hair fall in front of my face. My breath comes out shakily. How can I tell him I am nervous? How can he stand to touch me after everything I've done? After everyone who has touched me after him. A wave of shame brings the blood rushing to my face.

"Hey, my love. My love. It's okay."

His hand slides down to cup my chin. I fall forward into it and splay my hands across his bare chest. He feels so solid beneath me. I touch my forehead to his and shut my eyes. There's nothing to be done about the past. Now, it's just us. I nod silently before tilting my face down to kiss him.

Between us, his need throbs. My own desire to be even closer to him shoots through me when our kisses become more aggressive. At one point, I taste blood. I don't know if it is mine or his, but I catch a metallic flavor when I suck his tongue as it delves into my mouth.

I wrap my hand around him when I sit up and slowly guide him into me. It feels like my soul leaves my body. It feels like I'm whole again. I don't know how to describe it other than having him inside of me is one of the best feelings in the world. Our mouths break when I fall forward and he buries his head into my chest. He groans.

There is no pain as I lift and drop my hips against him, savoring every inch of him. He fits me perfectly, like he was made for me. He strokes a spot inside of me that makes my legs shake.

"Good girl," he purrs.

He leans his head back and pushes the hair fallen away from my face. He slides down into the chair and I lean my hands back onto his thighs. It's one of those feelings that's so good it hurts. The gentle touch to my face falls to my hips and he grabs me, hard. He forces my hips down every time I rise up. A breathless smile touches my mouth and I eye him wickedly.

"You look so fucking beautiful riding me."

It's enough to push me over the edge. I tighten around him, only managing a few more thrusts before I come. He pulls me forward at the peak of my orgasm and thrusts hard and fast, drawing it out so that the only thing I can do is hold tightly to him, digging my nails into his shoulders.

We are both soaked with how good he makes me feel. I let out a shaky breath.

I've hardly come down before he wraps an arm around me and stands us up. The room changes from blue to dove gray when he tosses me on the white linen bed. I pull him to me for another taste. He's so fucking sweet.

I moan into his mouth when he enters me.

There isn't anything like our connection, our lust, our love for one another. It doesn't just feel good. It feels right. I grab his ass and pull him into me, needing him to be closer.

There's a wickedness in his eyes, pure carnal need that sends fire shooting through my body. I arch into him as another wave hits me and I scream.

He slows the pace, making the strokes agonizingly delicious. He does over and over again until I lose track of the times he makes me come. I can hardly breathe and I'm shaking. Still, I can't get enough of him.

He pulls one of my legs up, fitting my ankle into the crook of his shoulder. He leans his face against my foot and kisses the soft skin there with closed eyes.

"I love you," I say.

His eyes flutter open. They look darker at this angle, but when he smiles, it brings the light to them again.

"I love you, Leah."

He takes a hard grasp around my thigh before leaning forward, pushing my leg back so he can kiss me. When I can't take much more, I break away to catch my breath. His lips fall to my shoulder and he bites me. Hard. I tighten around him at the same time he releases, milking every drop.

By the time he finishes, I am crying. I don't let him go in fear that he is going to disappear. It was like I remember it, but *more.* The fire between us more powerful and dangerous. I take a breath like it is my first and throw my head back into the pillows before finally releasing him. He runs his sweaty forehead from the crook of my neck to my forehead and lets out a shaky breath of his own.

A smile cracks across his face and he lowers himself, rolling beside me and pulling me against his chest. My hand finds the place over his heart, my head beneath his chin, sweaty hair sticking to his sun-kissed skin.

"I'll never let you go," he says.

"Don't you dare."

***

I startle awake when I feel myself slipping. No!

"I'm here," James says. "I'm still here."

His flesh is firm beneath my nails as I dig into him under the darkness that has fallen.

"Thank God," I say.

He pulls his arm from under me and I turn over, pressing my backside against him. I've always needed to be touching him to sleep well. He shifts a bit more before finally settling around me, slipping his arm beneath my breasts and pulling me to him once again.

"What did you say?" I ask sleepily. It's more of a sound he makes than actual words, but I hear something.

"Just how incredibly lucky I am."

We spend the next couple of days reveling in each other. I don't keep track of how many days pass, but I take note of when the sun falls and when it rises behind the window of our home. We cook and lay together after watching the sunsets through the back window. Most of our time is spent in bed, though. Between having sex and just holding each other, it's all I've craved for years. To be able to touch him again and know with absolute certainty that it really is James. My James.

"What are you going to do now that you'll finally be free?"

There hasn't been any talk between us about Orias's offer since our first night together. The wording of the question strikes a chord in me. It reminds me of the day in the compound when it was just me and Sebastian standing there. I think he was about to kiss me on the mouth before his lips touched my cheek.

"I don't want to see you get hurt when you finally have the opportunity to be free."

Oh god. Sebastian.

There was no freedom then and there is no freedom now. Freedom is a made-up word implemented by men a long time ago to give us false security. But why did that just make me think of him?

"What's wrong?"

I shake my head. "I don't know if I can do this, James. I don't know if I can have you and lose you all over again."

He sits up on his arm, facing me. "But I'm right here."

"For how long, though? And it's not just that I think Orias could be lying..."

I look down at the sheets tucked under our feet.

"Go on."

"There's someone else I have to think of. Someone other than myself."

He sits up and looks down at me. "Are you really worried about that monster? Raum?"

I shake my head again. "No. It's the person he's possessed. Sebastian… James…" I look up at him. God, why does he look so betrayed? "He's still alive. Raum has kept him the same way Leyak kept you in the beginning. Except…" I sit up, too, and throw my head in my hands.

"Except," he presses.

"It's different."

There is an uncomfortably long pause before he says anything else. "Do you love him?"

I meet his eyes. "It's not like that. I just... I *abandoned* you when Leyak stopped letting you out. I didn't know you were still in there when I left. I can't abandon someone else. And Raum, it's different. He lets him out. He doesn't force him or use him. At least, not the way Leyak did you."

The light changes in James's eyes, looking a little bit darker, a little bit harder than they were a second ago. "It doesn't matter if the way he does it is different. He is still holding this man—Sebastian—over you to keep you around."

I nod. I can't argue with that. It's not like I have a chance to ditch him anyway while being trapped in Pethaino.

"You know I wouldn't have left you if I'd known, right?"

His face falls. "I do."

It feels like I'm losing him all over again. In a way, I guess I am. He doesn't have to know that I won't be coming back.

I owe Sebastian my life, and I can't abandon him over someone who isn't truly here. As real as our time has felt together, I know deep down that James isn't *really* here. All of this is a giant illusion meant to distract me. Maybe Orias knew it would break me. Or maybe, by the skin of my own teeth, he had been telling the truth and this is a peace offering.

It's not enough.

"I need you to do something for me," I say. I can't keep the tears out of my voice.

"Anything," he says. He takes my hands in his and fuck does it hurt. It hurts so fucking much to have him touch me. I want him to stay.

"I need you to leave before Orias comes back. I'll take his offer, but I don't want him to tarnish you in any way. It's better that he doesn't know you exist."

The hurt in his eyes might as well have been a slap in my face. "You want me to go? I've missed you…"

I press my hand over his heart. "Just for a little while. I'll have to step out of here to make our deal and, when it is done, when Raum is dead, I'll come back for you. I'll find some way to take this place."

You should never have to leave your love twice.

James found me at a good point in my life and he stayed with me when the whole world turned to shit. We weren't just lovers, we were twin flames. We were best friends. He was… *is* the best thing that has ever happened to me. I never imagined a life without him and yet I have been surviving it. A little more banged up than before, but stronger because of it.

It's time I stop running. Though it would be so much sweeter running into his arms and never letting go.

"Do you promise?" he asks hopefully.

I press my forehead into his, then our noses and lips follow. How sweet and warm he tastes. How very human. He tastes like love.

"I promise."

***

A day goes by before the house begins to lose its color. Dust drifts in through the cracks of the windows and piles on top of the furniture. I haunt the hallways at all hours. I become the thing that goes bump in the night. Absentmindedly, I leave cabinet doors open or the faucets running. More days pass and the urge to look for James becomes unbearable. I force myself not to think of him. If I think of him, he'll come back, and I'll never be able to leave him.

Not ever again.

A door closes somewhere in the house. The fear that comes with every demon's presence fills the room. I turn to face the shadow I know is coming for me. Orias steps into the frame of the living room. He is fashioned in leather boots tucked under the hem of black pants and a button-down to match. His twists are pulled back with gold locks between every other strand.

He doesn't say anything. He doesn't have to.

"I'll do it."

XVII

"On one condition." I look around the empty house. White sheets now adorn the furniture instead of dust. I open my mouth, but I can't bring myself to deny this place. It feels so real. I let my hand drop to the back of a chair. It feels just how I remember it.

"It's yours," Orias says. He strides forward, extending his hand.

If I stay, how long will it take before I go mad? Every choice comes with a sacrifice, and I cannot leave Sebastian in Raum's claws.

I turn my nails into the seam of the fabric, staring. "I want your name."

The silence that follows makes me even more anxious. He withdraws his hand, curling his fingers into a fist. He smiles a little, but I know it's not because he's amused. It's the crazy look someone gets before they're about to snap.

"My name," he says steadily.

If I'm going to break the deal, I might as well get something out of it. Maybe it would make Raum a little less angry about the fact that I had considered betraying him.

"Would you not trust me to keep it safe the same way you intend to keep me?"

"I offer you everything and you return with this." His eyes look more red than black when they meet mine. Hungry.

"I am giving you everything. I think I am of equal value to your name."

He laughs. "Your value will never come close to anything of mine." He nods, shakes his head the other way, and then twists his neck as if he wants to crack it. The air in the room has grown warm. The damp fabric of my shirt clings to my back.

I ignore the snub. We both know my gift is anything but worthless. "I want it with your original offer, too. My freedom and your name in exchange for my services."

"Services," he mocks.

I focus on him, every bit of him to eliminate any thoughts he might pick up on. It's not until he extends his hand a second time that I ponder the consequences of what might happen when I break our agreement. After a while, the threat of death becomes redundant. Torture still sounds scary, but what else can they really do that I haven't already suffered?

"I will grant you this. Your gift for my name and immunity."

"I'm not shaking until I have your name."

Orias slams me back into a wall that wasn't there before. The impact makes my head throb. His fingers encompass my throat like the collar he intends to put there.

Tension fills the sliver of space between us.

"My true name is Oriasan."

His thumb and forefinger dig beneath my chin as he leans back, his eyes holding mine.

"Oria–" His grip constricts as I try for his name.

"Make the deal," he hisses.

The thing about deals is they need your permission to be made. It's the one thing a demon can't force on you. They can trick you into it, but they can't force you. A deal with a demon is free will.

I blink in acknowledgement.

His lips cover mine, inhaling the rest of his name sharply. He takes my breath with it in a giant gulp. I latch onto his face. If someone walked in, they would probably think we were in a passionate hold, not that one of us was being suffocated. My eyes roll and I fall into him, his arms winding around me above the floor. Try as I might, I can't close my mouth. An invisible force keeps it pried open while some part of Orias invades me.

The touch withdraws so quickly, ripping all heat away and replacing it with frigid cold. I snap my teeth, latching them over his lip. He catches my head as it falls back, and I gasp for air. One knee at a time, he finds the floor and lays me out onto the pillows and silks that were there before. His body stretches outside mine. The top buttons of his shirt have come undone to expose just below his collarbone.

A loud ripple jets across the room. There isn't any sound, but it's more of a feeling. It makes the hair on our heads fly up. Orias recoils from me, looking between me and the cushions. What the hell was that?

A second shockwave brings both of us to our feet. In the same instant, the sheets and cushions fall out from under our feet and a blue light fills the room.

"Sire." Onna materializes in the room and drops to her knees. Dagon falls behind her. They look equally fierce in their all-black attire. Onna's sharp eyes burrow a hole through my head when she looks up. I get a streak of satisfaction at the twist of her face. No doubt she thought I'd come out far worse than when she left me. She'll not like the conversation Orias is surely to have with her about my new role either. Even if there was a chance for us to be allies, I don't think there is a cell in her body that would allow it. "Forgive the interruption, but this matter could not wait."

Orias licks his lower lip and touches it when he tastes the blood welling. The corners of his mouth turn up with twisted amusement. "What is it?"

"The prisoners... someone let them out, but they've been beheaded. All of them."

It becomes very still between us. "What are you talking about?"

Onna looks over at Dagon awkwardly. "The humans are dead. All of them. I saw with my own eyes; their heads were stripped from their bodies and have been stacked in the courtyard. And Pethaino is crumbling. Waves beat down our walls as we speak."

On cue, another shudder rips through the room. I set my feet apart to steady myself. I lay my hand against Orias to right myself, and it is as if my touch alone ignites something within him.

He slings his arm across the room, sending a clatter of nothing into the void. "Where is Raum?"

"We could not hold him."

Orias motions to me and I turn with him, staying close to his side as we step through a gaping hole of darkness.

The void gives way to an actual room that looks like it was meant to be decorated as a haunted house. Black tattered linens hang from the ceiling lined one in front of the other. I pause when I catch a glimpse of a single wall composed of a black-glassed mirror. Is that where I've been?

On the far wall is the blue waterfall of fire of Orias's room.

Somehow my clothes have changed again, and I am in all black like the rest of them. The sleeves of my top are tight and plated with leather scales, with buckles crisscrossing over my chest. Over my equally fitted pants, with fastenings across the thighs, are boots strapped just beneath my knee and belted at the top with brass buckles.

It matches Onna's leather attire beneath her thin-sheeted armor and blades.

"Leah is now under my protection. Under no circumstances is any harm to come to her. And do not let Raum get his claws on her."

Onna balks mid stride. "Of course," she forces out.

"She is our key to acquiring the power in Babel." The way he looks at me is full of disgust, as if he doesn't need me as much as Raum does. As if we still don't have a deal to make.

A powerful rush fills my head, washing the sound of his voice to make way for another.

Where are you? Come to me. The dual voice roars like thunder demanding, calling to me. It resounds like a mantra. The chord tying me to the voice is taut. I resist the urge to follow it by digging my nails into the palm of my hands.

I'm here.

But the voice doesn't hear me. It continues in a ravenous way.

Onna pauses behind Orias as he leans out the window.

"I need one of you to go to the aviary. Send for Raguel."

"You brought Raguel into this?" Dagon snaps. He searches the ceiling as if the name will materialize the being into the room.

"Yes, I did," growls the king. "And you will be glad of it. We needed the alliance and, now that Raum is here, we will rely on it."

"Who is Raum, really?" Onna fidgets with the hilt of her sword. She looks at Dagon subtly then Orias, tilting her head down. "I was in the pit when everything happened. I don't even remember the names of the cyn who ruled in my time."

Orias's jaw clenches and releases. His hands grasp the ledge before he pushes off abruptly.

"We have been loyal to you, Orias. No one questioned you when you named Raum a king, but there have been whispers. When I left Tartarus, Baal was cyn of Eurynomos, not Raum. What is going on?"

Orias looks like he is on the verge of slipping. His eyes dart about the room erratically, looking for anything tangible he may grasp hold of, but the only thing within reach are his guards and me. Thick veins stand out when he clenches his fists. He runs his hand over his still bleeding lip. When he sees the smear, he spits.

"Baal *was* cyn. Raum killed him and ascended the throne. I was sent in the first wave to make way for the rest of you. For all of Tartarus."

"And you thought to not mention this," Dagon grits, then curses with a hiss.

"Baal," Onna says softly to herself, her brow scrunched in struggle. "I remember him. He was one of the first angels."

Orias's lips curl. "He tore through Vélos. He refuses to make it clear whether Bishop lives or is dead. I myself only saw two of their bodies."

Onna's eyes go wide with horror. Her cool countenance breaks apart at Bishop's name. Her eyes fall to me and the grief, for there is sadness there, burns in the wake of her anguish. Her nostrils flare and the cold warrior she was before is back with a vengeance.

"You have let a wolf into our den with the power of fuck knows how many cyn." Dagon runs a hand through his hair and a sharp sound, like a bark, escapes from the back of his throat. "Pethaino will fall."

"It will not!" Orias exclaims. "He cannot touch us. Not when we are linked." The air thickens and an intense pressure builds in my head. Both demons shake their heads in response, like they feel it too, as the words flow from Orias's mouth. The desperation, the breathy way he speaks has me unhinged. "I know all of his tricks, his weaknesses. There is nothing he can do that I do not already know. Why have you not sent for Raguel? Make sure the best of our Legion are guarding this tower."

"None of us are cyn. It does not matter that we share power when at the flick of his wrist he can flood us. We are not strong enough to withstand that force." Dagon tries to speak reason over Orias, but the king turns away, pointing to the window as he gives another command. "You knew he had the capacity to destroy us and still you shifted the lands like some human in a pissing contest."

Orias whirls on Dagon. "You will not speak to me when you are beneath me! You will obey me! I am your cyn! I am king!" His long talons catch the demon by the throat. He shoves Dagon, forcing him back a stumbling step.

"You have damned us," Dagon bites back.

"Enough," Onna snaps. Her eyes have not left me. The crimson heat of her gaze is damning as it seers into me.

Orias, the mad king, is spiraling farther. At this rate, I don't think he will wait for Raum's death before marking me. There's nothing stopping him from taking me right here in the middle of Dagon and Onna. I clench my sweaty palms and look past Onna, searching for some path to escape.

Orias's voice startles me back to attention. "He will not win! It is not a matter that he has inherited their power, but that I now have something he wants. We need him dead. All of us." Orias looks at me pointedly, sticking his finger in my face.

The powerful voice within my head grows louder, igniting an invisible fire beneath my palms that makes them itch. I level my gaze into Orias. The king isn't just mad, he is afraid. That is what this whole show has been about between him and Raum. An act.

Raum, so boastful about his power but never showing it. Until now, when the moment is right. It is all one giant game to them.

At least in this game I know who the real winner will be, and it is not the one that extends his hand to me now. Raum's voice goes out when Orias grabs my forearm.

"Forget what I said about you killing him. Our deal will keep you alive long enough after Raguel kills him for me to mark you. We need to keep you safe and out of sight until then." Dagon steps forward, shoving his hulking form between me and my would-be abusers. "Let me take her to the aviary. I will call Raguel and she will be safe there."

Orias looks between us then nods. "Yes. Good. Yes, she will be safe. Our bargain will hold long enough."

I shy away as Dagon reaches for me, but he is faster and latches hold to my forearm when Orias lets me go. "What about our deal?" I inhale sharply as Dagon twists my arm between my shoulder blades, sending a searing pain down my back.

Orias spins abruptly, looking between me, the ceiling, and the windows. "It is done. Go now, take her. Quickly," he snaps.

"What are you talking about?" Unless something has changed, a kiss is not how demons sign their name. There is no way for Orias to know I didn't have any intention of following through my end of the bargain.

Onna takes a step forward when Orias stops her. "No, I need you with me. We need to find Raum."

"What are you talking about? Orias," I demand.

"Get her out of here," Orias growls.

Dagon drags me away while I try to throw out Orias's real name, but it doesn't come out. The sound gets lodged in my throat. I know it. I can see it in my head, but I can't say it. Every time I do, I feel his fingers around my throat.

No. This isn't right. What has he done? What is happening?

The doors to Orias's chambers slam shut with a loud crack as soon as we are through. Dagon lets go of my arm. It tingles as the blood rushes feeling back into it. Sweet relief.

Come to me. Where are you? The voice sends a jolt of anticipation through my blood.

"Move quickly and don't say a word," Dagon says, silencing every question racing through my mind. He moves in front of me, leading me down a corridor then several flights of stairs until he comes to a sudden halt.

"What's wrong?"

He looks over his shoulder to me before I see it. The stairs are submerged beneath a dark layer of water. Dagon reaches down, placing his hand delicately over the water. With a deep breath, he lays his fingers on top. When nothing happens, he lets out a sigh.

The water seeps into our clothes as we submerge ourselves in the dark tide. Though the energy in the air is urgent, Dagon moves with caution. He takes slow, even steps as not to stir the water. The desire to run writhes in my legs, but I keep behind him. At least in the water we will be able to hear if someone approaches. Not even Dagon is able to quiet the sound of it.

The water spills out into what I believe to be the square. He pauses again, looking carefully outside of the entrance before motioning me along. Once we are outside, he moves behind me again, his hand clasped firmly to my shoulder, and pushes me forward. Between the gruesome posts are the stack of heads he had mentioned. Someone had dragged a table in the middle so installation could be seen over the water. They have been haphazardly stacked. Nothing about it is meticulous or artistic in any way. One of the heads has fallen off into the water and floats nearby, turning left and then right in the soft current. Poor man.

Abruptly, Dagon grabs hold of my other shoulder and forces me into an alley, pushing me back until the main road falls out of view. He shields me, though it feels more like he is about to attack me than protect.

"How long were you in the talon?"

"The what?" I keep my voice shushed like his.

"The mirror—the room we brought you out of."

"I don't know." I glance past him when a ripple of water stirs behind him. "What is happening?" I wave my hand beside my face. "Raum is shouting at me, and I can't stop it."

"He's missing. There hasn't been any sign of him until today, when he slaughtered the humans."

"You're sure it was him?"

Dagon gives me a pointed look and I hold up my hands in defense.

"And no one tried to stop him?"

"No one knew what he had done until a few hours ago. Ipos went to check the guard standing watch and found Cassius missing. The heads must have been placed late in the night. He came to warn Orias immediately.

"You've been gone for two days. I assume he did it as a stunt to draw Orias out. Onna couldn't wait until Orias had finished with you." He steps back to inspect me. "And I didn't want you in there any longer. We had been standing guard at his quarters' entrance, but when

I didn't see you in the room, I knew something was wrong."

I shake my head. "I thought it had been a night. Orias wasn't with me the whole time, so I don't understand what you mean. He was there when I woke up but… in there, it was weeks, months maybe before I saw him again. I don't know. Time fluctuated." I thought I'd misheard them before when they said it had been two days. I'm surprised Raum waited that long to do anything.

Dagon's face turns ashen. "What did you see? What happened?"

His voice takes on that hollow coolness Liam would get when his darker side was taking over. It sends an unnerving chill down my arms. It's crazy how much twins have in common. It's even eerier that a demon, though he may be good if there is such a thing, would choose to keep so much of the human.

I shrug. "Whatever I wanted. It doesn't matter. I need to find Raum." Before I can move past Dagon, he forces me back. "Get out of my way." The pull is stronger now, his voice louder.

"You do realize what's going to happen if you don't keep your end of whatever bargain you struck with Orias? You'll be cursed. Let me help you."

Cursed, possessed, used as a weapon. It's all the same, isn't it?

"Orias offered me immunity if I help him kill Raum."

His lips curl back. "I don't believe that. He has his head so far up Raum's ass that when he offered himself instead of you, he lost it. He's been raving over the ways to kill you. Why would he suddenly change his mind?"

"Have you forgotten the bargain Raum refused to strike with him? Orias found another way. Me. He thinks I'm a weapon. And clearly Raum does too or, according to you," I motion to him, "he would have disposed of me a long time ago. It is why he is looking for me now."

Dagon is mumbling over how I don't exactly have the power to kill Raum anyway. "What sort of weapon?" The words are barely out of his mouth when he takes a startled step back. He looks at his hands as if he has burned. "Fuck." There's nothing that gives any indication that I've hurt him.

"Will you explain what the hell is going on?"

"There are two daughters of prophecy that are to have a hand in the war between Heaven and Tartarus. The other heir is already in Tartarus. She is the reason we are here, why we were able to set foot on Earth. Are you really Solomon's heir?"

You've got to be shitting me.

"Orias believes I am. When I used Onna's true name, it was too much of a coincidence that she would obey."

Dagon pauses a moment then nods. "What do you believe?"

"Orias gave me his name, but I couldn't use it. It's like he did something to keep me from actually saying it."

His lips curl back again. "Which would be something he slipped into your deal without you knowing it. It's smart, but stupid on your part to have accepted."

"We didn't have time to seal the bargain before Onna burst in."

Dagon waves his hand dismissively. "If I give you mine, will you show me?"

I let out an exasperated sigh. "Yes."

"Do you promise not to use it against me?" he asks hesitantly. His eyes flick back and forth between mine, searching. He wants proof, but he's afraid.

I let out another breath, softer this time. "You've been good to me. You have my word."

Dagon nods. "Dalagon," he says quietly.

What is something demons hate most? Something they would refuse to do regardless of their intentions.

"Dalagon," I command. "Kneel."

An angry flash passes across his eyes. He looks as if he is going to fight me, his muscles tense, and the veins stick out in his neck and forehead. He trembles, as if he is struggling to stand, but then he bends his knee. He drops to the ground with a thud and looks up at me with round, wide eyes.

"What do you think?" I ask shakily.

He swallows. "I think," he says steadily, "that they are right about you, and you are indeed a weapon. I also believe Raum will kill every last one of us until he has you back."

I nod. "I think he will do it regardless."

Did Leyak know? I dismiss the thought as soon as it enters my mind. It's doubtful. Even if he had heard the rumors, he wasn't the smartest to put two and two together. I was just a plaything. He couldn't have understood my worth because he never even saw it. To him, I was nothing.

I extend my hand to Dagon. He doesn't take it but stands at the motion. He looks at the water between us and brushes his hands again to rid my touch.

"What were the details of the bargain?"

"If I helped him kill Raum, he would give me immunity. After Babel, he was going to give me the option to stay at his side or go. I had the opportunity to think it over, but I couldn't. When he came back in the room—the talon—I told him I would do it. I agreed to his conditions and matched it by asking for his name. But we didn't seal the deal. He kissed me."

A loud splash into the water makes both of us jump. When nothing else happens, Dagon holds out his hand and I pass him to follow. We slink farther into the alley, coming around the backside of another singed wall. It would be easy to get lost in here. Everything looks the same, like a giant black maze.

"For your sake, I hope you're right."

We walk farther into the city, taking multiple turns down what I assume are back paths, so we won't be noticed. I look hesitantly at my companion when we stop just shy of the aviary.

"This is the safest place," he says more to himself.

He lends his hand as we move down a slight incline, deeper into the water. It rises just shy of my butt. Movement catches my eye. At the top of the battlement closest to us is a line of demons on patrol. At their hips are long swords and at their backs sheaths full of heavily tufted arrows. He slows with me, watching them until they are completely out of sight.

The water seeps from my pants as soon as we climb the steps to the aviary. There must be some magic or demon spell for quick dry. It's a strange sensation as it climbs down my leg with each step to the top. I don't know if it's the water or something else that gives me the feeling of being chased, but a sense of urgency grips me. A dark wave curls up and hits me from behind and I slam into the big red door.

"Hurry," Dagon says.

I dart past him as the air begins to swell for what I think is going to be another hit. Instead, there is a loud bang as I cross the threshold. I turn just in time to see Dagon drop a huge metal beam onto the hooks extending from the door, locking us inside.

XVIII

Unease settles in the pit of my stomach as Dagon raises his hand. Beneath it, a red line follows, binding the seal of the door to the metal frame. Once the entrance is melted together, he moves to the second and does the same. I scan the stainless windows, but there isn't much to be done about those. They're bound to shatter if something really wants to get through.

The water that spilled in behind us dissipates. It rises into little droplets that collect above the angels, making everything look crystallized. By the time the transfer is finished, the floor is dry marble and the droplets have turned into a dark gray cloud with a black eye in the middle. Like a mini hurricane.

"You still on my side?"

Dagon ducks his head. "I am. But I'm about to provide the distraction you need to find Raum. For now, the safest place for you is at his side." He jogs up a small flight of stairs beneath one of the arched windows. He taps the glass with the nail of his index finger. "Do you see the bodies there, along the south wall?" He doesn't look to see if I approach or not, just keeps pointing. "There is a man and woman intertwined. You'll have to crawl through the bodies, but behind them is a gate. That is your way out, if the city does not flood before then, or if someone comes for you before Raum."

I step up beside him to peer through the orange tint. I can see the mass of bodies, but I have no idea which couple he is talking about. Without a demon escort, I'm going to stand out like a sore thumb. I pause.

"What are you going to do?"

He looks up at the ceiling cautiously.

Raum missed the ones in here. I look at Liam's sister hopelessly. I promised her I would find a way to free her, to free them all. I have power that does not even allow me to save them. *I'm so sorry.*

"I'm going to pray." His lids flutter as he looks to the angels. "I gave all of them the option to run with my bite or to die painlessly. It was the only two freedoms I could offer. It was that or torture. The things they've done... I've done," he corrects. "I couldn't bear it anymore. Your kind is safer with our venom so long as the mark isn't completed. It makes you stronger. You'll heal quicker." He grimaces. "The madness is inevitable, but it gave them a shot. I tried to save as many as I could."

I reach out, my fingers hovering in the air before I finally rest them on his arm. He doesn't smell of sulfur like the rest of them. There's still that earthy scent a lot of demons have, but there's no rot. Nothing that turns my stomach being so close to him.

"I doubt there is another like you."

He smiles again, softly. "We are few. Be careful who you trust, Leah. Even the best of us have ill intentions. And those who pretend have even worse."

I know it's not Orias he is referring to.

He pulls away from me and descends the steps back to the middle of the room. "I don't know what is going to happen when I start praying. It is best you find somewhere safe, and when you see your exit, run."

He takes a stand in the middle of the room and, very hesitantly, gets down on both knees. He rests his palms over the top of his thighs, tucking his chin in so that his fringe covers his gaze. While he finds his place, I take another step back, determining that where I'm standing is good enough. I take a seat on one of the steps, looking cautiously to the angels when he speaks.

"Father."

The name reverberates through the dead space.

"Hear me. I call out in anguish to You. I ask forgiveness for falling from Your grace. That I set foot on Earth and took hold of a body that is not my own. I reveled in my power, in all our glory being apart from You. I was blinded by foolishness. I beg William's soul would be taken from me and restored. I ask forgiveness for everything I have done since the Fall and... for my soul," he finishes.

The silence falls across the room, shrouding me like a weighted blanket. It chills me. Even when the temperature rises, gooseflesh spreads along my arms. The only sound in the room is my own breathing and the shaking remnants of Dagon's prayer.

Scratching comes from the other side of the wall. Heel to toe, I creep closer so whatever it is won't hear me. As I approach, a large shadow skirts out of sight on the other side of the glass. A few feet of where it had been slinks an even bigger shadow. Everything is muddied with color, but it didn't look like one of the horses. It's bigger.

The storm cloud that twists above our heads reaches across the ceiling with gray tendrils. Pushed by some invisible force, the angels sway. One of the women, I swear I see her toes curl, looks to be reaching out as she swings forward, her wings holding her adrift briefly before falling back against the invisible chord that holds her aloft.

A creak pulls my attention just past her. It takes slow, even steps across the roof. I retreat quickly to Dagon's side, not taking my eyes off the ceiling. "My Creator," he is saying. I touch his shoulder when a very large, very red eye alight with embers peers in from the outside. The creature lets out a guttural growl as it twists its head away, allowing me to see a mouth of dangerously sharp teeth.

"I thought no one came here," I whisper.

Dagon's voice softens when he opens his eyes. He looks around hesitantly as more and more shadows gather on the outside of the building. Dust filters from the ceiling as another monster is heard crawling to the top.

"What are they doing?"

Dagon's prayer falters. "They are looking for a way in so they can kill me. God, let my suffering be just."

I face him. "Dagon, I can't ask you to sacrifice yourself. This isn't what I thought you meant by a distraction. The whole reason I didn't take Orias's offer is because I couldn't bear someone else dying because of me. Raum has possessed someone I care about and I couldn't leave him."

Dagon frowns. "He isn't like me."

"No," I agree. "But, in a way, Raum does care for me. He'll protect me. It's why he keeps the man,

Sebastian, alive. You can't do this, Dagon. I cannot ask you to do this."

Glass shatters from across the room. Black talons retract only for another set to slip in to pry the metal apart. It bends with a groan.

"It's already done." Taking hold of my shoulders, he stands and turns me away from another breakage. "He will kill you once he is done with you."

Something slams into the door from the outside. It shakes the whole building. The angels shudder, their chords creaking in protest.

I don't know where the sudden strength comes from when I lock eyes with him. "I have every intention of taking Raum with me if that happens again." I'm not afraid to die anymore. Once you've experienced death, you find it silly to be so afraid of nothing.

Dagon uncurls the fist I've made and places his lips on my palm. His warm breath caresses my wrist as he pulls away and lays my fingers protectively over the kiss. The gesture is intimate, so human, that I grab hold of him before he can pull away. He shakes his head and gives my arm a squeeze.

A vicious growl brings our attention to the window the demons have been working. The head of the beast hangs loose over the arch, staring down menacingly. "Naughty, naughty little man." Its voice is like gravel. "I am going to devour you."

"I don't suppose Orias has had time to announce your immunity," Dagon whispers. He pulls me across the room when another bang comes from the door, but this time it bends, and a trickle of water fills up the seam.

"God help me."

"May He keep you safe for His bidding."

There is a loud roar before the ceiling breaks apart. The angels swing higher and higher until their chords finally snap. One by one, they fall. Their rotting wings extend behind them and, just before they hit the floor, the spell breaks. They scream.

Liam's sister is the one that draws my attention. Her voice breaks loose the same time her invisible chord snaps, and it's her brother she screams for. William's name is halfway out of her mouth when she hits the marble, her head splitting apart like the rest of them. Pieces of her scatter across the floor like paint spatter.

Thick blocks of concrete rain from the ceiling to make room for the first beast to climb through. It slinks down the wall with odd grace like a panther. The long serpentine tail whips behind it, flashing a pointed tip.

Without taking his eyes from the intruder, Dagon unclips the belt at his waist and passes it to me. I wear it like a harness, knowing too well it will slip over my hips. I relieve one of the sheaths of its knife. The weight of the hilt feels good against my palm.

"Quickly," he says. "As soon as there is a clearing, run."

Another throttle to the red door sends it flying open, with a wave of water to follow. I spring to the steps on the far side of the chapel, leaving Dagon alone as a second monster wades into the room.

The few glimpses I've caught of a demon's true form are nothing in comparison to the two beasts with their very large heads attached to their even bigger bodies. The one from the ceiling touches down on paw-like feet with talons that crack through the stone steps. Its taut skin is oily black flesh stretched across its powerful body larger than any draft horse. The spikes along the back of its neck bristle when it growls. The front of its elongated face is split open, and instead of skin there is bone the same gray as the spiral horns protruding from the back of its head. Neither of the two have tusks like the ones in the courtyard, but they have the same giant maws loaded with flashing teeth.

Dagon's transformation is quick but violent. The human flesh of his host tears apart and he, the demon he really is, crawls out of the man like he is nothing more than a costume. The seam splits apart at the start of his forehead, separating the skin down his back like a zipper. Bits of flesh and muscle that were not peeled away fly off his body with a shake of his head, splashing into the water. Red stains swirl around his black legs.

"Almighty, stay with me," he says, his voice more baritone than before. Dagon does not have horns, but he does have shredded stubs on his back that could have been wings but have either been cut or torn off.

The demon in the water shakes its head. "You dare call upon the Enemy. Traitor!"

"Beginning and the End, let Your fury rain upon us," Dagon continues.

"Silence!" the other screeches.

The demons convulse every time he says a name of God. Their movements robotic, glitchy. Despite their protests, more monsters crawl through what is quickly becoming ruins.

None of them see me. Or perhaps they're too focused on Dagon to notice. I make my move as soon as one rushes him and jump from my position. I falter when the one guarding the red door flashes forward and the end of its tail snaps my way. My foot slips when I duck, but I regain my balance, only falling part way into the water. A thunderous roar stops me in my tracks.

Three more monsters have found their way in and hang to the ceiling. The storm cloud falls, spreading like smog at their feet. Beneath their open-mouthed maws, three demons are tangled together, thrashing wildly in the water. It doesn't take long to determine which of them is Dagon. The two rip into him with bloody teeth and claws, forcing him underwater with each strike. If he does not bleed to death, he will drown.

The bodies that have fallen are stepped on and tossed aside like toys that have gotten in the way.

Dagon latches hold to the throat of a demon when it overreaches. It's all the leverage he needs to pull the beast down with a vicious shake of his head that rips black, stringy flesh and muscle free. Dagon's rise to his feet is only temporary as the rest of the demons fall on him.

The waterline has dropped significantly as it continues to rise in the form of droplets. Dagon roars and the rising water shoots up like a jet fountain. The remaining windows shatter, spewing fragments into my skin. None of that is what really sends me running.

It's the sheer power that enters the space, as if Dagon has commanded it out of thin air. At some level, you can always feel a demon's power. This is something entirely different. The magnitude of it shoots a type of fear I've never experienced. I hide my face, yet I know as sure as day that the *power s*till sees me. And it knows exactly who I am.

Get out!
Get out!
Get out!

The voice that sounds like mine comes like the crack of a whip. I don't need to be told again, but it continues to berate me until my ears ring. I run so fast the steps down to the main part of the city become a blur. The water is parting beneath my feet, opening a broad path somewhere beyond me.

A bright flash of white erupts behind me as I reach level ground. I turn in the split second the lightning strike retracts and a loud clap of thunder breaks across the sky. There is no wood or straw to catch fire, only stone and iron. Brick by brick, the aviary goes up in flames.

"Find her!"

The rage within Orias's voice is like an explosion. I have half a mind to round the backside of the aviary, but maybe I'll get lucky and they'll think I've perished in the flames. I move off the path to wade into the water. I slip down to my knees and pull myself behind a building just as Orias and a handful of guards come down the line. Onna's eyes are wide at his side and she comes to a stumbling halt. With a wave of his hand, Orias cuts off their path and lets the water pour into the aviary.

Ipos and another demon I don't recognize rush forward. I can only imagine what it looks like now, the carnage. Bodies rush down the steps in pieces. Dense splashes sound through the air as the demons search the ruins. The storm cloud, if that is still the same one, has dispersed into the sky that is now full of smoke.

Ipos walks out with his palms open.

"She cannot disappear! Find her!" Orias snarls. "Find Leah!"

As the small band of warriors turns to leave, Orias grabs Onna roughly. "Did you know of this?"

She balks before regaining her composure, her expression hardening. "I did not. I have always been faithful."

"So was Dagon, but it is his prayers still ringing in my ears. I will not be taken for a fool twice."

Onna lifts her chin, exposing her throat freely. "Never, my lord. My life is yours."

Orias flexes his hand at his side, curling talons instead of fingers into an awkward fist. He thrusts her away, so hard that she stumbles.

"Find Leah, and don't you fucking lay a scratch on her. We need her."

"If I may, what is so special about her?"

The shift of Orias's human face to monster is instantaneous. A long snout with flashing teeth erupt. "Find her!" The two words reverberate through all of Pethaino. I feel them in my bones and in the chills that spread on my skin.

Gracefully, Onna kneels and comes up in a fluid motion. She pushes past Ipos, no doubt making sure he hasn't missed something that she'll be able to pick up on. As soon as Orias turns his back, I flee.

I have to find Raum. But why hasn't he come for me yet?

"Raum," I call quietly.

There's no answer. I don't recall when the sound of his voice stopped, but it's not there now. I know he wouldn't leave me, but I can't help feeling that I've been abandoned.

Again.

XIX

The bodies all look the same. There are plenty of men and women that could be mistaken for a couple embracing. Dagon seemed so certain when he was pointing them out to me, though, I know I'm missing something. The hairs on the back of my neck stand up and I look behind me. There isn't anyone there, but it feels like I'm being watched. Hurry up.

As quickly as the panic starts to set in, a soft nudge of reassurance pushes it away. I let out a breath of relief. He's close. I lay my hand to my chest to steady myself. I take another look around, but I can't see him. It only makes finding the door that much more urgent. Let me locate it so as soon as Raum finds me we can get the hell out of here.

I take a couple of steps back to reassess the wall. They're somewhere right in front of me.

"Going somewhere?" Onna's cool voice coos.

I tighten my grip on the knife as I face her. She takes a hesitant step back then catches herself, lifting her weapon. If I didn't know any better, I would say she is as afraid of me as I am of her.

"You can't hurt me."

"Not intentionally," she says, her voice even more icy. "I'm not responsible for what happens if you resist. I told him you couldn't be trusted."

"I'm not running from Orias," I lie.

"I know about the gate. Don't make me come get you."

She still hasn't moved.

It's almost satisfying seeing her like this. Almost, because I know how unpredictable someone can become when provoked by fear.

"Sake-Onna, let me go."

The revulsion that ripples across her body looks painful by the grimace on her face. "Your commands are temporary."

Strong arms wrap around my waist, trapping both of my arms, and spin me around. Ipos's stern face twists when he shoves me back, nearly impaling me on a sword that sticks out from the wall at my shoulder. I jerk one of my arms free, dropping the blade into that hand, and in the same instant I bring my knee up, I hack for his neck. Ipos shoves me again to the side, so the blade sinks into his upper bicep.

I pull it free, and on the recoil, he grabs my wrist and presses his body to mine. Fighting him is like pushing against a brick wall. It doesn't matter the size of a demon, they're all strong. Ipos is especially sturdy.

"Onna—"

Ipos forces his hand against my lips and an explosion of bitter dirt fills my mouth. It fills up the back of my throat, and I give in to him in an attempt to spit out the contents. I can't get any of it out without inhaling it. My throat feels like it's on fire and my lungs burn even worse. I hit his chest and lean forward, spitting up what looks more like black soot than it tastes.

Ipos steps to the side as Onna approaches. I try to keep an eye on her as I gag. The dirt keeps coming. Every time I feel like I've almost got it all out, another cough fills my mouth.

The heel of her boot cracks into the center of my forehead like a sledgehammer.

"Orias said—"

"She fell," she cuts off. She crouches in front of me. "I don't care what sort of deal you made with Orias. Eirini is over and I don't serve you. He is *my* king, and I will do anything for him. Even if that means cleaning up a mess before it can be made." She grabs me by the cheeks and squeezes.

I spit out another clump of dirt. Her face twists, and she swipes the spit-up across my face mid slap. I roll over, face down, and cough up what I can. The dirt is a little less than before. I run my tongue over the grit behind my teeth and breathe.

My nails bite into the earth much like I want to sink them into her. I imagine her skin might taste like the grime in my mouth, foul. All wickedness is foul. Onna can threaten me all she likes, but I know she is afraid of me. I can smell it. A drop of blood rolls down in my line of sight, turning everything red. Turning her red.

She lunges at me, and I push up on my palms to meet her. Onna's weight crushes me back into the ground, and the impact on my chin snaps my teeth together. Past her hip, a black mass lands where she'd been standing in smoking form. She hoists me with her protectively, half dragging, half pulling me to my feet.

"Come and get her," she snarls.

The monster turns around, tail snapping savagely. On its back extend the remnants of burnt and tattered wings. Its bottom jaw hangs open as a slew of demonic words drip from its tongue.

"Da vocht ra mé."

Death has come.

Onna pulls me to her as she turns to take the blow of its lashing claws when it lunges for us. The force of the impact catches my breath and I stumble to my knees with a splash as their weight falls on top of me. I reach for the extended hand and allow them to pull me out of the tangle. Minutes ago, I had been willing to fight Ipos and now I'm grateful he runs at my side, pushing me along. These beings might not be my friends, but if they believe me to be useful, they'll keep me safe.

It's impossible to sprint through the water when it sucks around our legs like a vacuum. The water is too murky to see where my feet are landing. One wrong step and I'm down. A third set of footsteps crashes behind us. I glance over my shoulder, dark hair stinging my eyes, to see Onna is after us, but barely. She holds onto her arm that is held together by the few strips of fabric of her top. There is enough blood on her face that she's got a serious head wound that's bled over, or half of her face is missing.

"We need to get out of the city," I yell at Ipos.

"Not while Pethaino still stands."

But it is falling. It just needs a little extra push.

When Dagon prayed, did he reach anyone? Was it Heaven that responded with the lightning strike or God Himself? Or was it Dagon's power that had finally snapped and caused the fire to turn stone to ash?

"God, bring your fire down again. Please," I say breathlessly. "Bring your fire down on us."

Something grabs the back of my arm and sharply spins me out of my run. "You will not bring that fury upon us," Onna snarls. Indeed, half of her face has been torn apart. Below her eye are three papery strips of flesh curled over. She slams me into the nearest wall.

"What are you doing?" Ipos screeches. He backpedals.

"We need to split up," she barks.

"We *need t*o protect her."

"I won't let anything happen to her." She turns her good eye toward him. "I severed his wings. The last he saw of her was with you." She looks back at me with a hand pressed over her cheek.

Where is the monster? I look past her shoulder, but there is nothing but our own ripples in the water.

"Raum, hear me," I whisper.

"No," Ipos growls. "She'll never make it back to Orias if I leave you with her."

Ipos takes a step forward, but he doesn't make it farther than that. Demons pride themselves on the old ways, using blades and the occasional arrows as their choice of weapons. There is a coil of smoke from the end of the pistol Onna pulls out. I didn't register the crack being the bullet leaving the chamber. She's already shot him. A dark circular hole gapes in the middle of his forehead.

And she turns the barrel down and cracks the butt of the gun into the side of my head. The crack is *loud*. It splits right behind my eye socket, and I keel over, wheezing. She's taken the breath right out of me.

She's so damn fast.

The world spins into a murky blur of black and red. I hear Ipos's body fall. I don't. I stumble to the side, but something keeps me upright. I press my hand into the stone wall to get some sort of stability.

Onna scoops me by the underarms and pulls my weight against her. "If you even think of using my name, I'll snap your neck." She stoops to hoist me onto her shoulders. She turns and looks frantically behind us. I can feel him, too. He's furious and he is close.

As soon as she starts to run, my head clears. My vision becomes sharper and the intense pain inside my head lifts. At her side flashes a hilt. I grab it, second guessing the length of it when I pull it free, but make the decision to follow through anyway, though I know my mark might be off. It tapers off at the end like a needle. From tip to base, it has a mirror shine to it, like chrome. I turn it inward and shove it into her back. It pierces the back of her armor with a soft *pop*. I do it again and again, slamming my fists together.

She throws me from her shoulder, ripping the dagger from my grasp but leaving it firmly thrust somewhere in her rib cage. I cover my head as a stone wall comes up too fast. She stumbles in through the door she's tossed me and forces it shut. Her foot slips out from beneath her and she collapses against the door, her nails digging into the wood to keep her from completely falling.

"I'm on your side," she gasps. Onna lets out something like a groan and turns against the door as she reaches to pull the blade free. She stops momentarily and holds her tattooed hand out to me. "Please. Please don't use my name. I'm begging you."

She knows it's on the tip of my tongue.

"You've done everything short of killing me. And that, too, you nearly did."

Where are we? The air is musky and stale with old blood. It's colder in here. It's a giant room of nothing save for the wide-set stairs that disappear under the dark water in the back.

"I am Orias's right hand. But before I was his warrior, I was an archangel. It is in my blood to fight." She twists her hand far enough to grasp the blade and jerk it free. She holds it against her chest like it's her preservation. "Dagon was foolish in the way he exposed himself. He nearly exposed *all* of us. I told him he would bring down destruction." She shuts her eyes and breathes deeply. "I'm on your side," she repeats.

"You don't actually expect me to believe that, do you? That you want salvation. Or that, what? Dagon is the one that started all of this." I wave my hand, not once taking my eyes off her. I don't trust her, but I'm willing to hear her out.

Her eyes snap open. I swear they're more red than black, full of fire. "He was too indifferent. You cannot play both sides and be lax. He wasn't as close with Orias as I have been. I have played my part at Orias's side, distracting him when needed. You have to be willing to get your hands dirty, and that is something Dagon grew weary of. So, yes, I do blame him for what is happening now. I blame the rest on you. On Raum." She shifts her weight, pressing her back completely against the flat of the door. "You being here has pushed a series of events forward that should have taken another six months. Orias has been wasting power to prove he's stronger than Raum."

"He's not," I snap.

Onna's lips crack apart, flashing her pointed teeth. "No."

"If you're on my side, why did you keep me from the gate?"

"Ipos was a loyal follower," she snaps. "Dagon and I were the last of the Believers."

I don't bite. This is all too convenient, an easy out for her. At the very least, it's an attempt to lower my guard.

"The Believers?"

"We still follow God."

Her fingers twitch over the hilt, they dance down the blade. Her lips move, but I can't hear what she's muttering. I trust her less now that she's on edge. I'd be smugger if I knew she was just afraid of me, but there is something else. Something bigger. The electric feeling she gives off makes me anxious.

"If all of this is true, then tell me where Orias is."

Her fingers stop.

Before, my priority had been to run, now it's to find the king. If we don't kill him before escaping, he'll just come after us. He'll hunt us down until he takes me from Raum. I don't foresee him giving me a choice to make the deal and, though they can't be forced, I'm sure he would find some way to push me. He'd taken me from Raum once already. Who's to say he wouldn't be able to do it a second time?

"I can make you, but I'm giving you the chance to tell me freely."

Her countenance falls and she lets out a deep breath. Her hesitance leaves me wary. I could use her name, but I don't think I would be fast enough before she tossed the knife she covets into my throat. There's nowhere to run or hide except wherever the stairs may lead, and that'll take a lot of swimming. I never was good at holding my breath under water. I'd be lucky if I made it twenty seconds without wanting to gasp for air.

Onna shies away from the door she's been guarding. I can feel it, too. Feel him. The angry power reverberates through the air, seeking. I turn my palm out.

I'm here. I'm OK.

She looks at me with nothing short of disgust. She twists the knife again and, albeit reluctantly, extends it to me. "Take it as a sign of good faith."

This is the biggest game of trust if there ever was one. Once I'm within reach, she'll turn against me. A loud snuffle comes from the other side of the door. She doesn't move away from it, but her back stiffens.

"He's in the Great Hall. It's the most fortified place in Pethaino. In the event of a fall, it cannot be penetrated once sealed. Please, take it."

I nod. The blade still sits in her hand, but something is wrong. Steam, or is that smoke, comes from her palm that grips the blade. I reach for it, my hand suspended over it before I finally rest my fingers over the hilt. Nothing.

As soon as my fingers curl over it, she withdraws her hand and presses it firmly to her chest. The smell of burnt flesh wafts in the air. She'd held it before, though, and been fine. I touch the blade gently, but it doesn't burn me the way it did her.

"Once it's done, how do we get out? Where is the gate?"

"I'll mark it for you."

Something heavy throws itself against the door and lets out a deep growl that creeps down my spine, bringing chills across my skin. I have good sense to be afraid of it, but I can't stop myself from walking forward. Onna shies away from me, stumbling slightly to the side.

"What's wrong?"

"Nothing," she lies. "But Leah."

I lay my hand against the door. We weren't running from just any monster.

"Leah."

I look back at her. She's breathing hard. Her hand has found its way behind her back to stop the blood trickling down.

"Make it quick. He's still my king."

That won't be a problem. We have wasted more than enough time in Pethaino. Raum will slit his throat and then we are out of here.

Onna slips her good hand through the ring of the door handle. "He'll kill me if he sees me."

I nod. "Thank you."

She pulls at the ring breathlessly. The water swirls as the door opens, sucking and pulling, making her efforts more difficult. She hadn't faltered when half her face and arm were hanging from her body. It was this knife that wounded her.

The beast on the other side snarls.

The blade slides like silk and smoothly turns in my hand as I twist it toward her. It pierces her leather before finding a resting place beneath her rib cage. "I'm sorry," I tell her. I grab her shoulder and she falls into the door. I can't take any more chances. I pull the knife free and slide it in again. And again. And again.

Blood clots the sound of her growl.

In the same moment she falls in the water, the door flies open. I jump back quickly, looking for her to reappear above the murk, but a hulking head swings in through the door before I can spot her.

Like all the others in their beastly form, the demon is massive. It stalks into the room, turning its head to focus me with an eye sunk so far into the socket it appears eyeless. The monster reeks of sulfur and rot. It forces its way in, advancing on me so fast that I don't have enough time to move. My feet are cemented into the ground and, as it opens its huge mouth, I know that I'm done.

The jaws close above my head. The shock they make rattles every bone in my body.

It laughs.

The sound starts deep within its belly and rolls up its long throat before slipping through its leathery lips. When the sound escapes, it sounds like music.

"Still afraid of the dark?"

XX

The first initial crack that breaks through the air makes me jump. The beast shifts forward as one of its legs buckles. Another snap of bones breaking tears through the air. The transformation looks more painful as the demon shrinks. Its shoulders roll and new skin falls into place, golden tan skin.

My heart slams into my chest. I want to run. To him. Away from him. But I'm still too dumbstruck to move.

The beast throws its head violently, splitting the skin that runs down its spine. It happens so quick and it's so dark, but it looks like the monster turns in on itself. Long limbs and broken wings bend awkwardly under a series of bone-chilling cracks and what can only be described as a torrent of blood. I step back, but it's everywhere. The warmth of it spreads to the water. I can smell it.

I catch a glimpse of his face as it's thrown back in the dim light. The wave of emotions is overpowering.

One second, I am running to him and the next Raum has his arms around me, lifting me from the ground with crushing strength. I run my fingers through his hair to reveal his face. I dig my nails into the back of his neck when he tips his face to mine.

Kissing him is like an unfettered wildfire. The taste of him is the spark that ignites the tinder of my flesh. His breath fans the flames, sending waves of heated chills along my body, and then he consumes me all at once. The burning of his power dries the tears from my face. He runs his thumbs along the dirty trails they've left behind, smearing blood along my cheeks.

"Ozien," he whispers. "I've got you."

And I you.

Mine.

Ozien.

I press my forehead into his and breathe him in. Beneath all the blood, I catch hints of ash and wood fire. I pull away before I lose myself, knowing that somewhere danger lurks.

"I stabbed Onna, but I don't know if she's dead."

Raum sets me down and turns, looking across the water the same time I do.

"Come," he says. I follow him as he takes my hand. He's much more confident than I, though I sense his caution underneath.

"Wait." I touch his arm as we step through the threshold. "Sebastian?"

"Still here," Sebastian answers. They give my hand a squeeze. "I'm not that easy to get rid of."

A smile darts across my face when he answers. I made the right choice.

"Quiet," Raum hisses.

"There is a gate on the south wall. It's our way out."

Neither answers. Their grip tightens on my hand and the way of our escape falls farther behind us.

"We're going the wrong way."

"Quiet," Raum hisses again.

Though we still walk through water, it seems to part for him. It recedes to our ankles, rising again in our wake. It's then I notice they wear nothing but skin and blood. Perhaps we are getting supplies first. We also need to take care of Orias. He won't be too keen once he realizes I've crossed him.

I have to tell Raum what has happened. They both deserve to know. I could leave James out of it, though. That's none of their business. Raum needs to know what Orias has planned. He needs to know I chose him.

I recognize a few of the buildings we pass. We're near the stocks. I glance at the gallows, taking a better hold of Raum's hand for reassurance.

I slip to a light jog as their stride lengthens as soon as broken jail cells come into view. The doors have been ripped clean off; most lay scattered to the floor, but there is one that still hangs from its hinges. There is more than enough blood to tell this is where Raum slaughtered the humans. No doubt this is where they were being held, and so he made it their final resting place. Bits of nails are chipped across the floor where some attempted to crawl away.

It should go without mention that there is blood everywhere. It's spattered across every surface. Raum did this. I chose this over Orias, yet I feel safe at his side. How can I feel safe when he slaughtered over a hundred people?

To save you.

"No one will look for us here." Raum breaks into my thoughts as he closes a door, sliding a wedge beneath the handle for security. How did we get here?

I turn, taking in the room full of chains and weapons. In the middle of the room is a table with scattered papers and a gun. Behind that is a lit fireplace with a pile in front of it in the shape of a nest. Has he been here all this time? I slip Onna's knife beneath my belt.

Raum lets me go to cross the room, snatching a piece of cloth from the ground quickly. He rubs his skin with it, wiping and scrubbing the blood that has dried from his body. I watch the flakes fly off into the hearth. Once he has rid himself of the filth, he bends down again to step into a pair of black jeans.

"I know what you did. To save me." I glance at the closed door. Those poor people.

"It had to be done." He looks at me beneath his lashes. He pulls a shirt over his head and locks eyes with me again. "I could not go another second wondering what Orias must be doing to you." His eyes drop and rise back to my face. "Though you are in better condition than I expected." I touch where Onna hit me with the gun, but it's already healed. It's good being with him again.

"Orias didn't want to hurt me. He wanted to make a deal with me. One I didn't take," I say quickly.

"What sort of deal?"

"Your life in exchange for my immunity and his name."

The fire crackling in the background is the only sound. I hold my breath, willing myself to keep cool. The rise of emotion in my chest is one that threatens tears to my eyes. I'm not upset, just angry.

"He told you then." Raum tsks. "I wondered if anyone else would figure it out. Your Leyak certainly didn't."

It takes everything not to address the snub of Leyak.

"Were you going to tell me? If Sebastian hadn't said anything before fighting Onna, would you have? I could have died."

Raum tilts his head to the side and rolls his eyes.

I slap him. "You son of a bitch." My anger tapers as quick as its head rises.

A sly smile pulls Raum's lips back, but only one fang flashes when he smiles. "Do you feel better?"

How dare he.

"The less you knew the better. It was for your own protection." He turns his back to approach the fire.

"My protection? You don't think knowing I can control a demon—any demon—with its name is helpful?"

"So, it's true," Sebastian says.

"How long have you known?" I round the table until I am standing between him and the hearth.

"From the moment I met you," Raum says smugly.

"You fucking liar."

"It's true," he cuts me off. "That mark above your throat is the only thing that has kept you alive."

The image of him turning my head up sharply in the cave. At the time, I thought it was a quick inspection. And to a point, it was, just not in the way I expected. A wash of joy washes over me the moment he sees the cluster of freckles. How had he been able to contain his excitement then?

I swallow the tears building in the back of my throat. "I chose you. Chose to spare you and Sebastian. He can't help his situation, but *you*." The word is like venom dripping from my tongue. "You have done nothing but lie to me. Why did I do that?"

Raum takes my hands, letting the cruel mask drop for a moment. "Because we were made for each other. Look at you," he gives a hard squeeze, "stepping into your wisdom."

I want so badly to scream. I know he is trying to manipulate me, but he's right. He is good for me. Everything Raum has done for me has been to keep me safe. He spared me.

"Now, tell me the rest of what happened. You have been gone a long time."

I pull my hands away. "You can't see it?"

"No."

"There is a wall around you," Sebastian says. "It looks like a mirror and the only thing we can see is ourselves looking back. There is no door to get in."

A chill runs down my spine. For not being able to see what's in my mind they're spot on to where I had been.

"Orias made his conditions, and I came back with mine. I asked for his name. I told him I would accept only on that condition, and then he kissed me." I look into the fire, remembering the sick feeling that gripped me when he took hold of me.

"A deal is not met with a kiss."

"I know," I say a little too sharp. "Onna and Dagon interrupted to tell him what you had done. Dagon took me to the aviary," I trail off.

Raum shakes his head.

"What is it?" Sebastian asks.

"Orias said we made the deal, but we didn't. There wasn't opportunity or time to seal it."

"You were gone for two days." Raum's tongue darts between their lips. The behavior is too strange to belong to a human.

"How is a deal made?" Sebastian presses.

I press my fingers to the bridge of my nose. "You have to have intercourse."

"Did he fuck you?" The fire reflects in their eyes, looking hotter than the real one burning within the hearth.

"Me standing here should be proof enough that never happened."

"Then what happened for the time you cannot account for? I tore the city apart looking for you." A wave of power strikes me in the chest, forcing me to reach out to the hearth to steady myself. Beneath the surge of anger is sadness. I bite the inside of my lip when the pins start to prick behind my eyes. He'd been so worried.

"I don't know. When Dagon took me to the aviary, he said I'd been in a talon. It was a place like the one you described seeing in my head. But on the inside, it could be anything I wanted. We talked, I had time to think, and then I lied and said I would accept his deal. The pact was never made."

I turn out my hands. Raum has his own reasons not to trust me, but to say I'm a liar is calling the kettle black. Why is it so hard to prove your loyalty to a traitor?

"I can prove it." I pull Onna's blade free and tilt it into the light. Raum recoils. He looks from the blade to me, his muscles stiffening. "I don't know what this is, but I know it nearly killed Onna. Maybe I did kill her. And I know for my end of the deal to be upheld that I have to kill you."

Not that Raum would let me. Though the idea of stabbing him crosses my mind, every muscle in my body holds still. I couldn't do it if I really wanted to. Instead, I turn the blade inward, extending the hilt to him the same way Onna did.

"If I don't follow through, something will happen to me. Right?"

Neither of them takes it. Sebastian whispers something, but it's muffled behind their lips, making the words indiscernible.

"You have tried to kill me before," Raum says.

I nod. "And this time I chose you. Through Hell or high water. I am yours, Raum."

His lids drop back to the blade again before reaching out. Instead of taking the hilt, he pushes it back against my stomach. He has always taken my weapons. For whatever reason, he can't touch it.

XXI

I nestle against him in front of the fire. I don't know what we are waiting for. Surely Orias is tearing the city apart much the way Raum did to find me. How long will it be before they find us? What is Raum going to do? I'm so tired.

"Where did you get that?" I don't know which one of them has asked the question. The knife sits on the table where I left it. Looking at it now, it feels vile. It had felt good in my hand, but the thought of holding it again makes me shift uncomfortably.

"Onna gave it as a peace offering." I'll regret it if I find out she was being honest. But too much had been lost already to give demons the benefit of the doubt. Poor Dagon.

They move their arm down to clasp my bicep with a gentle squeeze. "It is a weapon of Heaven," Raum says.

"She was an archangel before."

Raum hums. "I recognized her tattoos. Strange she brought it with her. A messenger's weapon is one of the few things that can hurt us. It is the one thing that leaves a scar."

I look back at them. He favors himself more than Sebastian now. His eyes are wider than before, the shadows cast by his brow bone darker. "I can't believe you were all once angels."

They flash a tight-lipped smile. "Something like that," he says.

I wonder how much more beautiful they were before they fell.

"What happened?" Sebastian asks.

I smile involuntarily. It's good Raum let him stay. And all without the torment. At least, if he has tormented him, it's been lenient enough that Sebastian can handle it. It appears he has a grip on his sanity, at the very least. I remember the pain all too vividly of what James went through.

Is this how it's going to be from now on, though? The three of us, like this.

I want to be closer to Raum. Thinking about it sends a repulsive shiver through my body. Now that I know Sebastian is truly alive, it's an incredibly vile thought. It's *his b*ody.

Raum lets out an exasperated sigh.

"I mean, is it what religion tells us?" Sebastian presses the issue of the angels.

"We had a disagreement with God. Some of us were thrown out while the rest of us left voluntarily. There is nothing more to it than that."

I roll my eyes. Forever with the vagueness.

"Which were you?"

All at once the sadness I felt before falls across me like a shroud. The feeling is so sharp it makes my chest ache. I press my fingers against my heart absentmindedly to fidget the pain away. The story of their fall is a vivid flash in my mind.

"I left."

When he told me the story of their fall, he said he had known what it would cost him. Hearing him dodge Sebastian's inquiry, I don't think that is true. In fact, I wonder if he is being honest at all about his banishment.

Sebastian asks something else about a war and the devil. There has never been much said about the devil since the Possession. He is another one of those things we've all wondered to be real or myth. There wasn't much talk about him, or it, when everything went to shit. I don't know what the devil is. I've only ever experienced demons.

I squint. Is the fire going out?

Their hand drops to my lap when I lean forward. No, the fire is still burning bright, but the flames are... blurry? I dig my index and thumb into my eyes and rub them around. It must be the lack of sleep. My body feels drained. I sigh, closing my eyes. A bit of rest would do me good.

They're arguing now.

"You expect me to believe that everything in the Bible is a lie," Sebastian retorts.

"Everything you think you know about God is a lie," Raum responds. "You humans think you know everything because you read the words of dead men."

"If she's Solomon's heir–"

"Just because the characters are the same does not mean their stories are."

"I think you're full of shit."

"Ever heard the phrase, 'Do not concern yourself with the angels?' Our matters are not for you."

"And yet here we are, right in the middle of a war your kind started. You always act so high and mighty."

I'll never be able to sleep with their bickering. Raum's stories of Heaven and Hell have always bothered me. Everything I'd ever heard was false according to him. It's never sat right with me that people could have gotten things wrong for so long on so many levels. Surely there is some truth buried in there somewhere.

There is a faint haze in my vision when I open my eyes. The fire is dark. It *has* to be going out. Did I doze off that quickly that it's gotten lower? Confused, I reach out.

I hiss as my fingers touch the flames.

"Leah?" Sebastian asks.

"Something is wrong." I lean forward, feeling the stone tiles. They're getting darker, fading away quickly. "I can't see."

The darkness that surrounds me is more frightening than when I was dead. At least when I was dead there was nothing. The harder I strain to see, the quicker it goes. The fire shrinks down to the size of a pinhole and then it pops out of view and it's absolutely black.

"I can't see!" Something grabs me by the hips. Logically, I know it's Raum and Sebastian, but I balk. I lurch and slam my shoulder into something hard, probably a table leg.

Stirizo. Stirizo. Stirizo.

"Leah."

Tears spring to my eyes as I feel around haphazardly. A hand takes hold of mine and pulls me back, turning me around on my knees. I lay my other hand on their chest. "What's happening? What's that voice?"

"What voice?" Sebastian asks.

Copper bursts within my nose. The warm rush of blood falls down the back of my throat and I cough. I feel around blindly, looking for it. Where is it?

I shake my head. "Stirizo! I can hear it." I swallow another gulp of crimson. Where's the knife?

"Uphold. She made a pact. Leah, what happened in the talon?" Raum asks. He grabs my wrists when they brush the leg of the table I know the knife is on. I need something sharp.

"What is a talon?" Sebastian asks.

"Let me go," I growl. I push and then snap my arms into my chest, trying to break their hold, but it doesn't budge.

"It is a spell room of dreams crafted with mirrors. Within, there is no time; it can be a few seconds or years. Though the master of the spell is in control, those trapped have a hand at the events that unfold." They brush the tears from my face. "What did he do?"

I shake my head. I can't tell him. Why won't he let me go? I need to cut this thing out of me. If I put the blade into it, I'll be able to see again. By cutting it out, I can stop the blood flow.

"Tell us," Sebastian says.

"How did he torment you?"

I shake my head again. "He didn't! Give me my knife."

"Can you not help her?" Sebastian presses.

"I need to know what happened. I can sever the bond he made, but I need to know exactly what happened. If there was anything in the fine print, I do not want to sever their bond incorrectly." I can tell by the tone of his voice Raum is speaking directly to me now.

"There was no print, no contract. It was James. It was just James."

His name tastes like ash on my tongue. There wasn't anything malicious about the talon. It was kind and gracious. And yet it feels so wrong. I can still see his face smiling back at me, his green eyes crinkling at the corners.

They don't exactly let go of me, but everything feels like it stops. They don't pull with me, just become strangely still. For whatever reason, it takes the urgency out of finding the blade.

"You know there is no such thing as ghosts. When you die, you go to death. You go to sleep." Raum speaks as a stern father would, but there is a coldness in his voice that seeps into my bones. His words cut deep. "Do you hear me? James is dead."

"If it is a spell, then maybe it wasn't a ghost," Sebastian says, his voice cracking. I can feel his touch beneath Raum's hard exterior.

"Talons only account for the people who are in them."

No. His eyes were green.

"If it was just Leah and Orias…"

Green eyes.

Light skin.

Brown hair.

"Orias wasn't with me."

"Leah–"

"No! It wasn't him. It can't be."

So, you'll do it?
Yes.
Black eyes.
Dark skin.
Black hair.

"You don't understand. It *can't* be. It had to be James. It *was J*ames. Where is my knife? I need it!" I pull violently against their hold. Something snaps so I pull again, ignoring the pain that shoots up my forearms.

Everything about him was as I remember it. The feel of his skin against mine. The way he touched me was unlike anything I've ever experienced. There has only ever been one James and there will never be another like him. Our bond was ethereal, like we were twin flames. Soul mates. James was my soul mate. I would know if it had been someone else wearing his skin. I would know it because he is mine and I am his.

"It was James."

If I put the blade in deep enough, this will all stop. I need to cut it out of me.

Orias's face takes shape behind my blind eyes as I desperately hold onto James. It was real. His wicked smile falls over what should be James's mouth. "I can feel this," he said. Even as I realize it is Orias that kissed me, I still feel James.

"Don't take him from me again," I cry. "Just let me cut it out. Let me keep him."

"I am sorry," Raum says. Their hands cup the underside of my chin.

"Raum, don't!" Sebastian yells.

Their strong fingers twist around my chin, their other hand sliding around to the back of my head. The pressure is so intense. So fast. The pain is like a spark, and then it's snuffed out as Raum twists my head too far. I hear my bones break before there is nothing.

***

"When is she going to wake up?"

Raum hums. "Not much longer now."

I'm lying down, caught between the heat of a body and the warmth of a fire. Their arms tighten around me protectively. I know it's with good intention, but it makes my skin crawl. It doesn't feel right. It had felt right with James, and that was a lie. I want to rip my skin off. I reach to tear at my face, but my arms don't move. It's not their restraint that holds me still, though. Be it some power or my own exhaustion, I just can't move.

"What was she raving about? Cut what out?"

"Me." Raum clears his throat.

Dull pain radiates from the base of my skull down to the middle of my spine. The headache is the worst part of the pain, though that seems to be receding, too. I fade in and out of consciousness, their words slipping in and out, moving through one ear and out the other.

"How are you so calm?" Sebastian asks.

Raum laughs from somewhere in his chest, breaking the somber mood that's cast over all of us. "If I let my rage come to head, you will be snuffed out. Your death will further wound her."

"I saw James, or what was left of him, when those demons came to our city. I thought that would break her having to kill him. To kill them both."

"Leah cannot be broken."

"And yet you've stolen memories from her."

Raum's only response is nuzzling his face into the crook of my neck. He breathes me in. On exhale, that same breath shudders. "Everything I do is to keep her safe."

"Until she is no longer useful."

"I care because she is Leah." There's something like reverence in his voice. It is the voice of someone who has killed for me and would do it again until there wasn't anyone left to hurt me.

Finally, my eyes open. Orange flames dance beneath the hearth. There is black cloth beneath my body, separating me from the cold floor. Their arm is wrapped around me, beneath my breasts with their hand clamped to my wrist. It is such a way that James would hold me in his sleep.

I blink and the image remains.

The room spins slightly as I sit up, sliding away from the embrace so I can look directly into the fire. This body doesn't feel like mine anymore. It has been abused more than once, brutalized more than that. I wish I could change skins as easily as the demons do. I would nestle into someone new, start over, and be someone brave and untouchable.

It's not fair.

"You broke my neck."

A rustle sounds behind me as they sit up.

"A deal allowed Orias to skirt around my mark. You would have remained blind and spoiled from the inside out until you upheld your end of the bargain. Until I was dead. It was the only way."

I nod, wincing. My neck feels so damn tight.

"How did he do it?"

They run their fingers through my hair, starting at my scalp, down to the back of my neck. "A talon only reacts to the person it has been made for. You set the stage and he stepped in to play the part." Raum's touch softens. It's strange that I am starting to understand when it is him or Sebastian, or both.

"You're saying this is my fault?" I choke. There was nothing I could have done to prevent it. I didn't know what a talon was. I didn't know Orias would trick me. He seemed so certain I would take his offer. I thought he had gone.

"He took advantage of you."

Of my weakness. I hear the unsaid insult in his tone. I rub both my arms to fight off the tears, to fight off the pressure building in my chest. It would have been so much easier if Raum had left me dead.

"There was someone else in there. There had to have been at first. They changed their face to people of my past and his." Did Ipos play the part when Orias showed me the power of the talon? Was it Onna?

A flutter of panic quickens my breath. I turn quickly. They stiffen behind me, but no one makes a move. The knife is just where I left it.

Raum's countenance is unreadable when I look back. He clamps a hand over my shoulder and squeezes. "He will suffer for this," he promises.

I look a moment longer before turning my attention back to the flames. At least my intuition had been right not to trust the king. That the lesser of two evils is Raum, even if he is more powerful. I still believe that. Even with Orias wielding Pethaino's power, I know Raum has the upper hand. Orias's spiral is evidence of that. If only there was a way for him to harness Pethaino, too.

A flash of James's smile lights up behind my eyes whenever I close them. It twists into Leyak's nasty grin before widening into Orias's. I throw my head into my hands and sob. The images replay again and again in my head. It goes on like that until a gentle touch, a soft pressure to the back of my head, quiets me.

They've taken everything from me. Even this new power I have been introduced to will be used against me. They'll take that, too, if I let them.

I lean my head to the side, resting it against their palm. Their hand turns to cup my face. Their rough thumb grazes my skin, lulling me from my tears.

It starts as a gentle prick, like someone has tapped the top of my head. It spreads like ivy, curling down across my eyes, past the skin and tissue of my body until it wraps around my bones. It feels good, this touch. Too good.

"Don't." The numbness doesn't fade, but it doesn't spread. "I don't know if that's you or my mind playing tricks on me, but don't. Let me keep this."

Their thumb stops the gentle brush-like strokes.

In some sick way I want to hold onto James even though I know it wasn't him. I need to hold onto this anger, feed it. They'll never take from me again. He didn't deserve such wickedness to happen to him. Neither do I.

I turn around, taking their hand before they can pull it away.

"You've always said how powerful you are, but I've only experienced this," I touch my temple, "and the fire. Can you destroy him and Pethaino?"

Raum smiles, deepening the laugh lines of his borrowed face. "I can."

"Then let's do it. Now."

That smile falters. "Leah, are you alright?" Which one of them asked that?

"I am not." I stand, unsteadily. It doesn't matter who spoke. Of course I'm not alright. They rise with me, extending their arm for support, but I brush it away. "I am done being the piece to a game I don't know all the rules to." I snatch Onna's dagger from the table before Raum can touch it. I know he won't, but I don't want him even considering it. "If you're so powerful, prove it. Let's go after him and let's finish our path to Babel."

"Leah," Sebastian says hesitantly. Their brows furrow and force a strange look across Raum's countenance.

"Don't Leah me." I slip the knife through my belt and take a step toward the door. I want to feel Orias against me again. But this time, when his throat is within reach, I'm going to rip it out. I am going to sink my teeth into his neck and the knife straight into his heart. I want his blood to flow until the whole kingdom is painted red with his death.

"I have had everything stripped from me. Everything!" The screech of my voice sounds more animal than human. My vision—I catch my breath for a second. It's not fading this time, only the color has changed. Everything is red rimmed. I exhale. "I have his name. I will not be played again." I point at them, at Raum. "Never again."

Raum reaches for me. He touches the air by my face in an attempt to brush the hair away at my cheek, but instead he brushes smoke to the side. The dark bands curl out from under my skin as he grips my biceps. "Never again," he confirms. "My little fury, you are not a game piece. You are a weapon." He holds my eyes. I can see some part of Sebastian disappear behind the lacquered gaze. "Let's show them how powerful you are."

I think I hear Sebastian saying something, but it's muffled. It sounds like he is telling me not to fall. Not to listen to Raum.

But there is no one else but Raum.

Us.

"Let's show them how powerful *we* are," I say.

Raum flashes his teeth, his canines long and pointed atop his lower lip. "As you wish."

XXII

The door groans with restraint from the water pressure on the other side. Raum has instructed me to stand behind him, because when the door opens it's going to break free, and he doesn't want the water sweeping me off my feet. I touch his back, signaling that I'm ready.

At first, nothing happens when he pushes against the door. Water trickles in through the crevasse and then it's a full-on funnel. It rushes against our feet until the door is completely open and then–

A wave of power erupts beneath my fingertips where they still lay against Raum and blows out into the city. Like a curtain, the water draws back, opening a path that has walls well over three stories high. But it doesn't stop with a path. Raum steps out and throws his hand up, and with his other, he curls his hand into a fist and pulls. For a millisecond, the water stops moving before another surge of power forces it up.

It's much the same way the water transferred in the aviary. But this feels different. I can't put my finger on it other than it is powerful. The water rolls back in giant waves, exposing the ground of the city and buildings that had been submerged. It tilts back over the walls, leaving everything shiny and glistening. The wall of water towers higher than Pethaino, looking more menacing than the swords and bones that thrust from the stone.

I feel invincible at his side.

The hallway leading to the Great Hall remains empty. The hollow darkness casting uncertainty over my shoulders like a cloak leaves me on edge. Where is everyone? I didn't expect anyone to be outside with it being flooded, but here? There is no sound.

"Perhaps Onna was lying," I say.

Raum touches his finger to his lips. I strain to hear whatever he can when he cocks his head, but there is nothing other than the sound of my own breath. This feels like a trap.

"Let me go in first," I say. I hold up my hand before he can stop me. "Orias thinks our deal still stands. Let me talk to him."

"I am not letting him anywhere near you again."

"Let me do this. Just don't let anything happen to me this time." I give his arm a gentle squeeze.

"Leah–"

"Trust me. I can do this." I touch the hilt of Onna's blade. I'm more confident with this than anything else I've ever wielded.

Raum looks over my head, his throat moving so the veins stick out beneath the collar of his black shirt. His brow furrows and then he drops his head and shakes it. "Be quick. I will not wait long." The black orbs of his eyes flash deadly.

I nod. There is nothing else to be said. I clasp his wrist tightly, willing his strength into me, asking for it. Don't let me falter.

Two large doors stand wide open, the great entrance to the Hall. The amount of heat that flows from the entryway is as unsettling as it is stifling. The air is thick with humidity. I cautiously enter the haze, more on edge and with less confidence than I had moments ago.

I strain to listen for any signs of movement, but there is nothing. Is that a mirror through the haze? My stomach tightens. Could he have moved the talon in here? If Orias means to trick me again, I won't make it. I can pretend to be brave all I want, but if this is a talon and he uses James against me, I'll not be able to fight him, let alone kill him. It's not just James I'm afraid of, though. If what Raum says is true, Orias could turn into anything or anyone in my memory.

I step to the edge of where I first noticed the glass and shut my eyes. I reach out into the void, searching for him. It's impossible to find someone you're not tethered to. Perhaps if our deal was still in play, I could sense him better. A heavy chill spreads over my body, roving like tentacles that leave me feeling slimy. He can't win.

I open my eyes and step over the threshold.

The Hall looks different now. Black glittering dust flits through the air, the tables and foliage completely gone.

There is no sign of Orias, nor can I feel anything, but I know he is here.

"Oriasan," I call.

Something moves in the middle of the room; like a hulking silhouette, it slinks amongst the shadows of the smog. As much as I ache to do so, I refrain from pulling Onna's blade. There's a chance he'll notice the weapon anyway, but best to keep it hidden just in case. I finger the denim of my pants instead to steady my fidgeting.

"Orias, I need your help."

Something else moves in my peripheral, setting every nerve of my body on fire. When I turn to look, it is gone. Whatever it was, it was big. It's bigger than any demon I've ever seen and far bigger than the monsters my imagination can concoct.

"And yet you ran from me," he whispers against my ear. I spin around, my hand still aching to reach for the blade, but he isn't there.

"I ran. Not from you, but from the monsters chasing me and Onna. She seeks to kill me."

He chuckles somewhere to my left but the space there is empty, too. The haze has softened to an off-white, enough to see through, to reveal the bloodstained landing where I nearly died and a row of empty pews. I look up to the rafters, terrified that he is about to drop down on me.

Hot hands fiercely grab my hips and pull me back into him. Every muscle in my body goes rigid and the sweat against my brow cools. He chuckles as he slides around me, releasing me so he can stand in front of me. His solid black attire has a faint blue sheen to it that somehow makes him look bigger. The grace in which he moves, his muscles tensing and releasing with each step, reminds me so much of a panther. The light traces the outline of his dark skin when he comes to a stop, standing so still he might as well have turned to stone.

Orias's lids flutter as he judges the distance between us. And then he strikes.

I throw my arm up. Too slow. His hand nearly encircles my entire throat as he hoists me up, briefly, before slamming me into the ground. "You think I cannot feel what you have done? You're right!" He leers over me, his hot breath burning against my face as he blows purposefully against it. "There is nothing binding us now that Raum has broken it. I don't need your permission to shackle you."

I heard somewhere once that the devil needs permission from God before they can harm a human. What God would allow such wickedness? Is it to teach us a lesson? Or is it to punish us for our lack of belief and faith? Such a strange thought to have as Orias snaps his teeth in my face. His fangs protrude from the gaping holes in his upper gums, sliding out, ready for blood.

"You do. It's why you tricked me the first time. You couldn't get it from God, so you had to get it from me."

"Ah!" He waves his index finger in front of my face before turning his hand quickly and pressing his thumb over my eye. "An heir of Solomon inherits his wisdom. The only way to trap you was to use your heart against you." His thumb presses into my eye and I gasp.

The hilt of Onna's blade kisses my hand and I pull it out and stab, meeting something soft. Liquid warmth touches my hand, and I withdraw in the same instant Orias pulls away. I cover my eye, opening it slowly behind my palm as the shock of pain radiates from the socket. My vision is blurry when I remove my hand, but at least my eye is still intact.

There is a gaping puncture wound in Orias's shoulder that he touches. Alarm settles over his face, his lids fluttering quickly, and he jerks his hand away. He rubs his fingers together before turning it into a fist.

"You little bitch."

I take a half step back and duck when he charges. Instead of his fist flying at me, his knee comes up, catching me in the nose. I reel back, but he follows and grabs me by the top of my hair to pull my head back down. He slams his knee into my face again, and that cracks my nose wide open. Blood fills my mouth; it pours across my lips. He drops me as soon as I start sputtering, and I hit the ground with no time to catch myself. The only thing that keeps me conscious is the clang the blade makes when it strikes floor and that, somehow, it's still in my hand.

"It didn't have to be this way. I was going to take care of you." His voice is oddly calm. He takes two large steps forward and kicks me in the stomach. "Tell me, were you a Believer before or after we came?"

Is he talking about God?

"Neither," I groan. I spit blood onto the floor and suck in a breath of air. The break in my nose sends a stab of pain that goes all the way up into my forehead.

Orias smiles a wide grin that shows too many of his teeth, making him look like a scary cartoon. "Then there's still hope for you."

I push up on my hand slowly, enough to get my face off the ground. Blood drops like little crystals, glinting in the light. It hurts to breathe. I think he has cracked one of my ribs, multiple more likely.

He turns his head slightly to the side, listening to something. I think I hear it, too, a wet slithering sound. I try to hold my breath. The wet sound stops when I do, but the quiet sliding noise continues. Orias takes a step forward, turning his head the other way.

As soon as he turns around, I bring the blade up and slash it across the back of his ankles. Onna's blade cuts through the back of his boots like butter, sliding all the way down to his Achilles tendons. He doesn't even make it a half step before he falls forward, catching himself with his palms. I jump up, falling quickly and rising again before he can beat me to it. His braids make it easier to lock my grip against his head and pull it back. Even though he is stronger than me, at this angle he won't be able to get up, not quickly at least, with his legs twisted beneath him and his feet useless.

I press the tip of the knife into his chest, daring him to move. I'm already expecting him to disarm me. Small, weak little Leah. Not this time.

I blink until the room stands still. The pain in my face is numbing, and my whole body screams as I put every bit of my strength into holding him still.

"You will not move, Oriasan."

He chuckles, sending vibrations up through the hilt. "You really think I gave you my true name?"

The confirmation of it bites more than I anticipated. "Not after I found out it was you in the talon. Do you not recognize this sword, though? She's dead," I say. "I killed her with her own blade."

I feel him tense, though I can't see if he notices the sword. He must because he isn't laughing now.

"Raum is going to kill you once he has Babel. If you had taken my offer—you did not even have to kill him. All you needed to do was trust me and I would have protected you."

"You raped me." My throat constricts as I force the words out. "You're going to pay for what you've done."

As if on cue, Raum enters the room and, with him, power and smoke. The smoke moves like water at his feet, flits of ash and embers sift in the air of his wake. It gives me strength when Orias trembles. I tighten my hold through his hair, turning my knuckles stark white as my demon approaches.

"Brother," Orias strains. "I was only trying to be like you."

The flash of his hand is like a viper striking. Raum catches Orias by the jaw and squeezes. I dig the knife in deeper. I can feel his heart slamming against his chest beneath the point, threatening to burst.

"You are nothing like me. I *am* power while you scavenge on others to have yours. I *am* cyn of Eurynomos, but you served me long before then. And let me remind you, since you have forgotten your place, that you are on your knees at the mercy of a woman you raped while she stands with me freely. A woman who has more power than you could ever acquire simply by being human. I did not gain my power or loyalty because I stole it. Everything I have has been won."

It's then Orias tries to break free. The force of his strength is explosive, and when I pull him back into my chest, my breath catches. It's only with Raum's help that I'm able to hold him.

"You were never a cyn. You were just a shadow to one and thought that made you his equal." Orias jerks his head to the side, attempting to catch Raum's hand between his sharp teeth.

"Leah," Raum says, his voice hoarse with controlled rage.

I meet his eyes. Whatever he is thinking won't work, but it's worth a shot. It had worked before, for Orias. Why wouldn't it work for me?

Outside the window, the water casts a menacing shadow over the city walls. Every demon within Pethaino must be standing out there now. A hiss winds up through the air as they glare up at me in unison. Why hasn't Orias sent them in for us? Why are they just standing there? Perhaps he is afraid. Can they see the knife I hold over his heart from where they stand? Do they know? Why are they not protecting their king?

"Legion!" I call.

The silence the single word casts is chilling. Orias strains against my hands to look out the window, his crimson tongue flashing between his fangs. "What do you think you're doing?"

"Tear down the city."

In the first few rows, I can see a few of the demons look at each other. Somewhere in the back there is a ripple effect, some of them turning while the rest just stand, their black eyes boring into me.

"Legion! Tear down the city!"

Orias chuckles. "Too bad. That would have been a good idea."

"Legion!" This time my voice echoes across all Pethaino. There is rich power as I call out with an authority I didn't know I was capable of. "I command you to turn on your kingdom. Break down Pethaino brick by brick until the water swallows you whole. Let it drown each one of you."

As if a blanket falls over them, it becomes deathly quiet, and they listen. They turn on not only the city but each other. Some fight and claw through the others to reach the wall. The largest of the demons throw their bodies into the walls, impaling themselves on the spikes and sharp blades. One runs headfirst, splitting its face open upon impact. It stumbles back, its movements unsteady. It charges again.

Another of the demons in the front row steps forward, more cautious with his order. He looks up at me, his face full of rage, and he reaches forward to a sword that protrudes from the wall closest to him. He tosses it into the army behind him and goes for another. A couple more step forward and start doing the same. They toss the bodies impaled to the ground next. The brawl reaches those more reserved and soon they, too, are wrapped up in the blood lust. One by one and piece by piece, the demons start to break down the wall. In the midst of it, they are torn apart, too.

"My name is Legion, because we are many," Raum mocks.

The clamor raises in volume as the demons become more aggressive with their movements. One of them pulls a sword free and slashes it at his neighbor before shouting what I recognize to be a vicious slur for humans. It doesn't matter. I commanded them and they listened; they don't have to be happy about it.

"Loyalty," Raum says. He lets the word hang in the air. "I know what you did to Leah. You used her adelfi against her, and still she chose me. How does it feel to know you are still nothing?"

Orias slams an elbow into my gut, but I keep my hold locked. Whatever he broke is already healed. When he tries a second time, I slide the knife's edge up and against his throat. The scarlet line ripples like a ribbon, so delicate and faint. He swallows a sound of agony.

"There is something about you that has always excited me, though." Raum follows the line with his finger. "What is it like to steal from your brothers? What does it taste like to reap of the Fallen?" His grip softens to stroke the underside of Orias's chin. The touch is too intimate, something he would never... has never done to me.

Orias trembles beneath me. His terror seeps into my bones enough to weaken my hold but he doesn't fight. There is nowhere to run except into Raum's fangs, and he knows it.

"I would like to see what that is like."

Wetness slips across my hand. Too cool to be blood. Too soft to be anything but tears.

"What does your soul taste like?"

XXIII

The knife edges across Orias's chest as Raum digs his fingers farther into the underside of the king's jaw. He uses his free hand to latch hold of the back of the king's skull. Orias lets out a blood-curdling scream that jolts me from my daze. I hold the knife steady, too afraid that if I let him go on my end that he will somehow be able to hurt Raum.

The weight of his head falls against my hand. Raum climbs on top of him before I have the chance to move out of the way, and my leg gets caught beneath their weight and forces me to the ground. I pull the knife away and stumble back to my feet.

Outside, chaos brews as the demons become more hurried with their actions. We won't need a gate to escape through once they tear down the wall. The water still stands high, blotting out the sun that should be moving to the west, getting ready to set.

The dead: I can smell them again. Through the stink of rot that pollutes the air and smoke, their heady stench burns its way into my lungs. My stomach turns as the corpses are disturbed and buried beneath the falling rubble. Faint sobs, a final cry for help as those still half-alive are discarded. I thought they had all been dead, those impaled.

Another command sits on my tongue. They won't hear me, not over all the clamor they make. Two demons have started to work on our tower. If the rest notice, they'll get the same idea. Then it will be Raum and me beneath the rubble when the stones fall in on us. They're doing what I commanded by their own terms. It's a fault I should have caught.

The thud of a body pulls me back to matters closer to me. Two bodies. Orias and Raum lay motionless next to each other. I walk slowly. Something should be happening but it's not this. I risk another glance out the window, but the water still stands. That means Raum is fine. Right?

He groans and I take his face in my hands when I drop to my knees.

"I've got you," I say.

The flash of white catches my breath when he blinks. The light is too muted to tell for certain, but I know his irises are rich brown. He turns his face into my palm and groans again. "Everything hurts." He turns his head back then forward to me, bloodshot eyes straining. "What's wrong?"

"Sebastian..." I feel frozen. It's really him. Demons can't fake a possession; they can't fake the eyes. That means–

Orias's body lays still, his chest rising and falling with life's breath. Again, I look out the window, but the water still stands. Sebastian's warm hand on mine snaps me out of my dreamlike state. I press my palm more firmly to his face.

"It's you," I say. He starts to shake his head then stops. He lets out a gasp as he sits up, so I have to drape my arm around him to help. "He's in Orias."

"Is that possible?" he asks, leaning his head against my chest. His whole body is shaking.

"I have no idea. Look at me." I turn his face up to get a better look at his eyes. They're entirely clear. No murk or dark hides in the whites of them. Sebastian's face still looks distorted while it shifts, and I realize why he is trembling.

"You can't change back."

A more violent shiver runs through him. "What are you talking about?"

I shut my eyes. Don't let Raum's relinquishment be the death of this man. The slow, steady beat of his heart gives me encouragement even though I'm unsettled. If Raum wanted Sebastian dead, he would have done it already. It could be a cruel trick, to let nature take its course to keep the man's blood from his hands, but I must think the best.

"When Raum possessed you, your body had to adapt to him. He's bigger than you, he looks different." I touch his hand when his hand flies to his face. "You're you, but I don't think the rest of your body is going to change back. Or maybe that's what is happening now."

"It doesn't feel like anything is changing," he says through gritted teeth. "It just hurts."

I look back at Orias, who is supposed to be Raum. Why isn't he waking up? And why would he do this after what Orias did to me? I adjust my grip on Sebastian to keep him from sliding while I reach for the other body. I trace along the veins of his hand. One of the tendons flexes when his finger twitches and I let out a subtle breath. I slip my hand in his and squeeze.

"What is all of that noise?"

"The demons are destroying the city." I smile stiffly when he gives me a confused look. "Legion is their collective name, and I told them to tear it down."

A painful grin touches Sebastian's face. "I knew there was something special about you." He sits up when he notices my hand in Orias's; his heart beats faster before it's cut off when he pulls away. "Why didn't you send them back to Hell?"

I blink at the question. Why hadn't I? The only thought I'd had was for them to destroy the city. I wanted Orias to watch as everything was stripped away from him, everything he built and thought he had won; gone. And, truthfully, I didn't want to send them back. They could be useful once we reach Babel.

"Leah."

Rationally, I know none of this makes sense, yet at the same time it makes perfect sense.

This is what *I* want.

I shake my head. "I don't know. It's nothing. Let's get you up. We are going as soon as he wakes, and I'm not leaving you here."

"I can't go to Babel with you." He stands awkwardly, pressing his palms into his knees as he takes a broad stance. I regretfully let go of Orias's hand to help him. He waves me off unsuccessfully.

"You have to. I can't do this without you." I slip my arm through his to help him straighten his back. Sebastian retains Raum's height, though his build is not as muscular. That much is his original form.

Naturally, I could do anything without Sebastian. I don't want to. We can't part after all we have been through.

Sebastian's eyes widen, and I follow his gaze to the demon. Orias's arm twitches, his fingers extending and retracting as he stretches. His shoulders roll back, the arch of his back coming off the floor, and then he rolls to his side. He continues to stretch and flex. One of his arms reaches across the floor and he pulls himself closer to me in a slithering motion that truthfully creeps me out. He turns his head up at an unnatural angle. His neck would have to be broken to twist like that.

"Raum," I say cautiously.

Beside me, Sebastian takes my hand and gives a gentle pull.

The creature snaps his head in his direction. He reaches out again, slapping the top of the ground in front of our feet so we both jump back. I clutch the front of Sebastian's shirt to keep him from falling.

"Ozien," Raum says. He slams his palm into the ground again and pulls himself forward. There's something incredibly disturbing about the way he moves. A series of pops come from his spine when it suddenly curves out to the side, turning his body into an S.

Every cell in my body tightens as the darkness of the room becomes heavier. Its weight sends me into a panic, and I pull Sebastian back with me as the creature continues its slow progress. The slow but loud slaps of its palms jar me each time. The head twists farther and the body follows. It comes up on one arm, still reaching for us with the other, its chest curving toward the ceiling and its face looking directly at us. The mouth splits open wider than it should, into a sinister grin.

"Raum, what are you doing?"

"Legion," they mock. "Legion. Legion. Legion." The voice is not one I've heard before. It is grotesque and pinched, higher than a demon's normal baritone, and the words are all mushed together.

"That's not Raum." Sebastian holds onto me now, trying to force me behind him.

Another series of cracks splits through the air as the body continues to twist. It turns over, its back completely broken and twisted grotesquely. It rises, extending its arms, and lets its head drop down. The shoulders move back and forth, the head bobbing to the side in the opposite direction.

"Leah. Leah. Leah."

A sharp pain rips through my entire spine so violently I fall to the ground screaming. It's so blindly fast that the sheer force of it sends me into blackness, only to wake up again to the same pain violating me. I turn, trying to twist my body in any sort of way to alleviate the pain. Meanwhile, the creature turns with me, rolling so that it feels like my back is breaking. It thrashes, slamming its head to the ground, and mine follows suit.

"What's happening?" Sebastian grabs me by the shoulders, and turns me over, wincing when I cry out.

"Raum," I grit. My throat feels constricted, like my neck is about to be broken again.

"It's not Raum."

"Orias."

The creature is both, death-rolling in the body until one of them gets the upper hand. I can feel someone else's skin sliding over mine, trying their best to latch hold so they can constrict me. When it does, the coil is so tight around my gut that it forces the air out of my lungs. I latch hold of Sebastian in desperation, my slick palms sliding down his arm. The pain of it sends me reeling, and I reach for his face next, clawing for anything I can sink my nails into to numb the pain. When the compression weakens, I inhale only to feel a sweet burning sensation fill my lungs.

Sebastian jerks his face out from under my hands. I reach for his shoulders, digging in deep. Raum is doing the same, his talons sheathed in Orias's belly in an attempt to disembowel him. I kick my legs in response.

"Leah, you're hurting yourself." Sebastian grabs my wrists to hold me still.

Somewhere, my knife is discarded, but I don't know when I let it go or where it has gone. Another scream tears through my body as Sebastian forces me down and a sharp crack rips down my spine. Red hot pain runs into the top of my thighs.

"Kill him." I force it through my teeth. It comes out guttural and reptilian.

Tear him apart until there is nothing left.

The creature turns so it is on both hands and feet, its chest to the ceiling and its face pointed back in my direction. The mouth is stretched from ear to ear with rows of teeth instead of the single line on the top and bottom. Its nose is pointed, and the skin has started to peel back. A horrible sound tears through me as something breaks within me again, and it feels that not only are my bones breaking, but that I'm being flayed.

"Stop!" Sebastian yells. He stands up as if he means to approach the monster. In the midst of my pain, I can smell his fear. He reeks of it. "Take me. Raum, come into me. Please!"

I reach for him, for anything, as my vision starts to go and a coil finds my throat.

Sebastian drops back next to me and pulls me into his lap. "Come into me! Possess me, Raum. You're killing her!"

He looks around quickly and takes Onna's discarded sword. I reach for his shirt. The fabric slips through my erratic grasps until I finally get a hold of a corner and hold on for dear life even as another twist sends my body rolling. He can't kill them. If he does, then it's all for nothing. I'll be gone, too.

"Dios escúchame. Please help us." He holds the knife over me for a split second before looking back at the creature that stops as soon as he speaks.

It slowly rolls out of its contortion. Whoever is wrapped around the other loosens their hold, and I gasp for air as sweet relief, though painful, washes over me. I can feel my spine realigning itself, the vertebrae crunching together as they slide into place. The creature shifts, the body becoming more human than monster as the skin repairs itself and the limbs become more natural.

I grab hold of Sebastian's shirt with my other hand and pull myself into his lap, not taking my eyes from whoever is controlling the body. I can feel Raum, but I can't be sure. The pain isn't receding as fast as it should if it is him, and everything feels foggy. I shut my eyes for a few seconds to allow myself to adjust to the transition.

"Leah."

My eyes snap open to Raum's voice. He sways when he stands, taking a half step forward to steady himself. His skin is lighter, but he still bears the striking resemblance of Orias. I reach out in an attempt to crawl to him, but Sebastian lays his arm in front of me. I'm too weak to fight him. At the subtle shake of his head, I don't try to.

"Just give me a minute," Raum says. He takes another step forward, catching a band of light that illuminates the sweat on his body. He tips his head down and looks at me. Briefly, he looks at Sebastian, but it's so quick it's like the man isn't even here. "Are you alright?"

I open my mouth to speak but I know I'll start crying if I do. Every lash of pain is worse than the last. How do they always manage to inflict more hell than I've already been through? I shake my head. Even that inflicts pain that shoots a white light in front of my eyes. I close them to wish it away. Blindly, I reach. The stone surface meets my hands as I steady myself enough to get on my hands and knees.

Darkness stoops in front of me. I can feel the hulking form just before me. I shudder.

"Leah," Raum says softly. His fingers gently touch the side of my face. "Look at me, please."

Please.

When I do, his eyes are moving back and forth across my face, searching. The light refracts in their depths.

"I'm sorry," he says. He strokes his thumb over my cheek, smearing a little bit of blood that has splattered there. My face doesn't feel as swollen. It is always better when we touch. "I could never hurt you like that.

I did not know." He looks past me to Sebastian. "Help me lay her out. She has several bones that need to be reset. You will need to hold her still. I can hold most of the pain but, for a split second, she'll feel it. Healing is different when dark power is used."

He takes my head and shoulders when Sebastian supports my back and hips to lay me on my back.

"Ah!" I cry out when something pierces my back. It shoots up into the back of my head, bringing fresh tears.

Raum's skin is still too dark to be his, but the shape of his face has changed slightly, his forehead higher, brows thicker. Though his hair is still in braids, it doesn't look as coarse and has the blue sheen of his thick locks.

He takes my nose between his fingers first, quickly crunching it into place. My eyes water instantly, and I inhale a deep breath through my mouth. When the swelling recedes in my face a bit more and I can breathe through my nose, Raum slides his hands beneath me, his fingers cupping the back of my neck.

Heat pools beneath his hands and seeps into my skull. It flows down my neck and shoulders, rippling through my body until the fever encases me entirely.

"Her spine is broken in three places, her neck is fractured, and her left lung is pierced." Raum's face is twisted in a tight grimace.

"My god," Sebastian chokes. "How was she able to move? She got up and–"

Raum's voice is thick when he speaks. "It was through me she pulled her strength. I did not know the damage, or I would not have allowed it. Ozien," he says reverently. "This is going to hurt once and then it will be over. It has to flow through you before it comes into me."

Sebastian straddles me, looking at Raum hesitantly before pinning my arms down.

I blink in response and breathe. That's when it happens. The pain that tolls like a knell erupts within. Where the heat had fallen over me so sweetly, the sheet is snapped away to expose the damage, pulling my skin off with it. That is what it feels like when the power rips through my body.

I scream. Loud enough that my voice goes hoarse. Sebastian slams me down when I rise involuntarily. I arch back into Raum's hands. *Make it stop,* I convey.

His face twists as the pain furls within, like it's trying to twist its way out.

He pulls his hands back suddenly and everything is gone. There is only a tingling sensation that spreads through my body. Even still, I'm too afraid to move. I wait until Raum nods before I breathe again.

Sebastian leans forward with relief and gently lifts his leg to the other side. "Thank God."

Raum grunts. His hands are replaced by Sebastian's to touch my face, like he is checking for a fever. He looks up hesitantly at the demon.

"Is he dead?" I ask.

"Yes," Raum answers a little too quickly.

"Have you ever possessed a demon before?"

I turn slowly, leaning into Sebastian's hand, and brace myself on the top of Raum's thigh to sit up. The room tilts slightly. I focus on one of the windows until everything around it settles down. Smoke still lingers, though I doubt there is anything else in the room we have to be worried about.

"Yes," Raum repeats. There's something in his tone that makes me look at him, but whatever it is, he doesn't give away. He grips the underside of my arm as he helps me to my feet.

"Did he suffer?"

There's a pause before he answers. "At your expense."

I shake my head. "If that is what he felt, then I'm glad to bear it."

Raum smiles stiffly. "It was more."

I nod. Good. Partly, I wish Orias had endured a longer torture, but I'm glad it's over. A crash comes from outside the window, followed by a reverberation that shakes the room we're in. We will be lost here if we don't get out soon.

Raum lets my hand slide free, but I keep our fingertips together and follow him to the window. The rest of the army has started on our fortress. They took my order literally, but they will kill us in the process. I'll not forget the fine print next time.

I face them. "Why aren't you with them?"

Raum chuckles. "Ozien," it's almost enduring when he says it, "I am Raum."

The name, *his* name, is like a confirmation, yet I know it is a lie. He is not a part of the Legion, but neither is he Raum. Even now he is taunting me.

He grips the edge of the sill and leans farther out. I follow suit as the mass of demons turns in a wave to look at something. It looks like a man, another demon more than likely, moving quickly through the crowd. Raum stumbles back from the window so quickly I nearly bolt with him, but Sebastian's weight at my back keeps me immobile.

The demon meets my eyes as soon as he looks up. His face is awash with light that comes from I don't know where. Demons don't radiate light. Sheer power, of course, but light is something that flees the moment they are within its presence. It strikes me that I've seen him before, but it had been the back of his head. The only thing that makes him recognizable is the red braided Mohawk.

Skin so pale he looks sickly covers his body. His face is just as strange as the rest of him. It's too angular with high cheek bones and a short forehead and slanted brows that cover eyes set too far back into the skull. He's tall, taller than Raum I would guess. In a way, I suppose he can be considered beautiful like the rest of them, but there is something terribly unnatural about the way he looks that unsettles me more than any of the demons I've met before.

There is a power that shrouds him I can feel from the tower. It pushes the rest of the demons back. They lower their heads like dogs, as if something on the ground has become far more interesting than the work they had been doing moments ago. Whoever he is, he exudes real power.

I push Sebastian back and turn to Raum. I scan the ground until I find the archangel's blade and tuck it safely at my side. Its weight gives me the courage I need to ask the question I'm afraid to know the answer to.

"Who is that?"

"Raguel," Raum says hoarsely. He looks around wildly, his thoughts spew against my shieldless mind like fireworks. Fear, anger, rage. They all meld together with blinding heat that send me reeling. For an instant,

I think Raum is going to flee, but the feelings are wrangled and he becomes like hardened steel. Raguel is nothing. Raguel cannot touch him.

"He is an angel."

XXIV

I shake my head. "That is who I saw Orias speaking with before. I know it was him, but I couldn't see his face. Why would an angel be working with Orias?"

"Maybe he can help us get out of here," Sebastian suggests.

A sound barks from Raum's throat, not quite a laugh. "Angels do not help their fallen brethren. Whatever business he might have had with Orias was for his own benefit, not for the good of Tartarus. You two," he points to us individually, "are expendable. He does not need to see a mark to determine you are bound to me. What did he say when you saw him?"

I shake my head. "Orias insinuated that the key was here but wouldn't tell Raguel what it was. He didn't want him to steal it." To steal me. I wonder at which point he realized who and what I was. "He knows you're here, too," I add quickly.

Raum's face curls like he has a bad taste in his mouth.

"Angels are avengers of Heaven. He would help *us*." Sebastian looks at me pointedly.

Based on the urgency to fly, I can't say I agree with him. I know even less about angels than I do demons.

I've never even seen one, let alone heard of them being real, before now. If they really are avengers, then I agree with Raum. Mark or not, it looks like we are all in cahoots. Especially if he did have some sort of deal with Orias, which makes even less sense.

"What does an angel have to do with Orias?"

"We will find out shortly. He draws near. Quickly, cover the boy's eyes."

"Wait, why?" Sebastian takes a couple of steps back.

"You are going to portray me while I play Orias. We cannot do that if your eyes are uncovered." Raum looks to me. "Raguel's presence has already broken your command. If we were to take a stand now, we will not be able to take an entire city and him. I am not foolish enough to put your life in danger again so quickly."

My hands shake as I cut the bottom of my shirt into an uneven strip that I use to tie a blindfold around Sebastian's eyes. I guide him to the middle of the room and give his shoulder a squeeze that is meant to be reassuring. Maybe there is some truth to Sebastian's words, too.

Angels are of Heaven, so they would be on our side. Right? But again, why would he have met with Orias in secret? It must have been in secret because I haven't seen him since. Anyone who meets in shadowed alleyways are up to no good. None of this makes any sense.

"What if Sebastian is right?" I ask hesitantly.

Raum's head is tilted back. His face shifts, taking on Orias's features instead of his own. It doesn't take long since he already favors the king. The most noticeable change is the darkening of his skin and lower brow. When he looks at me, it seems that he looks at me with... pity?

"You are a weapon, Leah. Do you really think anyone will keep you alive on either side once your duties have been met? You are an asset in acquiring Babel. Whoever gets there controls the power. All of the power of Heaven and Tartarus and everything in between. Not even an angel will spare you."

He's not taunting me now.

It's hard to look at him with the face of my enemy. I know it's Raum behind the king's face, but I can't control the sick feeling that coils in the pit of my gut.

"Boy, you are not to speak whatsoever. If anyone believes that you are not me, none of us are getting out of here alive. That is not a threat, it is a promise. Keep your tongue quiet." Raum nods to the blade at my hip. "Use it to hold him steady."

Raum takes my chin between his thumb and forefinger. His eyes drop down to my lips and then he is turning, leaving me with an unbearable desire to kiss him. I follow him silently, pushing Sebastian along with the sharp point of my sword.

My chest is tight as I lead Sebastian through the dark corridors. I try to stay as close as I can to Raum, but it's hard to push Sebastian any faster when he can't see anything.

"He's using me as bait," Sebastian says, his voice hitching.

That might very well be the case, but I don't believe it. I can't believe Raum would spare him just for this. He had no idea Raguel was here, though I suppose Sebastian's expense would be convenient. He has never given me reason to believe otherwise, but I hold onto the belief Raum will spare him.

"Quiet," I instruct.

Raum holds out his arm to stop our flight. The hairs on my arm stand up as an electric jolt strikes me, powering through my bloodstream like lightning. Part of me wants to run. The other knows it would be cowardly to flee now when we are so close.

Raguel steps around the corner. My fear is heightened at the sheer sight of him. The power he exudes is magnified as he turns his sharp eyes to me, and I catch my breath. Those eyes. They're more human with the white cornea, but instead of one iris there are two in each eye, bright as crimson stains.

"Leah Jo Corrine," he says, his voice a high clear note that hangs in the air. "When you mentioned the key to Babel, this is not what I imagined." His strange eyes flicker to Raum.

"And now you see why," he replies as Orias.

I have not heard, let alone thought, my name in years. No one ever mentioned it. Not Leyak, not Raum. The last time James had used it, I had been Leah Glaser. His name. We could not get married during the fall of humanity, but we didn't need to. Him claiming me, and me accepting, had been more than enough to bind us. Even now, if Raum were to peek inside my head, he would hear the name Glaser ringing, not Corrine.

No one knows my real name. Is Dagon's story about the prophecy true? I struggle to regain my thoughts and master control before this precarious situation can slip further out of hand.

Raguel's lip curls. Even angels have fangs. "Of course." The strange stare of his eyes settles over Sebastian. "Have you culled him?"

"I can cull any of you," I say evenly. A flood of pride swells in my chest. I keep my eyes trained on the angel as his countenance shifts to one of amusement. I have no idea if my power works on all angels, or just those that are fallen.

"I suppose you are the reason for the chaos below." The light of his arrogant smile does not reach his eyes. The irises of them drift apart. Two of them are looking at me, but the other pair separate, looking above me at Raum's imposter. "Kill him." He jerks his chin to Sebastian. Raum tips his head and holds out his arms flamboyantly, mimicking Orias's overdramatic style perfectly. "Would it not be in everyone's best interest to source his power?" He holds a finger in the air and turns to me.

I haven't let my breath out. He's using Orias's voice, his mannerisms—he *is* Orias. I grip Sebastian's shoulder a little tighter for reassurance, but there is something in the way Raum is looking at me that makes me want to bolt. Of course he would take on Orias. It's an act. I try to rationalize it all, but it doesn't steady my fast-beating heart.

"He's mine," I say quickly, regaining myself. "I will do what I want with him. We have our agreement," I say, looking at Raum quickly. "The only one sourcing his power will be me." That last bit is for the one who marks me. Whatever plans he has for Sebastian, he can toss because I'm not letting anything happen to him. He's mine, too.

Ozien.

Raguel blinks. "When your head is clear of him, you will think the same of Orias." Our eyes lock. The way his burrow into me make my knees weak. "Come here." The two words have power.

I hold my breath. *Don't do anything stupid,* I beg silently. Sebastian's jaw ticks. I can feel his frustration, but he doesn't speak.

Raguel can't see the blade I hold to Sebastian. He doesn't see that I place the hilt in his hands that are clasped behind his back, only pretending to be tied. Sebastian's knuckles turn white as if he holds onto it with dear life. I pray he doesn't have to use it.

The way Raguel's red eyes rove makes me feel like some sort of livestock ready to be sold for auction. He doesn't touch me, or circle around me the way demons do, yet he makes me just as uncomfortable with his appraisal when I approach him. The strangest part is that I notice his individual irises flicking in separate directions. It's so subtle, because they're so close together, but it looks as if they're vibrating while making their assessment.

He extends his hand, letting it hover in the air before laying it to the side of my face. The pain is white hot. His eyes narrow when I flinch from under him.

"I would like to see your power for myself. Will you command him now?"

I look at Raum hesitantly. "I don't know his name."

Raguel tsks again. "And yet here he stands, restrained without temper. Raum is not foolish enough to attack me, but he would be fighting to be free of you were he not under some... spell."

I look at Raum for guidance, but there is nothing reassuring in his gaze. I turn slowly to Sebastian. The line of his jaw is so sharp you could cut butter on it. I lick my lips hesitantly.

"Do it," Raum says.

Raum isn't his name. No one would believe it if I used it now. "Raumal," I say, albeit a little too warily as I pull the made-up name out of the air. "On your knees."

Sebastian drops. There's only a slight grimace when his knees crack into the ground. I know from experience how painful that must be. He'll be able to run when we need to, but it'll be with difficulty. Sebastian is a big man, bigger after Raum's invasion. All that weight will at least leave bruising.

"Good," Raguel says. He looks at Raum, his countenance looking repulsive. "We have no need of him, though. Kill him and, when you're done, you'll possess her. If our theories are correct, we do not need her conscious to use her ability."

Raum cocks his head. "She'll die without him." He says it all a little oddly, like it doesn't sit right on his tongue. "And her soul is to be untouched."

"Her soul is already tainted by his mark. I can smell him in her." Raguel curls his lips. "She's given us enough proof that a pure soul means nothing. Possess her, lock her in a box when you're in there for all I care. But bite her in a million places to make your mark."

I heard stories long before the Possession about angels saving people's lives. They bring messages of good news. They praise the Lord and keep watch over His children. That's what the Christians say. How wrong they have been about everything.

Whatever Raguel is, he is not a guardian. His voice is cold and emotionless. There's a clear strip of malice when he speaks. "She'll live," he says.

"Afraid to get your hands dirty?" Raum mocks.

Raguel's movements are inhuman; they're too fast and stiff. His head jerks to the false king. "It is enough that I oversee the likes of you. I'll not possess her myself, but it is a necessity that we work together."

A flash of silver catches my eye. I take a half step back into Sebastian as he pulls me into a defensive embrace. His hold is loose, still weakened by Raum's expulsion. He's not strong enough to hold me, and he certainly isn't strong enough to take either of them.

"You're not touching her. Either of you." He points the knife to the hollow of my neck.

"What are you doing?" I hiss.

Raguel takes a half step forward then stops. The upturned leer that had been on his face drops. "Your eyes." He turns in the moment Raum pulls a long blade through the air. Raguel throws up his arm, letting the blade split his flesh to the bone.

A flash of bright light erupts, forcing me to my knees. It pushes us all to the ground. Sebastian's grip is shaking when he pulls me along, dragging me in the opposite direction.

"Run!"

On instinct, I listen. The blood rushing to my ears sounds like waves crashing. The light expands behind us and threatens to put me into the floor again, but Sebastian is there, hoisting me by my hair when I stumble.

My heart races as I follow him, my stride extending so I can catch up to him. It's when we near the exit that something else rushes over me. I grab the back of his shirt and shove him forward, throwing him off balance into the nearing wall. Everything was going perfectly, and he had to screw it up. Stupid human.

Sebastian pushes himself away from the wall and shoves his palms into my chest, slamming me back violently. "Get it together," he snaps. He points the blade in my face before I have the chance to rush at him. "He's using you."

"Raum had everything under control," I grit through my teeth when he forcibly grabs me.

"And now he knows he can possess you without killing you. He will take your power."

A loud crash comes from the way we have run. Sebastian grabs me by the collar and forces me forward. He's breathing too hard, though. He hangs onto me while he tries to gain his balance by leaning his weight into the wall.

I twist from his grasp, and he leans forward, his hands grasping the tops of his knees.

"You're not a hero."

My words sound empty when I see what would have been our escape. The entrance is blocked by the rubble of a fallen tower. There's a small crevice toward the top that none of us are small enough to fit through. I know that if I even try to wriggle through, there is a chance the remaining debris will crush me. The gap is too close to what used to be high ceilings. I can see parts of the arch broken beside it.

I hold up my finger when Sebastian starts to speak.

He turns toward the direction of my gaze and curses under his breath.

Relief washes over me when I see Raum run around the corner. There is a nasty sheet of red down the side of his face that makes the mask he wears more terrifying. I've seen the look in his eye before, at the cabin. It's not just fury but fear splayed clear as day across his face.

"Do not stop running now," he snaps.

Before I can move, he grabs my arm and pulls me along with him. Sebastian grabs my other hand, but I pull him before he can drag me the opposite direction. He's going to get us all killed.

It's not algae or natural slime that makes the rocks we climb so slippery. Something soft meets my hand as I follow behind Raum. The sheer panic that runs through me is all it takes for me not to look down. At least these people will have some sort of burial now. Sebastian pushes against my hip when my foot slips. Perhaps he means to encourage me, but all it does is heighten my urgency. He's terrified.

"Where is Raguel?" I ask when Raum stops.

"Close. Hurry, come here."

The hole is bigger than I thought. It'll be a tight fit, but I can make it. The men, on the other hand, I'm not so sure about.

"Go," Raum says. "We are right behind you."

There isn't time to worry about what might happen if they don't make it. I take hold of Raum's hand, squeezing it to comfort us both. I look at Sebastian, too, and have a terrible, sinking feeling that this is the last time I will ever see him. Raum lays his hand on my butt as I crouch down to get leverage. He gives me a gentle push through the opening while I pull myself through, grating my palms on the rough edges. Something soft touches the underside of my belly when my shirt tugs up.

My hair obscures my vision as I come out on the other side. A strong wind cuts through the strands and, as I fight to push my hair back, I get a clear view of the army of Pethaino waiting at the bottom. In the front lines, one of them holds a bow with an arrow poised directly at me. My foot slips as the bowstring pulls taut and a wave of rubble careens to the bottom.

XXV

"Don't shoot!"

The voice comes somewhere in the back, hoarse and thin.

In the eerie sea of bodies, Onna strides forward with an awkward gait. Pain is laced across her face and, with every step she takes, it becomes more apparent that she suffers. I knew there was a chance she lived but I hadn't expected to see her again.

She holds up her hand to steady the fury building amongst her men. The daggers she shoots with her eyes cut through me to the crawl space behind me. "Is it done?"

"Onna, let me go."

"What have you done with my king?"

Tension runs through my body as she says those two words: my king. The look in her eye as she searches for him, the hopeful switch in her stride. It is not loyalty alone that drove her to Orias's side. I understand that now.

"Let me go," I repeat. I can use her name, but I'm giving her the chance to prove me wrong. Dagon can't have been the only one.

Dark pressure brushes against my backside. I shift as Raum crawls through, keeping my eyes focused on the fallen archangel as she climbs the rubble.

"My lord!" Onna breathes, liquid in her voice.

"Don't let go, Ozien," Raum whispers. He takes a firm hold of my forearm.

Looking back, I can catch a glimpse of what's about to happen. I let out a breath as Sebastian slips through the crevice next, keeping his head down and eyes out of sight.

I turn back in time to see Onna's face fall. She stumbles forward and clenches onto the rocks. "Orias. Orias!" His name is a battle cry on her lips.

A loud roar overpowers her anguish. I twist my hand to grip Raum's hold and let him pull me into his chest. Sebastian is on his other side, crouching within the other half of Raum's embrace.

As the swell of the transition takes us, the archer lets his arrow fly. The shaft splits my scaled armor apart and sinks into my shoulder. It shoves the breath from my lungs, but I don't make a sound. They will never hear me break again.

Onna climbs faster. She's screaming for her king, her voice rising like a banshee's. She holds out her hand and pulls me down. She doesn't touch me, but I fall out from beneath Raum's grasp. The tug, it comes from my waist, at the sword belted to my hip. I reach for his ankle, anything that will keep us together, when I hit my knees. With my other hand, I hold the blade in place.

"They're here!" she yells.

A bright ball of light hurtles from the top of the slope. It breaks apart just behind Raum's head, bringing our transition to a crashing halt. He spins Sebastian out of the way as another ball erupts. He must have a shield around us because this one also breaks apart, but this time when it dissipates, I can see Raguel behind it. His pale face alight with bright hot fury.

We are trapped.

"This will not end well for you," the angel snarls.

Sebastian moves behind me and pulls the arrow free, sending a rush of blood down my arm. I roll my shoulder and pull Onna's knife free. The blade, where it had been no longer than a dagger, extends to the length of a sword as I turn, holding it between her and me.

"Sake-Onna, don't!"

Her hand is out reaching still, calling the sword into her grasp when the tug stops.

Another blast and the invisible ward cracks. Raum throws his hand up and curls it into a fist. The top of the tower falls. It collapses just behind Raguel when he jumps down beside us. The roar of the stones falling isn't what catches my attention, though. It is that one of the walls of water comes crashing down with it.

"You do not know the power you face," Raum says. The soft resonate thrum of his voice is unlike anything I've ever heard. The strength of it cuts through the water that takes out half of Pethaino and drowns out the screams of the demons that are overtaken by the massive wave.

Sebastian darts between me and Onna. The female shows her teeth, but she doesn't move. Her eyes flit down to the rising water, to the smoke that curls into the air as her comrades burn in the wake of a clean current. A few have managed to draw themselves out, or escape the wave altogether, but there are still three other walls of water remaining that Raum can drop at any moment.

Onna hesitates. Even though she cannot balk against the command, there is nowhere for her to run. Her snarl widens and she lunges forward, latching her long fingers around Sebastian's calf. I sling my arm over his chest, and she takes hold of me, too, grabbing the wrist of my sword arm and pulling me forward. The three of us tumble a few feet closer to the water.

I twist, losing my footing on a dislodged stone, and fall to my side. Sebastian is on top of her in an attempt to pin her down. Every time he reaches for a knife at her hip, she bucks. She throws her hips up then twists her legs. It's as if her body coils free of him like a snake and she kicks the man to the side.

Above us, Raguel and Raum are locked in a fight for power. Raguel has drawn his own silver blade and hails his force upon the demon, the sharp edge hacking into the torn shield.

We need to get to Raum.

"Drop another wall!" I shout.

Be it timing or him actually listening to me for once, a second wall of water crashes down. This time the wave cuts through the backside of the tower. It shifts the stones and throws Raguel on his back.

"Sake-Onna, help us. Fight for us!"

Her fist has curled over a jagged bone jutting from the ground. "Don't," she says, her voice strained.

"It is done."

"If Raguel touches me, your command will be broken. You cannot hold me."

I motion forward. "Fight him until then."

"I will have my revenge for this. And Orias," she bites.

Then she is on her feet, stumbling to Raguel. Blood pools down her back where I stabbed her. Her own sword had done that, the same one that Raum wouldn't touch. Does it work on all angels or just the fallen? It's on my lips to call her, but I think better of it and keep the sword in my hand. I might need it if she fails, or worse, she comes back for it.

I knew my gut had been right not to trust her. I should have ended it when I had the chance.

One of the demons that has survived the chaos scrambles toward me. I block its attack of curled talons with the sword. It recoils as the sheared edge slices across the knuckles and I follow it down, forcing it into the water, and cut into its neck with a satisfying *thwunk* when it hits bone. Another one is half-shifted, with the body of a man and limbs and face of a monster, as it charges me.

Sebastian, having found a sword of his own, holds his blade between the teeth of another demon. He twists the sword with a bellowing yell and shoves it forward, the tip of the blade exiting the back of the demon's head.

They fall upon us like locusts. I step in front of Sebastian when another demon leaps forward. His momentum carries him too fast, and I twist, misjudging slightly but still hitting him in his torso all the same. For as inexperienced as I am, the touch and force of the blade make up for it.

"Stay behind me. The blade is poison to them."

Sebastian nods and takes a step back. He turns, putting us back to back as we try desperately to stay alive. I was right in assuming he was skilled in combat. Despite the drawback of his possession, he is far more talented than I am with a blade. He is as quick as the demons, turning and striking before they can lay blade or talon on him.

But our chances shift when more climb from the water with smoking and peeling skin, in a rage. There are too many, and we are mortal.

"We can't stay here much longer," I yell.

Sebastian nods and, in that moment, his reserve collapses. His body is drained, broken. He falls to his knees every other step as he climbs. I rush beside him and throw his arm over my shoulders, hoisting us up to keep him going. We won't make it in time with the way we are struggling. We won't make it to safety.

Raum has Raguel in a hold with his teeth fastened to his neck. His throat flexes as he drinks the angel's blood. At his side is Onna, with a blade wedged beneath Raguel's shoulder. He pulls away with a flash of fangs as he rips the angel's neck open.

Onna doesn't move. She stares down at Raguel, her eyes wide and hopeful until he rolls away on his stomach. Her lips part in an attempt to call for him, but nothing comes out. As long as he doesn't reach for her, she can't hurt us. But how had he broken the spell over the Legion?

"Get us out of here," I breathe when I reach them.

Sebastian moves me between the two of them and wraps his arms around Raum's back, and the demon's arms come around him.

The transition is easier this time with them surrounding me; it doesn't feel as painful, though the air is sucked from my lungs. I pray for Sebastian's safety, that he will make it with us wherever we are going to land. It feels like fire engulfs us and, though I know we are already hovering over Pethaino, I could swear we are still there, still standing close to each other.

Dense pain clamps to my ankle as soon as the remaining walls of water come crashing down. Onna's body is nearly ripped free when a wave hits her. She sinks her talons in the flesh of my calf and then anchors herself to my thigh with the other. She screams when the water hits, her lower half outside of the shield going up in smoke.

"Let go!" The words scald my throat as the fiery air fills my lungs.

Her eyes are wide with desperation and her mouth is parted as she struggles to breathe. She reaches farther up and sinks those nasty curled talons into Sebastian's thigh.

The invisible flames grow hotter, and I feel Sebastian start to slip. His arm that had wrapped around Raum and me snaps around my waist from the intensity of the force that surrounds us. I cling tighter to Raum. If Onna takes Sebastian, he'll take me with him. She will drag us all down, and Sebastian won't leave me with Raum. He would rather us both die than for me to be left with a monster.

None of us can let the others go without falling.

Something hits us from underneath, though it is more like a turbulence than an impact. Onna screams and, as if something has grabbed her from below, is snatched from the air. Sebastian's weight pulls me back and rips me from Raum's arms. Golden light peels my eyes back, then blue, then gold again as the world spins furiously before my eyes. Sand spews out from beneath our weight, the impact breaking Sebastian and me apart as I crash into the hard ground.

"Ahh!" Sebastian cries out.

I roll to my feet, dropping to my knees once, twice, before I can stand, leaning most of my weight on my hand as I find balance. I can't press any weight into the leg Onna's torn apart. My pants are wet. Water or blood?

The world is still spinning, but we are here. Wherever that may be.

In all black and dark skin, Raum stalks past me. I follow his path, reaching out, but am unable to stop him when he attacks. He is on Sebastian like a wolf, fangs bared and muscles rippling. He kicks Sebastian past his extended hand, straight into his gut. Before Sebastian has a chance to breathe, Raum hoists him to his feet by his throat.

"I spared you for her sake. Put Leah at risk and I will not make the mistake again."

Raum isn't going to kill him. He's only threatening him. If Sebastian hadn't instigated Raguel, we would have been better off. He deserves to be disciplined.

He grips Sebastian's thigh, tearing another ragged scream out of the man's throat. The smell of burnt flesh fills the air. With another growl of disapproval, Raum drops him to the ground.

I turn away. The world still spins as I search our surroundings.

"Where's Onna?" My hips fall to the side and my butt hits against the sand as my body collapses beneath me. I press my hand to the largest wound on my thigh as I look for her. The sand is covered in blood, mine probably.

A quick look at Sebastian tells me Raum has healed him. At the very least, the wound in his thigh has been cauterized.

Raum turns, looking for her, too, but it is just the three of us. There is no wave of his hand, or touch from him. He meets my eyes briefly before turning to the shoreline. The blood stops running through my fingers.

She's not here.

Before me lays the ocean and behind me is nothing but sand. This is a true desert. I'm torn between excitement and worry as the expanse disappears in the distance. The anticipation of being so much closer to Babel outweighs any concerns I might have, though.

A wall of water moves rapidly across the ocean floor in the direction we have come. Somewhere in the wave's path is Pethaino. There will not be a stone left standing once it hits. The damage will be colossal.

I jump to my feet to get a better look at it all.

I smile. They'll all be dead. Every one of them. No one will be able to follow us now. No one will ever hurt us, hurt *me* again.

"Leah," Sebastian whispers.

I hear him, but I can't take my eyes off the wave. I wish I could see what damage it'll do. I wish I could have seen more of it while we were there. I wish I could hear them scream.

"She's dead. They all are." I look around once more as the shrill cry of Onna's scream rings back to me.

"I don't think that's Raum."

"What?" I ask, looking at him now. He, too, is fixed on the scene before us. He reaches to me when he attempts to stand, and I help him to his feet.

"I was with him long enough to know that's not just Raum."

"What are you talking about? Orias is dead. Raum killed him."

Sebastian's lips purse together. He shakes his head and looks cautiously back to Raum as he lowers his arms from the sky. "I don't think so."

Raum's skin has not softened to the gold complexion I have grown accustomed to. While I did not expect the length of his hair to change on its own, I imagined the texture would be finer. It's hard to tell when it's still twisted. Yet I can see his fire in the black eyes set between his thick brows. It is Raum's smile, looking more like a sneer that breaks his face apart.

I smile, but unease spreads beneath the warmth that envelops me. I knew with every atom of my body that James had been in my arms inside the talon, and I had been wrong. I loved James. How am I to know if the monster reaching out to me, pulling me in an embrace so he can kiss me, is Raum or Orias?

Acknowledgements

First and foremost, I want to thank each and every one of my readers. Because of you, Leah and Raum's story was able to continue. And let me just say, this is just the beginning. I want to thank Josh, my dear friend, for still listening to my rants and ideas to perfect this story. And to you and Mike, for your pride and love for me and what I do. I will forever cherish the friendship we have. Sheryl, for listening to me when you have no idea what book I'm talking about because I have multiple working manuscripts but you're enthusiastic all the same. Kelvin, the support, encouragement, and pride I have received from you is the reason I have pushed myself to be a better writer and person. I am blessed to have you all in my life. I love you.

About the Author

ALLISON PAIGE loves traveling with her camera, particularly in the Irish countryside, and has several ongoing projects that she writes out of her home in Charleston, South Carolina with her corgi. She fills her spare time working with animals of all types and is a fervent advocate of bee, ocean, and wildlife conservation.

Made in the USA
Monee, IL
21 July 2025